'Readable, fresh and witty . . . funny but also poignant.'
Independent on Sunday

'Funny and well-observed . . . another sure-fire hit.'
Heat

'Like Bridget Jones for the metrosexual.'
Loaded

'Gayle's chatty style sustains a cracking pace'
The Times

'Mike Gayle has carved a whole new literary niche out of the male confessional novel. He's a publishing phenomenon.'
Evening Standard

'Touching and funny.'
Sunday Mirror

'Ever wished you could see into the male mind? Here's your chance . . . Insightful and hugely witty.'
Cosmopolitan

Also by Mike Gayle

His 'n' Hers
My Legendary Girlfriend
Mr Commitment
Turning Thirty
Dinner for Two

About the author

Previously an Agony Uncle, Mike Gayle is a freelance journalist who has contributed to a variety of magazines including *FHM, Sunday Times Style* and *Cosmopolitan*. BRAND NEW FRIEND is his sixth novel.

BRAND NEW FRIEND

MIKE GAYLE

HODDER

First published in Great Britain in 2005 by Hodder and Stoughton
A division of Hodder Headline

The right of Mike Gayle to be identified as the Author
of the Work has been asserted by him in accordance with
the Copyright, Designs and Patents Act 1988.

A Hodder paperback

3

All characters in this publication are fictitious
and any resemblance to real persons, living or dead,
is purely coincidental

A CIP catalogue record for this title is available from the British Library

0 340 82540 5

Typeset in Benguiat by Hewer Text UK Ltd, Edinburgh
Printed and bound in Great Britain by
Clays Ltd, St Ives plc

Hodder Headline's policy is to use papers that are natural, renewable and
recyclable products and made from wood grown in sustainable forests. The
logging and manufacturing processes are expected to conform to the
environmental regulations of the country of origin.

Hodder and Stoughton
A division of Hodder Headline
338 Euston Road
London NW1 3BH

For monkey two

Acknowledgements

A huge debt of thanks is owed to the following: Phil Pride, Sara Kinsella and everyone at Hodder, Euan Thorneycroft and everyone at Curtis Brown, Jane Bradish-Ellames, the Monday-night footballers, the Sunday-night pub people, Jackie and Mark for the northern-based fact-checking, Emma and Darren for introducing me to Chorlton, Asif (because I missed you out last time), Danny Wallace (for being Danny Wallace), everyone at the Board, everyone who has dropped me a line in the last year (you've helped considerably), all my old friends and all my new ones too, my wife, Claire, and the rest of my family, and anyone whose sofa I have crashed on in the past (especially you, Dave).

PROLOGUE

(Principally concerning Eskimos)

A man, a woman and a discussion about Eskimos

'Do you want to hear an interesting fact?' said Jo. 'Eskimos apparently have over fifty different words for snow. Snow's really important to those guys – I suppose it's because sometimes the difference between one type and another can mean the difference between life or death.' She paused and laughed self-consciously. 'You know they've got words for dry snow and wet snow, fluffy snow and compact snow. They've got words for snow that comes down fast and for snow that comes down slow – they've thought of everything.'

'That's a lot of snow,' commented Rob as his eyes flicked to a scruffy-looking mongrel crossing the road in front of them, oblivious to the night bus hurtling towards it. It only narrowly missed being hit, but continued coolly on its journey to the bin outside the off-licence, which it sniffed studiously, then cocked a leg against.

'So, what's your point?' asked Rob.

'Well, it's like this,' replied Jo. 'If Eskimos can come up with fifty words for snow because it's a matter of life or death, why is it that we've only got one word for "love"?'

PART ONE

(Principally concerning a big move)

Rob waits for his girlfriend

The events that led up to Rob Brooks discussing love, Eskimos and snow with someone who wasn't his girlfriend Ashley McIntosh while sitting on a damp kerb outside an off-licence in South Manchester had orginated in a solitary event that had taken place roughly a year and a half earlier in a house in Tooting, south London.

It was Friday in July, just after nine o'clock, and Rob, a thirty-two-year-old graphic designer was sitting on his sofa in the house he shared, staring at the clock on the wall. He was waiting for his girlfriend to arrive from Manchester so that he could complete his transformation from part-time single bloke to dutiful full-time boyfriend. Rob had been working towards it – with him going to Manchester or her coming to London – every other weekend for the last three years. It was like living two lives, one in which he was a bachelor and another in which he was a fully paid-up member of the Couple Club. And although it had been fine in the early days, the older he got the harder it was to sustain the effort involved maintaining this type of relationship.

To Rob's mind, the Long Distance Relationship was for young people or, to be more exact, people in their twenties who had the kind of wired energy required for a cross-country love affair, which he hadn't for a long time. He was well past the age when a long-distance relationship was anything other than a big fat pain in the arse, and now he questioned the validity of any journey that wasn't a commute to work or a taxi ride to the airport for a weekend shopping trip to New York to buy (amongst other things) the kinds of trainers, T-shirts and clothing that would impress the more fashion conscious of his friends.

Rob was convinced that it wasn't just him who thought like this but people like him too. People who would rather spend an evening on the Internet trying to work out how to order food in than leave the comfort and safety of their homes for a real life all-singing all-dancing store. It might seem ridiculous to order groceries on a computer, but, in these cash-rich, time-poor days, it made so much sense to a busy man like Rob. So he couldn't help but wonder that if life was too short to spend time in the supermarket it was also too short surely to spend every other weekend on the motorway while the rest of the world relaxed. But he accepted the tedium of weekend travelling as one of many things you do for love.

The cordless phone rang on the table in front of him and he answered it immediately. Maybe it was Ashley, to say she was at the front door. He knew there was little chance of that – normally she didn't leave Manchester until after six – but he allowed himself to imagine letting her into the house, chatting to her about her day, making her a quick something to eat, then taking her to the Queen's Head in time for last orders.

'Hi, sweetheart,' said Rob, into the receiver, while he ordered himself an imaginary pint. 'Still got far to come?'

'I'm on the M6,' replied Ashley.

'Which bit of it?' he asked, trying to mask his disappointment.

There was a long pause. 'I've only just gone past Stoke. There's a huge tailback – roadworks somewhere.'

Rob did a swift calculation and worked out that his dream of last orders was dead. It would be at least midnight before she got to London, which meant that not only would they miss the pub but she would also be in a bad mood.

'Why were you late leaving?' asked Rob.

'Why are you making a big deal about it?' snapped Ashley.

'Because I told you last night that there were roadworks on the M6 outside Birmingham and that if you were late leaving you'd get stuck in loads of traffic.'

'Well, you were right.'

'I don't want to be right,' he said, no longer bothering to hide his exasperation. 'I just wanted you to take my advice and leave a bit earlier. If you had you'd be here, not sitting in miles of traffic.'

There was a click and the line went dead. She'd put the phone down on him. Rob watched the clock in silence. He hadn't meant to get annoyed so quickly. And the last thing he needed was for the weekend to get off to a bad start yet again. I'll have to call her back, he thought, but before he could, the phone rang again. 'Look,' he said, 'I'm sorry. Okay? Let's forget what just happened and start again.'

'Sorry for what?' said a gruff northern voice that Rob recognised immediately. It was Phil, his friend, house-mate and co-director of their two-year-old web-design consultancy, cIUNKEE mUNKEE.

'In trouble with the missus, are we?' asked Phil, laughing.

'Sort of,' conceded Rob, taking in the background noise at the other end of the line. He could hear talking, laughing and music – classic Friday-night-in-the-pub ambience. He felt strangely sad.

'What've you done wrong this time?' asked Phil.

'It's a long story. And it'll get even longer if she rings back and finds the phone engaged and that it's not me trying to call her back.'

'All right, Bobman,' said Phil. 'I was just calling to see what time you'd be down here.'

'How many times did I tell you today that I wasn't coming out tonight?'

'Ten or twenty,' replied Phil, between sniggers.

'So why are you tormenting me like this? Normally it'd be fine, you know that. But with things the way they are between me and Ash the last thing I can afford to do is fail to greet her after her long journey because I'm in the Queen's drinking too much and falling over, like the weekend before last.'

'You are so under the thumb,' said Phil, chuckling. The phone went muffled, and then there was a roar of laughter. Rob was imagining what he was missing – a pint, conversation, the feeling that the weekend had really arrived – when a male voice yelled down the line, 'Rob, you big girly tosser,' which brought him to his senses. It was his friend Woodsy, a.k.a. Peter Woodman, a.k.a. Rob and Phil's unofficial semi-permanent house guest.

'Are you all right, mate?' enquired Woodsy.

'I'm fine,' replied Rob.

'Phil says you're coming to the pub,' said Woodsy.

'No, mate, I can't. Ashley's on her way.'

'Oh, you have to come.'

'I can't.'

'Please.'

'I can't.'

'She won't mind.'

Rob laughed. 'Oh, yes, she will.'

'Hang on,' said Woodsy.

There was another long pause, filled with the sounds of the Queen's Head.

'Mate?' said Phil.

'Yeah?'

'About the pub.'

'What about the pub?'

'Are you coming, then?'

'I've told you I can't,' replied Rob. 'I don't understand why you're torturing me like—'

Another burst of laughter at the other end of the line prevented him finishing his sentence.

'Sorry about that,' said Phil, a few moments later.

Suddenly Rob felt even sadder about his lost Friday night. 'Is it good?' he asked.

'What?' said Phil.

'Is the pub good?'

'It's the pub,' said Phil laughing. 'How good can it be?'

'But I'm not missing out on anything good, am I? I mean, who's out tonight?'

'Everybody,' said Phil.

'Like who?'

'Okay . . . Ian One's here . . . and Ian Two . . . and Kevin called to say he'd be down before last orders – oh, and Darren's at the bar.'

'Really?' asked Rob.

'Yeah, really,' said Phil.

'And what have you all been doing?'

'What kind of question is that? We've been drinking mainly – and talking.'

'Talking about what?'

'Do you really want to know?' asked Phil.

'Yes,' replied Rob. 'I do.'

He could hear Phil repeating the question to their friends.

'Okay,' said Phil, back on the line. 'The boys have helped me do a quick recap. We've been talking about dangerous things we did when we were kids, will a socialist Utopia ever be possible, some new girl in Ian Two's office who's supposed to look like a young Sophia Loren, bands whose second albums were better than their débuts, work in general, Ian One's broken computer and finally, "In which video does Kylie Minogue wear those gold hotpants?"'

'"Spinning Around",' said Rob automatically.

'Are you sure?' asked Phil. 'Because I reckon it's "Can't Get You Out of My Head."'

'You are so wrong,' insisted Rob. 'You're a whole album out, mate.'

'We'll see about that,' said Phil. Rob heard him ask the others. 'Okay,' he said, after a few moments. 'I stand corrected. You're right – this time.'

'Of course I am,' Rob replied, desperately wishing he was there to be smug in person.

'So, are you coming down?' asked Phil.

'I can't,' said Rob. 'The first ten minutes of being together in a long-distance relationship are crucial. You haven't seen each other all week, you've both been under a lot of stress, you're tired, and maybe a bit grumpy. You're a ticking time-bomb waiting to go off. If World War Three isn't going to kick off, you both need to have your wits about you and I don't think I will have if I come down the pub.'

'Fine,' said Phil. 'But don't wait up for me and Woodsy. We're thinking about going to a club in town, then back to Ian One's because his missus is away and he's just bought the uncut version of *Enter the Dragon* on DVD.'

'*Enter the Dragon*,' echoed Rob, longingly. He sighed and glanced at his watch. 'Look, I'd better go. Catch you later, mate.'

If it had been up to Rob he would have spent the rest of the evening lamenting what he was missing but the second he ended the call the phone rang again. A small-voiced Ashley piped up, 'I'm sorry,' and started to cry.

'I'm sorry too,' Rob replied, then added, 'But, sweetheart, you can't cry when you're driving. You might have a crash. You've got to concentrate.'

'Is that all you care about?' sniffed Ashley. 'The car?'

Her response flustered him. Was he wrong to worry about her crashing? Should he encourage her to let it all out while she was in control of a vehicle travelling at seventy miles an hour in the middle lane of the M6? In the end he decided to ignore her comment because, most likely, even she knew that it didn't make sense. He had to say something to appease her, though. And he had to say it soon. 'I love you, babe,' he whispered. 'You'll be here soon and everything will be all right.'

'I love you too,' said Ashley. 'I'll speak to you when I'm closer to London.'

Four years earlier: How Rob met Ashley McIntosh

Rob and Ashley had first met at a leaving do for Ian One. In the time that Rob had known Ian One (whose real name was Ian Quinn) he had graduated from marketing junior to marketing manager with a team of ten people under him. At the pace he was climbing the career ladder, it was only a matter of time before he went to a bigger firm. Ian One's leaving do was the stuff of legend. His company coughed up for a free bar all night and he invited not just work colleagues and major clients but his friends too.

At the time Rob and Phil were both at the Orange Egg design consultancy in Shoreditch, working on print ads, corporate websites and general design, but they were thinking about starting up their own company. The rest of their friends were at the party too: Ian Two (whose real name was Ian Manning), Woodsy, Darren and Kevin. The six were standing together in a large group at the bar when Rob spotted Ashley coming through the door.

As far as relationships went, Rob had been going through a dry patch that was threatening to turn his whole life into a Sahara. It wasn't that he never met any single women, rather that he didn't meet any single women who came up to his self-imposed, stringently high standards. His last girlfriend, Trish, had been a part-time model and fashion student who, as well as being exceptionally easy on the eye, had a great sense of humour and, most important of all, got on with his friends. For the two years they had been together Rob was convinced that he had found the *yin* to his self-confessed difficult-to-fit *yang*. Then she had graduated from the Royal College of Art, announced that she was desperate to go to New York to get into fashion and wanted him to go with her. For several weeks Rob wavered, trying to make up his mind, and at one point sent his CV to a few design studios and advertising agencies in Manhattan. The crunch came, however, when an ad agency forwarded his CV to a small design studio in the process of setting up. They contacted him immediately and practically offered him a job over the phone. The second his east-coast pipe-dream looked like it might become reality, he had realised that he didn't want to go. He couldn't pinpoint why – it would have been a brilliant opportunity – but no matter how he looked at the situation it didn't feel right. When he had broken the news to Trish she told him she was the best thing that had ever happened to him and he'd live to regret not taking that chance. And Rob was sure she was right. A year later, he'd met loads of single women but hadn't been interested in any of them. As he'd explained to Phil, 'They're just not Trish.'

Then he met Ashley.

'Now *she* is amazing,' said Rob, to his friends.

'Out of your league, mate,' pronounced Phil.

'Absolutely,' added Ian Two.

'What is my league?' asked Rob.

'She's a nine,' said Darren, 'and you're a six and a half.'

'A seven tops,' added Kevin.

'I'm an eight and a half at *least*.'

'In your dreams, mate,' said Woodsy. 'You're a six and a half. Stick with what you deserve, mate.'

'Right,' said Rob. 'We'll see about that.' Without taking his eyes off Ashley he went over to Ian One on the other side of the bar. 'Any chance you know who that girl is?' he asked, pointing at Ashley.

'Don't know her but I do know the woman she's talking to,' said Ian One. 'If you ask me she's way out of your league, mate. She's young, attractive and well dressed – what could she have in common with a scruffy graphic designer like you who has more pairs of trainers than a sports shop?' He laughed. 'Nothing I'm saying's going to stop you, though, is it? You up for some smooth talking or what?'

Drinks in hand, the two men made their way across the room and Ian One opened with a kiss for his work colleague, Michelle.

'I can't believe you're really leaving,' she said, hugging him. 'You're like part of the furniture.' She turned to the woman standing next to her. 'Ian, this is my baby sister, Ashley.'

'Hi, nice to meet you,' grinned Ian One. 'And this is my mate Rob.'

Ian One, ever the perfect wingman, began to ask Ashley about herself to draw her into the conversation. She was twenty-four. She was a medical student at Manchester University Medical School. She'd come to London to see her sister for a few days. Then he made an excuse to take her sister aside, which left Rob with the perfect opportunity to break the ice with Ashley.

'So,' began Rob, 'you don't look like a medical student.'

'I'm not sure how to take that,' replied Ashley, smiling.

Rob winced. 'Why don't you tell me what I look like and then we'll be even?'

She laughed, then looked Rob up and down as though he were an item of clothing she liked but wasn't sure she

16

wanted to take home. 'You look like you work in a record shop,' she replied.

'I'm a graphic designer.'

With certain girls Rob had found that "I'm a graphic designer", with its implied creativity, had a certain cachet. Ashley, however, didn't seem to be one of them.

'What's that, then?' she asked.

'I'm like an artist,' explained Rob, 'only I work in the commercial world. I design things like ads, billboards, posters, book jackets, packaging, corporate logos, websites – that sort of thing.'

Over the next half an hour they talked, uninterrupted, about their lives. There was something easy about their conversation – it wasn't forced, just flowed naturally – but Rob couldn't escape the feeling that it was simply a means to an end. They didn't know each other, might not have anything in common, but they wanted to know each other so conversation was the only avenue open to them. As far as he was concerned Ashley might have been reciting the times table and it wouldn't have mattered. The result would have been the same because the conversation was just a jumble of personal details. It was the fact that they were having it that said everything – and primarily: 'The more we do this the more I want to do it.'

As Ashley was about to reply to 'What's your favourite film?' Michelle returned, without Ian One, and reminded her sister that they had a table booked at a restaurant in Piccadilly for nine thirty.

Ashley looked at Rob. 'Do you want to come?' Then she turned to her sister. 'It wouldn't be a problem, would it?'

'No, of course not. More the merrier.'

Ashley's eyes met his. 'So, how about it?'

Mike Gayle

'I'm afraid I can't,' he said. 'It's Ian's leaving do.'

'Oh, he won't mind,' said Michelle. 'The way he's going, he won't even remember.'

They all gazed at Ian One who, now jacket-free and tieless, was dancing exuberantly with a middle-aged woman.

'Yeah, I know,' said Rob, 'but I'm with the rest of my mates, too, and it's frowned on to leave parties early.'

'I could understand what you were saying if you were an eleven-year-old and you'd spent the day playing out on your bikes, but you're a grown man,' laughed Michelle. 'At least, I thought you were.'

'It's a friends thing,' explained Rob, 'and there's a certain etiquette with these things.'

'You make it sound like you belong to an exclusive golf club,' said Ashley.

'It's something like that. The fact is, if it wasn't Ian's leaving do – say we were just down the pub – it wouldn't matter at all. I could leave without giving my mates a second thought.'

'And why's that?'

'Because a night down the pub is a regular occurrence.'

Ashley nodded. 'But a leaving do isn't so you have to be seen to be doing the right thing.'

'Exactly,' replied Rob.

'Well, it's your loss,' said Michelle.

Suddenly Rob realised she might have a point. Some sort of masculine brain malfunction had caused him to talk himself out of having dinner with an attractive twenty-four-year-old medical student. What was he thinking? She was the first woman he'd been properly attracted to since Trish. And Ashley didn't even live in London – how would he get a second stab at making something happen between them if they didn't live in the same city?

18

'On second thoughts,' he began nervously, 'maybe I could get some sort of papal dispensation from Ian to make it all right.'

'No,' said Ashley, touching his hand. 'You stay with your friends.'

Rob thought about saying it was fine, but was all too aware that he was in danger of losing what little cool he might still have. Instead he replied, 'You're right. Friends should come first. Because without them what are you? But before you go I'd like to insist on one thing.'

'Which is?'

'Your phone number.'

Ashley and her sister exchanged a knowing glance.

'Have you got a pen?' asked Ashley.

'No,' replied Rob, digging into his pockets and pulling out his mobile. 'I'll just put it in this.' Ashley took it from him, carefully tapped in her number and pressed 'save'. Then she kissed his cheek, picked up her coat from the back of the chair next to her and went towards the door.

Alone, Rob checked her number as if it was the only proof in the world that the last half-hour hadn't been an elaborate dream. Was the number she had given real? He took a deep breath and pressed 'call'.

'Hello?' said a female voice.

'Is that Ashley?'

'Yes – who's . . . Rob?'

'Yes.'

'Rob that I was speaking to less than a minute ago?'

'Yes, *that* Rob.'

'What can I do for you?'

'Nothing at the minute. I just wanted to check – with you

19

being a trainee doctor and all – that you'll be available in case of an emergency.'

'Oh,' she replied softly, 'I'll always be there for you in an emergency.'

Thirty seconds later she walked back in and, without a word, they kissed. And that, pretty much, was that.

Ashley arrives in London

It was just after midnight when Rob heard Ashley's car pull up outside the house. He turned off the TV and looked through the curtains: she was reversing her convertible MG into the kind of parking spot that most people would have written off as a non-starter, which said volumes about Ashley's ability behind the wheel *and* her personality. Nothing was too difficult for her – whether it was life in general or precision parking. He put on his trainers and went outside to help her with her bags.

'Hey, you,' he said, as she unlocked the boot.

Ashley allowed herself to be kissed.

'How was the journey?'

She didn't reply, just rolled her eyes and hauled out her bags. As they went towards the house Rob asked question after question in a bid to coax her out of her dark mood, but her responses were strained and barely audible.

He dumped the bags in his bedroom while Ashley made herself a cup of tea. By the time he was back downstairs she was sitting in the living room with a steaming mug in her hand. Rob turned on the TV and they watched an old episode of *Have I Got News For You*. In the half-hour it was on, Rob laughed several times, but Ashley failed to raise so much as a smile.

'I'm really tired,' he said, stifling a yawn as the credits

rolled. He stretched in pantomime fashion – his code for, ''Do you want to have sex?''

'I'm shattered,' replied Ashley. 'The second I hit the pillow I'll be out like a light.'

'Me too,' said Rob, decoding her answer as a firm negative.

'I just want a big hug and then to fall asleep,' she said, cuddling up to him.

'Are you all right?' asked Rob.

'No.' She sat up. 'Actually, I'm not. I think we need to talk.'

'It's the long-distance thing, isn't it?'

'Yes.' She looked into Rob's eyes. 'You know I love you, don't you, more than anything in the world? But you must see that we can't carry on like this. I miss you too much, the travelling makes me bad-tempered and I feel like our life is on hold . . .' She pointed across the room to the armchair where a sleeping-bag adorned with a pair of green boxer shorts lay bundled up. 'And although I love Woodsy to death even he's getting a bit too much for me.'

'I know,' said Rob eyeing the boxers. 'I'll have a word with him about tidying up.'

'But that's not the point, is it? The point is, do you want us to live together?'

'Of course I do,' said Rob. 'I've told you that a million times.'

'So if you want to be with me, let's go for it. Come and live with me – or stay here, if you prefer. I'll start looking for a new job tomorrow. All you need to do is *say*. But we can't carry on the way things are. Manchester or London? The choice is yours.'

Rob nodded slowly. The choice was indeed his. He knew Ashley had been more patient than he deserved. She had asked time and again if she should apply for a job in London so that they could be together and he'd always said no. The fact was, he knew he'd have to leave London one day. It was too expensive. It was too grimy. It was too . . . London. And he was aware of what was at stake. He didn't want to miss out on a good thing as he had done with Trish because of geography. He knew Ashley was his one chance of living a proper life. He didn't want to miss out on the Buying-a-house Thing, the Getting-married Thing, the Being-a-parent Thing, even the Being-happy-for-the-rest-of-your-life-until-you-pop-your-clogs Thing. And it didn't seem fair that he might miss out on all that just because he wasn't ready to move city.

'Look, Ash,' he began, 'I know things can't go on like this, and one day I will move up to Manchester. It's just that . . .'

'What?'

'Things are different when they become reality. It'll mean a lot of changes, like moving my job. Phil and I have only had the company running two years—'

'But you've told me before that you could easily set up in Manchester and commute to London for meetings with Phil. It's only two hours on the train.'

Rob swallowed. She was right again. And, to make matters worse, he and Phil had had the discussion only a month earlier. Phil had suggested it might be a good thing as then they'd have the desk space to hire their first employee.

'Look,' said Rob, 'all I'm saying is . . . can't we just wait a little longer?'

Ashley shook her head. 'Not any more. Just give me a reason – one *good* reason – why you won't move.'

'I can't give you one,' he told her sullenly. 'There are too many to choose from.'

'And that's the last you've got to say on the matter?' she asked, as she untangled herself from his arms and stood up.

'This doesn't have to be a "Thing", okay? All I'm asking for is a bit of time.'

'How much?'

'Two years . . . three max.'

'No,' said Ashley, firmly. 'You've agreed we can't carry on like this.'

'You're right, but now's not the right time for me to leave London.'

'You've said that. But I still don't feel you're telling me the real reason why.'

'It doesn't matter.'

'Of course it does, because whatever's stopping you is affecting my life as well as yours. I don't understand you. You say you want to leave London but you won't make the decision to do it. Don't you want to be with me any more?'

'Of course I do,' said Rob. 'I love you.'

'Then what is it?' asked Ashley. 'What's stopping you?'

'I just need more time,' said Rob. 'A bit more and it'll all be sorted, I promise you.'

'Well, that's the one thing you can't have,' said Ashley, and with that she left the room and headed upstairs, slamming the door after her.

'Where are you going?' Rob called after her.

'Back to Manchester,' she replied, as she appeared at the top of the stairs holding her suitcase.

'It's late,' said Rob. Panic had worked its way into his voice. 'You're tired. I'm tired. Can't we just talk about this?'

'No,' she said, as she came down the stairs. 'We can't. Not any more.' She brushed past him and slammed the front door behind her.

Rob opened it and followed her along the path to the gate. 'What do you want me to say, Ash?' he shouted.

She was standing by her car now, fumbling desperately with her keys. 'I want you to say that you want to be with me as much as I want to be with you,' she said, evidently fighting back tears. 'That's not too much to ask, is it?'

Rob didn't answer. Instead he sat down on his neighbour's wall, closed his eyes and put his head into his hands. He heard Ashley start her car. As she slid it into gear and drove off, he exhaled heavily. He wished more than anything that he was in the pub with his friends. At least they would understand why he was finding it so hard to make the decision. They would see it his way. Unlike Ashley who didn't understand that at the age of thirty-two, there were only a handful of things that could genuinely terrify a man – and, ridiculous as it might seem, one was the idea of moving to a new city and making new friends.

Nine years earlier: When Rob met Phil

Saturday afternoon. Two o'clock. Fresh off the Luton Line
Express coach from Bedford, Rob entered the dilapidated
rented six-bedroom house in Kilburn that would be his new
home. He was carrying a large rucksack, a suitcase and a
cumbersome just-about-portable CD-player. As he stood in
the hallway, his mind was flung back to when the landlord
had first shown him the room. He studied the floor. Had the
hallway carpet always been so heavily stained? He sniffed
the air. Had the smell of dust and damp been so strong? He
examined the walls. Had there really been what looked like a
faded blood splatter by the stairs on his last visit? Had his
eyes been open at all when he was last here? He was
wondering whether it was too late to beg the landlord for
the return of his deposit cheque when he heard a noise from
the living room. He realised it was one of his house-mates
and decided to check it out. As he entered through the
heavy panelled door, he saw a bloke of his own age sitting
on a purple sofa wearing a pair of Blackburn Rovers football
shorts and a bright blue T-shirt that bore the words 'Pavement: The Slow Century'. He was reading a magazine that,
on closer examination, Rob saw was a copy of Mac User. 'All
right, mate?' he said, as he looked up.

   'Yeah, cheers.' Rob introduced himself: 'I'm Rob, Rob
Brooks.'

'Phil Parry. You must be the guy moving into Steve's old room.'

Rob nodded. 'I'm only here for six months, and after that I'll probably move on.'

'We all said that when we first moved in,' Phil told him. 'But no one ever leaves because, as filthy, flea-ridden and mouldy as this place is, it's cheap.'

'Well, someone's gone because I'm taking his room.'

Phil raised his eyebrows questioningly. 'Didn't it put you off, though?'

'What?'

Phil lowered his voice: 'You know.'

'Know what?' Rob lowered his too.

'Moving into a room where someone's just died.'

This news took Rob by surprise. 'You're telling me the guy in my room *died*? Of what?'

'Gullibility,' said Phil, laughing. 'Steve's not dead. Not unless you count moving to Milton Keynes to live with your bunny-boiler of a girlfriend as a form of expiry.'

As jokes went it wasn't the greatest, but Rob was pleased that the stranger had felt comfortable enough within minutes of meeting him to make a joke at his expense. Then Phil offered him some coffee and Rob followed him round the kitchen while his new house-mate pointed out things he thought Rob ought to know (One: 'This is the kitty jar for milk, coffee and tea. We all drop a pound in it once a week. IOUs will be frowned on.' Two: 'This is Katie our resident nutter's cupboard. Never steal food from her unless you're in the mood to start World War Three.' Three: 'This is my cupboard. Never steal food from me unless yours is well stocked so I can steal some back.').

'So,' began Phil, as they sat in the living room with their coffee, 'what brings you to London? Just finished university?'

Rob nodded. 'I've just got my first job in graphic design.'

'You're joking,' said Phil. 'Me too.'

'Where do you work?' asked Rob.

'An advertising and design studio called Worker's Play Time in Soho. What about you?'

Rob laughed. 'The art department at Ogilvy-Hunter on Charlotte Street.'

'Good company,' said Phil, grinning. 'Maybe we should work together one day.'

They were delighted to have so much in common straight away. Once the basic autobiographical details were out of the way they ventured on to music. They asked each other what bands they liked, and listened to the answers carefully, calculating whether they had sufficient crossover in taste, which, thankfully, they did. Rob felt as if he was a contestant on a TV game show. With each round of questions, the stakes were that much higher and the correct answers harder to come by. Over the afternoon they made their way through the world of graphic design, films currently on general release in West End cinemas, films in general, current TV series, TV series from the seventies, TV series from the eighties, Blackburn Rovers' current form, Luton Town's current form, music (again), gigs, magazines, people they hated on TV, women they fancied on TV, travel, newspapers, Formula One, stories about being drunk, stories about good-looking ex-girlfriends, and finally (by this time it was late evening and they had retired to the pub) stories about when they had nearly died doing something horrendously stupid (Phil, playing chicken in the middle of the road with a traffic cone on his head; Rob, potholing in north Wales while under the influence of a very heavy night). By the time they returned to the house – having stopped off on the way to get two kebabs and a large portion of chips – the pair were in no doubt that they had met their perfect match. It was like falling in love, but without the effort or sexual tension and with the knowledge that they would never have to remember each other's birthday.

Later they were joined by Ian Quinn (a.k.a. Ian One), an old secondary-school friend of Phil; Darren Usher, whom Rob met when Darren worked briefly at Ogilvy-Hunter; brothers Kevin and Ian Manning (a.k.a. Ian Two), whom Rob first met at their local sports hall playing five-a-side football; and Woodsy, whom Rob found asleep in the shower the day after his twenty-fourth birthday party. Over time they became much more than just friends: they were Rob's family too.

Meanwhile in Manchester

'Neil,' said Ashley, standing up to greet the man in front of her. 'How are you?'

'All the better for seeing you,' he replied, squeezing her in a hug.

It was mid-afternoon on the Sunday after her split with Rob and Ashley was in her local café-bar, the Lead Station, with an old friend.

Ashley had known Neil, another First Year three years her senior, since her first week at university. He had been out in Manchester city centre with a few of his friends and Ashley had been there with some of hers. The two groups had converged on a subterranean student drinking den called Corbières wine bar. During the evening they had got talking. Ashley had been attracted to Neil immediately. He had dark brown hair, stubble, and while his clothes – an old grey sweatshirt, baggy jeans and bright white trainers – were scruffy they also made him look cool.

At the end of the evening their friends had teased them so openly about the inevitability of them getting together that, without conferring, they opted not to say goodbye properly at the end of the night. It wasn't only embarrassment that had stopped them taking things further, it was the desire not to be so completely predictable.

Some weeks later when they eventually kissed, at a party

in Fallowfield, it was in a darkened bedroom covered with Joy Division posters (Neil's best friend's) and no one knew about it. They did no more than kiss and half-way through Ashley confessed that she had a boyfriend back home in Worcester and Neil said he had a girlfriend in Huddersfield.

For weeks afterwards they half expected a second kiss to take place but it never did, even at their most drunken moments. It was as if a window of opportunity had closed and neither wanted to reopen it. When they graduated it was clear to both that they had more to lose by taking things further than they stood to gain because somehow they had become friends.

Ashley had been there for Neil through a handful of serious relationships and several flings. She had been there for him when his father had been diagnosed with throat cancer two years after graduation and a year later when he died. They were close. In many ways she thought of Neil as an older brother, but there was more to their relationship than that. The flirting, though tempered, remained. And this contrast seemed to be the dynamic in their friendship.

'Can I just say,' said Neil, looking her up and down, 'that you're looking great?'

'You can,' said Ashley. 'Although I think the new hair, makeup and clothes are symptoms of a greater malaise than usual.'

'What's up?'

'Rob and I have split.'

'What happened?' asked Neil, concerned. Neil cared about her and Ashley liked that. While he'd never been a big fan of Rob he knew that Rob mattered to her. And that was important.

Ashley took a sip of the latte she had ordered and told him the whole story. 'That's why I called you,' she explained, at the end. 'I've had Christine, Lauren, Louise *and* Mia all working on an explanation but I need an expert on the male mind to sort this one out. So, what do you think? What exactly *is* his problem?'

'Friends,' said Neil. 'His mates.'

Ashley couldn't believe what she was hearing. 'Pardon?'

'It's a guess . . . and let's not forget I don't know him that well, but that's what I reckon. He doesn't want to leave his friends behind.'

'You must be wrong,' said Ashley. 'He's thirty-two, not thirteen. I've asked him to move to Manchester, not Outer Mongolia. Surely he can't have given up on what we had just because it would mean leaving his mates behind? You wouldn't do that, would you?'

'Choose my mates over you? Not in a million years. But he's not me and I know plenty of guys who would act like him.'

'But this is Rob's and my future we're talking about. Do you *really* think that's the reason? I wouldn't dream of not moving to London because of my friends. Not for a second! I love Rob and want us to be together too much.'

'I don't doubt you'd give up everything for Rob but it's different for men,' said Neil.

'Why?' asked Ashley.

Neil shrugged. 'It just is.'

'What should I do?'

'You want my advice?'

'You know that's the only reason why you and I are still friends after all this time.' Ashley smiled.

'Well, my advice is this,' said Neil. 'Do nothing. Rob's not stupid. He knows you're too good to lose.'

'Really?'

'Yeah, really. Don't ring. Don't call. Don't email him. Just let him stew. I guarantee that by the end of the month he'll have agreed to move to Manchester.'

Phone call

It was Friday night, two weeks since Rob had last heard Ashley's voice and he was dialling her number. He had missed her more than he thought possible. He hadn't expected the experience of being apart from her to be totally pain-free, but neither had he expected it to take its toll on him in quite the way it had. He had even begun to think wistfully about the Long-distance Thing. It occurred to him that their relationship hadn't always been like this – the rows, the frustration, the tiredness. Back in the early days their separation had meant that he would look forward to their weekends together. They used to be the highlight of his week. But there was no way he could get back that feeling now. That time had gone. Now change was not only inevitable, it was long overdue.

'It's me,' said Rob, when Ashley answered her phone. 'Ash, I've been doing a lot of thinking and I'm going to move to Manchester, if you still want us to be together.'

'Of course I do,' said Ashley. 'I didn't want it to come to this.'

'I know you didn't. This is my fault. I want to live with you. I want to live a proper life. I even want to leave London. I just – I just didn't have the guts to make the decision, that's all.'

'What if you hate it?'

'I'll be fine,' said Rob. 'Don't worry about me. Everything will work out okay.'

'I know I'm asking a lot of you,' said Ashley. 'I know that. But just give it a year. And if you're not happy then we'll move to London and make the best of it. What do you say? I want us both to be happy.'

'I know you do,' said Rob, 'and your plan sounds great. We'll give it a year and take it from there. I'm sure it'll be fine. I was just being stupid.'

When Rob put down the phone an hour later, having discussed in great detail their plans for the future, he felt good: he had finally done the right thing and, more importantly, everything would be okay. He had taken a step towards building a solid future for them. Yes, there would be obstacles to overcome and, yes, sometimes he'd feel like jumping on the first train to London, but the risk of losing Ashley was too great for him not to give the next twelve months his all. *I mean*, he thought, as he wandered into the kitchen, *exactly how hard could it be to make some brand new friends?*

PART TWO

(Principally concerning
Rob's first six months in Manchester)

Hit the north

Rob had never seen Ashley as happy as she was on the Saturday morning that he moved all of his belongings into her three-bedroom terraced house on Beech Road in Chorlton. To say she was ecstatic would have been a major understatement. She was – metaphorically – over the moon. Rob couldn't believe that her happiness was down to something as simple as him occupying space in her house and making it look more untidy than it had ever been while she had lived there alone. Even so, he was glad to be the source of such joy.

'I'm sorry about the mess,' he said, gazing at the chaos he had caused in her normally serene living room with its cream walls and carpet, and tastefully chosen furnishings.

'Don't mention it,' said Ashley. 'I love having your clutter here because it means you're here for good.' She clutched his hand. 'I know it might seem a bit pathetic to be so happy about it but I can't help it. It's how I feel.'

It was roughly six months since Rob had agreed to make the big move. It had taken this long because he'd been so stunned by the immensity of his decision that he'd needed time to come to terms with it. No more getting his morning newspaper from Mr Singh, the garrulous newsagent on Tooting Bec Road who knew not only his name and what paper he took but what type of milk he liked. No more using the theme tune of *London Tonight* as a means of knowing when it was time to stop work and head for the pub. And, of course, no more week-night visits to the Queen's Head with his friends. He was moving his entire life, everything that made him who he was, one hundred and eighty-five miles north to where the only person he knew well enough to ask out for a post-work pint was his girlfriend.

As for Rob and Phil's web-design consultancy, they had agreed that most of their work could be organised by phone and email, and that once the spare room at Ashley's had been fitted with a computer, colour printer, scanner and high-speed ISDN line Rob would, within reason, continue with much of the kind of work they had been doing at their studio in Wandsworth. Regular monthly meetings would keep them up to date with how the business was running, and Rob had agreed that if Phil required him to attend pitches to new clients he would come to London by train.

As the day approached for his move, Rob attended two leaving parties in his honour. The first was a surprise, thrown at the Sun and Thirteen Cantons in Soho. Phil and Woodsy had told him they would be nipping into the pub for a quick pint before a gig. As soon as he entered the bar, however, he spotted Ian Two's fiancée Becky coming out of the loos: she caught his eye and looked so guilty that it could have meant only one thing. It didn't matter, though: when he entered the pub's upstairs room Rob was still taken by surprise to see so many of his friends and acquaintances all crammed in to celebrate with him. There were London-based friends from his schooldays in Bedford; there were friends from art college and university; there were general friends and old house-mates from when he had first arrived in London; there were friends from his days in the art department at Ogilvy-Hunter;

and from the Orange Egg design studio. Then, of course, there were the boys – his core friends – and, last but by no means least, Ashley, who had organised the evening.

With so many people in one place to wish him well Rob was genuinely moved. He held Ashley's hand tightly as he went round the room greeting his guests, with a huge lump in his throat.

However, Rob's last night as a council-tax-paying resident of the borough of Wandsworth was a far more sedate affair. It was just Phil, Woodsy, Ian One, Ian Two, Kevin and Darren. And as the conversation kicked off – something to do with transfer rumours at Manchester United – Rob sat back, sipped his Guinness and savoured the moment. To Rob there were few things in life as satisfying as being surrounded by a group of men with whom he felt he belonged, even if they were all quite different. He felt as if an invisible bond bound them tightly to each other, although they never acknowledged it. And whether he moved to Manchester or Malaysia they would be his friends for life, he was sure.

As the conversation turned to a pending England match, the players' fitness and the England team in general, Rob looked to his left at Phil, who was currently holding forth on why England would never again win the World Cup. Sitting around this table listening to his friends talk reminded him of wandering into a newsagent's and taking his pick of the magazines in the 'Men's General Interest' section.

If Phil was a magazine, thought Rob, *which would he be?* After a few moments' consideration, he concluded that because Phil knew quite a lot about sport, music, fashion, entertainment, male grooming and which supermodel or actress was hot, he would be a general-interest publication like *GQ* or *Esquire*.

He was well aware of how pointless this train of thought was, but there was no way he was going to stop now that he was on a roll. As the conversation moved on to a debate about the best B-sides ever recorded, Rob decided to work out which magazine the rest of his friends were too.

Ian Two was sitting next to Phil. Although he worked with computers all day and sometimes all night he didn't like talking about them unless someone else brought up the subject. Ian Two could have been a magazine like *PC Monthly* or *Computer Shopper*, but his favourite talking point was films. Most of his conversation was based around films he'd seen, films he wanted to see, films in production. So he'd have to be a worn copy of *Empire* or, at a push, a dumbed-down *Sight and Sound*.

Darren was next to Ian. Of all Rob's friends Darren loved music most. He had a CD collection that ran into thousands, he knew about new bands before anyone else, and he still went regularly to gigs. Darren would be a glossy music magazine like *Q*, or an import issue of *Rolling Stone* – something that knows its stuff and doesn't mind telling you so.

Next to Darren was Ian Two's brother Kevin. He liked discussing politics, although he didn't express any particular affiliation. He thought all politicians were corrupt (secretly Rob believed that Kevin wouldn't be satisfied with any party unless he was its leader). Sometimes he sounded as if he was just to the left of Che Guevara; at others he was more akin to Margaret Thatcher (although it was unlikely that she would have punctuated every sentence with 'innit'). As a magazine, Kevin would be a dumbed-down version of *Private Eye* or possibly *New Statesman*, but with better jokes.

Ian One was next to Kevin, and straight away Rob thought he would be a football magazine, like *The Gooner*. Not that

Ian was uncomfortable talking about anything else – he was reasonably good on music, films, TV and life in general – but he seemed happier with football. The minute any conversation went that way he became more animated, like he'd suddenly found his top gear.

Finally, on Rob's right, there was Woodsy. Rob thought long and hard, but failed to come up with a satisfactory magazine for him. He agreed to get another round in, then said, 'A quick question.' He was taking advantage of a lull at the end of the B-side debate. 'If Woodsy was a magazine, which one would he be?'

Given the frequent inanity of their conversations, none of Rob's friends was the slightest bit fazed.

'He'd be one of those things that come in forty-eight parts with a ring binder,' said Ian Two.

'My dad collected one about steam trains,' chipped in Kevin.

'I used to get one when I was a kid,' added Darren. 'It was called the *Unexplained*, about the paranormal and freaky stuff.'

'That's it!' said Phil. 'That's Woodsy all over.'

'And what about Rob?' asked Woodsy.

In perfect unison they all said, '*Women's Weekly*,' and sat there laughing, until Rob was reminded to get off his backside and go to the bar.

At the end of the evening a sombre mood fell across them. The main group said goodbye, so Rob, Phil and Woodsy walked back to the house that would now be Phil and Woodsy's, rather than Phil and Rob's. Having spent months looking for somewhere else to live, Phil had decided that the best place for him was where he already was and promoted Woodsy from the sofa to Rob's room.

The next morning, Rob transferred his boxed and bin-bagged worldly goods into a hire van and said a final good-bye to Tooting and his friends.

'This is it, boys,' he said, as he climbed in.

'Send us a postcard from sunny Manchester, mate,' said Woodsy, as he waved Rob off from the front doorstep.

'Take it easy, mate,' said Phil, then he went over to the van and shook Rob's hand. 'Make sure you visit us soon.'

Rob's first Monday morning in Manchester

It was eleven o'clock on Rob's first Monday as a fully-fledged resident of Manchester. Having decided that he wasn't going to start work until the following week he had spent the morning setting up his new office in Ashley's guest bedroom and registering at the local doctor's surgery, then walking around Chorlton.

Rob had never lived anywhere like Chorlton in his life: it bore about as much similarity to Tooting as Clacton-on-Sea might to the French Riviera. The two places just didn't compare. Before Rob had started coming to Chorlton regularly to visit Ashley, he had never seen such a high concentration of vegan delicatessens, boutiques, café-bars, gastro pubs and restaurants outside places like Hampstead or Brighton. And, as far as he could determine, the entire area was populated chiefly by *Guardian* readers, actors, senior medical staff, vegans, journalists, musicians, BBC employees, Reiki healers and, that catch-all phrase for the educated and affluent, 'young professionals'. As Rob wandered aimlessly past the shops on High Lane, taking in the cool but crisp January day, he saw two actors from *Coronation Street*, a man in a woolly hat whom he was sure was the musician Badly Drawn Boy, a well-known club DJ *and* a local TV news presenter.

An hour later, having exhausted all of Chorlton's must-see

sights, including King Bee Records, North Star Deli and Chorlton Bookshop, he caught the 85 bus into the centre of Manchester. There, he visited Market Street, the Arndale Centre, the Triangle and the PrintWorks, then wandered up and down Deansgate and the area around King Street until he was exhausted.

As he left Waterstone's in St Anne Square, just after two o'clock, it began to rain heavily so he took shelter underneath the awning outside Dixon's. From this vantage-point he craned his neck to stare at the slate grey sky. People walking past him looked up too, as if they were expecting to glimpse a bird or a plane or even a suicide attempt from one of the roofs of the surrounding buildings. But there was nothing to see except the rain-filled clouds. And what had started as a pause to save himself from a soaking turned into a philosophical reverie.

He had only been in Manchester three days, yet he already missed London more than he had thought possible. He missed the familiarity of Oxford Street, the warmth of Covent Garden – even Londoners. Every now and again, as he stared at the sky, he overheard a passing conversation and the Manchester accent reminded him of all the times he'd been abroad and heard words spoken but had been unable to make sense of them. And for those few moments he was completely and utterly lost in translation.

Hanging on the telephone

Later that afternoon, back at Beech Road, Rob had tired of emptying boxes, setting up flat-pack shelves and finding new homes for his possessions, which had once had a perfect home in Tooting. At an all-time low, he picked up the phone and called Phil at work under the guise of finding out how Lee, the new graphic-design trainee, was coming along and to check up on the most recent project that had come in from a food-packaging client. On a social basis Rob and Phil rarely spoke on the phone for longer than a few minutes: one of Rob's proudest pub facts was that he and Phil had once called to arrange a drink and their conversation had lasted a staggering eight seconds and contained five words – a personal record.

Today, however, Rob established a new record – for endurance. Without even realising it, the two men were on the phone for over an hour (smashing a previous record of twenty-five minutes). Although they talked about work most of their conversation was taken up with matters they would normally have reserved for the pub. At one point Phil joked that, if they stayed on the line and opened a can of beer each, they could have a virtual drink together. Rob named their virtual pub the Telecom Arms and made himself landlord. Although it was a joke, he felt the same lump in his throat that he'd had on the night he had left London. Phone calls to Phil would never be the same as a pint and a chat with him in person.

'I'd better go, mate,' said Phil, at last. 'I've got a tonne of work still to do before I can think about going home.'

'Yeah, of course, mate,' said Rob, gathering himself together. 'No problem.' He paused, then added, 'Before you go, any idea when you and Woodsy might make the trip up here to sunny Manchester?'

'You're top of the list, mate,' said Phil, 'as soon as our workload goes down. The sooner you get your ISDN line the better.'

Rob laughed. 'They said it should be fitted by the beginning of next week, you slave-driver.'

'I emailed you a file this morning. Did you get it?'

'I've only just got the computer set up. I'll check it out in a minute. What is it?'

'Nothing much,' said Phil, 'but I guarantee you'll love it.'

'Right,' said Rob. 'And I'll send you the ideas I've had so far on the Voss-Pearce Consulting site.'

'Cheers,' said Phil. 'I'll take a look at them and mail you first thing in the morning.'

Rob pressed 'end call' and sank back into the sofa. He thought about unloading the dishwasher before Ashley got home but he couldn't be bothered. He thought about unpacking his suitcases but he couldn't be bothered with that either. Then he thought about the email Phil had sent him and suddenly found some energy. He took the stairs two at a time, ran into the spare room and turned on the computer.

Within minutes he was downloading the attachment on Phil's email, which turned out to be an MP3. As he listened to the track on his computer speakers, Rob found himself grinning, but as the song ended, he suddenly felt sad. He wouldn't have admitted it to anyone in the world, least of all himself, but he missed Phil – he missed him like he'd miss his right arm if he lost it. In fact, he thought, as he listened to the song again, I'd willingly give up a limb just to go for a drink and a chat about nothing with him. An arm. A leg. A foot. Pretty much anything.

Rob stood up, grabbed a blank CD-R from the desk behind him, dropped it into his computer tower and burned the solitary track on to it. Moments later he ejected the CD from his computer and clutching it in his hands he made his way downstairs to the kitchen.

Coming home

As Rob was going into the kitchen Ashley was pulling up outside the house. It had been a long, hard day at the hospital, but although she was exhausted, she was also elated to be coming home to Rob for the first time. She had been worrying all day about how he was settling in to being in Manchester – even while she was seeing patients – but had refrained from calling him for fear of overwhelming him. The fact was Ashley felt guilty. She felt guilty for having forced the issue. She felt guilty that he was now without friends. But mostly she felt guilty because while he had transformed his entire life for her, little in hers had changed. She was in the same house, doing the same job and could spend time with the same friends. She almost wished she could make a sacrifice equal to Rob's so that things wouldn't seem so unbalanced, but she couldn't think of anything that would come across as more than an empty gesture.

As she made her way up the path to the front door, rummaging in her bag for her house keys, she stopped and listened. She could hear music, which seemed louder the nearer she came to the house. She went inside and walked along the hallway to the kitchen. When she opened the door, the sight before her eyes made her laugh so hard and for so long that she felt as if she would never stop. Rob was standing on the oak kitchen table her parents had given her as a housewarming gift. Eyes closed, he was playing air guitar to a cheesy eighties-sounding rock song coming from the portable CD player on the kitchen counter.

Still laughing, Ashley walked over to the CD player and turned it down. Rob's eyes flew open and then he grinned at her. She was glad he seemed happy.

'Hey, you,' he said, still on the table. 'I didn't hear you come in.'

'Well, you wouldn't, would you, you nutter?' said Ashley. 'You wouldn't hear anything over that noise. What *was* that racket?'

'Van Halen,' he replied.

'Van Halen as in "Jump"?'

'The very same. Which is strange since I don't like "Jump" because it reminds me of school discos when everyone used to jump when they got to the chorus.'

'So what does *this* song remind you of?'

'It's called "Dreams" and reminds me of driving along Highway 61 in an open-topped Cadillac,' he replied. 'Not that I've ever done it, but I might one day.' He climbed down from the table and kissed her. 'Musically speaking, Phil's in a retro phase and he's been rediscovering the back catalogue of a certain Mr Eddie Van Halen. He emailed the song to me this morning saying, and I quote, "It rocked." He's right too. It does rock.'

'I knew he had to be involved in it somewhere,' said Ashley, putting down her bag. 'You two are like Thelma and Louise.' She smiled. 'Anyway, apart from listening to soft-rock anthems what else have you been up to? Highlights and lowlights.'

'My lowlight . . .' said Rob, and took a moment to think '. . . was getting caught in the rain in town today. I know it's

January but does it ever stop raining in this place? It's a wonder the United and City players haven't all got webbed feet. It's just so relentlessly grey here – it's as if it's in the air.'

'You get used to it,' Ashley told him. 'What about your highlight?'

A broad grin spread across his face. 'Opening my eyes a few seconds ago to see you standing in front of me.'

'That, my darling boyfriend, was the right answer.' Ashley kissed him again.

'How about you? How was your day?'

'My lowlight was shopping in the supermarket near the hospital at lunchtime. The queues were huge and there were no fresh vegetables. It was awful. I'm afraid it's just pasta for us tonight.'

Rob put his arms round her. 'And what was your highlight?'

'Oh, that's easy,' she replied. Without another word she took his hand and led him upstairs to their bedroom.

One day in Rob's life

It was three minutes past nine on the one-month anniversary of Rob's arrival in Manchester, and he was already swearing at his computer. It wasn't that it had crashed. It wasn't that it was no longer letting him do an important task. It wasn't even that he had accidentally deleted the last half-hour's work. He was swearing at his computer because he had just checked his email to discover that someone called Galactica2345 had outbid him on eBay, by a measly fifty pence, for a twelve-inch tall, boxed, fully jointed and posable Mr T doll.

He had intended it to be the jewel in the crown of the constantly evolving collection of items he had bought from eBay in the previous weeks. Before the move he had never had time to browse on eBay, but since he'd been in Manchester he'd become addicted to it. At first he couldn't think of anything he wanted but after he had come across an entry for a mint condition 1982 Action Man, he had decided that his 'thing' would be to collect toys from his youth. His hoard of what Ashley privately referred to as 'Rob's treasure trove of crap' now filled several shelves in his office. Rob looked forlornly at the space he'd cleared between his Six Million Dollar Man Transport and Repair Station (a bargain at £34.77) and his fully working Commodore 64 computer (not quite such a bargain at £122.98), then returned to his screen, deleted the offending email and opened up Dreamweaver.

It had not escaped his attention that there might be a direct correlation between the volume of items he was buying off eBay and the length of time he'd been without friends in Manchester. In fact, it had occurred to him that if he didn't acquire a social life soon there was a strong chance that he would end up owning absolutely everything he'd ever wanted in his life. And what would he do then? Why would he get out of bed in the mornings? How would he keep it together? eBay took his mind off how lonely he was. For the short period of time that he was logged on to the site he could forget his lack of friends and someone to talk to during the day and focus on things he could do something about: bidding against other socially challenged Internet geeks who, because they, too, were bidding in the middle of the day, must also work from home.

And that was Rob's main problem.

Working from home.

Other than fielding occasional work-related calls and emails from Phil, Rob was left to his own devices, which was the opposite of how his working day had been in London. In Wandsworth, Rob had spent his day taking calls from friends and arranging nights out for the week, holding meetings with Phil at the pub across the road from their office, occasionally dealing with a midday drop-in from Woodsy, looking for a companion and a lunchtime pint, as well as an awful lot of work. Now, however, his London friends weren't calling to arrange nights out, meetings were happening mostly over the phone, Woodsy was having his lunchtime pint alone and, with no interruptions, Rob was getting more work done than he'd ever done before.

Bad as things were, Rob took some consolation from the knowledge that at the end of the day he would be with Ashley. There were times when he felt as if it was only when she returned home that he could start living. So, when he wanted to go to the pub, he went with Ashley. When he wanted to go to the cinema, he went with Ashley. In fact, when he wanted to do anything outside the house but didn't want to do it alone, Ashley came with him. It wasn't just that Ashley gave Rob access to a social life, she *was* his social life.

As much as Rob hated to admit that he needed anything (until this point he had scoffed at the idea that 'no man is an island') the truth was that he did. And while Ashley was a great way of linking him to a social life on the mainland of humanity, Rob really needed some friends in Manchester whom he could call his own.

'I'm a Billy No-mates,' he explained to his mum, one Thursday evening when, to her surprise, he called her for a chat. 'I haven't got a single friend up here.'

She thought he was exaggerating, so he put her straight.

'I'm not making this up, Mum. And I'm not going to realise suddenly that actually, yes, I do have friends – like the old man who says hello to me in the corner shop, or the young couple who live in the house next door and smile at me whenever I get into my car. And your suggestion about the guy in the supermarket who always asks if I want help packing my bags? It's not true, Mum, none of these people are my friends. The old man who says hello in the corner shop can often be seen greeting various inanimate objects around Chorlton, including lamp-posts, mountain bikes chained to railings and the ancient Dr Barnado's box in the shape of a small child outside the newsagent's. The couple who live next door only say hello if, by mistake, they come out of their house at the same time as I'm coming out of mine. When they're on the ball they spot me first and either linger in their hallway, pretending to pick up the post until I've gone, or sprint down the path like Olympic athletes on steroids and drive off like the clappers. Honestly, Mum, it never ceases to amaze me just how far we English will go to avoid saying something as potentially embarrassing as 'Hello'.

'And as for the guy in the supermarket, I can tell by his voice that he doesn't care whether I want my bags packed or not. Why should he? He's probably got far more important things to worry about. So, to answer your question, have I made any new friends yet?, the answer is one hundred per cent, no.'

A night out with Neil

It was just after eight o'clock on the following Friday night and Rob was sitting at a table in the bar at the Cornerhouse Cinema on the junction of Oxford Road and Whitworth Street when he spotted his companion for the evening.

'Hello, mate,' said Neil, and shook Rob's hand formally. 'Good to see you.'

'Good to see you too,' said Rob.

'Have you been waiting long?' asked Neil, taking off his coat.

'No,' lied Rob, who had seen the same group of students wearing 'UMIST Hockey Club Pub Crawl Mania' T-shirts walk past the window twice.

'What are you drinking?' asked Neil.

'Carlsberg, if that's okay,' said Rob.

'Of course,' said Neil. 'I remember now. Ash once told me you're particular about your beer. So, you're a Carlsberg man?'

'I drink Guinness too,' added Rob, in an effort to make himself seem less picky. 'Although it depends what mood I'm in.'

'And you don't like anything else?'

Rob shook his head. 'I'm a bit weird like that.'

'Not at all,' replied Neil. 'If you know what you like why bother with anything else?' He smiled. 'I usually go for Tetley's but tonight I might join you in a Carlsberg.'

Rob watched Neil make his way to the bar and sighed. He was beginning to feel uncomfortable. He was well aware that Neil hadn't called out of the blue – he'd obviously been put up to it by Ashley. It was a pity drink, an invitation to go out based on nothing more than obligation to a friend. Rob had known this, yet had still said yes – out of politeness and genuine desperation.

Until now, the longest Rob had been away from his London friends was a three-week touring holiday he and Ashley had had in Canada two years ago and even then it had been almost too much for him. But the withdrawal symptoms he had experienced in recent weeks were much worse. Rob had days' worth of conversation stored in his head just waiting for an appreciative audience. One night, as he and Ashley lay in bed, basking in post-coital bliss, some of it had leaked out.

'Which do you think is U2's best album?' he had asked.

'Pardon?' responded Ashley, taken aback.

'You know,' he had continued, 'U2, as in the rock band. Which do you think is their best album?'

'Well, the only one I've got is *The Best of: 1980–1990*,' she replied.

'You *can't* count compilation albums,' Rob had chided. '*Studio* albums *only*.'

'What are you on about? Why are there rules to this conversation suddenly?'

'Never mind.' Rob had turned on to his side and decided that the answer to his question was a tough choice between *The Joshua Tree* (an obvious crowd-pleaser) and *War* (still obvious but not quite as easy to love). But there could be only one winner: which would he choose?

'Have I done something wrong?' Ashley had asked.

'It's just me.' Rob had sighed and turned back to her. 'I've got a lot on my mind.'

Ashley had reached across to her bedside table and switched off the light. Rob lay quietly in the darkness next to her; when her breathing had slowed into the rhythm of sleep he had closed his eyes to join her. And just as he'd been about to drift off, he'd whispered, '*The Joshua Tree* – definitely.'

The following evening, out of the blue, Neil had called.

'So,' said Neil, returning from the bar, 'how are you settling in? Weather not too much for you?'

'Everything's pretty good, actually,' said Rob.

'And you like Chorlton?'

'Yeah. It's a nice place.'

'It is,' confirmed Neil. 'Very nice indeed.'

There was a long pause and the two men simultaneously took sips of their beer. Rob was just about to ask Neil about his car, a four-year-old black Porsche Boxter, when Neil suddenly reeled off the first of a huge list entitled 'Questions to ask Rob should the evening get a bit tough'. It was bizarre. He enquired about the hardware and software Rob used at work, projects he was working on and the graphic-design industry. Then he moved on to music: what were the latest CDs Rob had bought, who did he think should've won last year's Mercury music prize, did Rob rate Badly Drawn Boy – Neil knew somebody who knew somebody who drank in the same pub as him. Then he moved on to films: what films had Rob seen lately; had he heard of various new releases. Neil went on like this, frantically covering topic after topic, as though the evening would fall apart if he stopped for a moment. But it wasn't a conversation they were having – at least, not in the sense that Rob used the word: it was an interrogation, brought on by the fact that the two men simply weren't clicking. Rob was a square peg and Neil was a round hole.

Just after ten thirty things started to get really desperate. The silences between them were longer and they were scouring the bar's clientele for inspiration, but as Neil was Ashley's friend and Rob was Ashley's boyfriend they couldn't even pass comment on the small number of attractive women around them. It became obvious to Rob that the evening would soon grind to a halt, leaving them both embarrassed and stranded in conversational limbo. However, just as he was about to excuse himself and go to the gents' for the third time in the last half-hour, Neil introduced a subject on which they both had something to say: Ashley.

They talked about her early days at college and exchanged amusing stories about her. They dissected her positive personality traits, and even a few of the negative ones. And for what remained of the evening, even though she was at home preparing for some up-and-coming exams, it was as if she was a third person sitting at their table.

Several times Neil made a few carefully-thought-out jokes about her, which were accurate enough to make Rob laugh, but not so accurate as to indicate that he knew her better than Rob. In return Rob made a few jokes about her that got a belly laugh from Neil, but made it clear – even though it hadn't needed pointing out – that no one knew her better than he did.

At the end of the night they went their separate ways without making a plan to meet up again. There was no doubt in Rob's mind that Neil lacked the potential to be a new Phil because the only thing they had in common was Ashley. And friendship, as far as Rob was concerned, would never grow out of that.

Party fears

'How did you get on?' asked Ashley. 'Meet any nice people?'

'It was a complete waste of time,' replied Rob. 'Honestly, we ought to go home now.'

It was quarter to eleven on a Saturday night in March, two months into Rob's new life in Manchester. He and Ashley were in nearby Didsbury at a party given by Ashley's work friend, Miranda, to celebrate her husband Carl's thirty-seventh birthday. Before he and Ashley had arrived at Miranda and Carl's, Rob had been reasonably optimistic about the party. He had still not made a single new friend and, dissatisfied by the sporadic contact he had with his London mates, had persuaded himself that this party was his big opportunity to find one. From the moment he had walked through the door until now he had worn his most welcoming expression, attempted to be at his most charming and generally sent out the most positive vibes he could muster to anyone who would have them.

'What went wrong?' asked Ashley. 'When I last saw you in the kitchen you were really positive about tonight.'

'Where to begin?' asked Rob, unable to hide his frustration. 'I should've known what kind of do this would be when Miranda kept referring to it as a "gathering" instead of a party. It's a gathering, all right. A gathering of the undead. Where's the fun? Where's the dancing? Where's the atmosphere?' Rob pointed to a balding young man in jeans and a T-shirt talking to a plumpish woman in denim dungarees. 'Look at him! He's drinking Pepsi Max.'

'How do you know?' asked Ashley.

'Because I've been watching him all night. And he's not alone. Half the people here are on soft-drinks.'

'And that's a crime, is it?' Ashley laughed. 'Who died and made you Minister of Boozing?'

'It's not a crime,' said Rob. 'At least, not yet. But the only reason so many people are on soft-drinks is because they've driven here. Why didn't they get a minicab like most normal people? I'll tell you why. It's because they're only here to prove to themselves that they still go to parties, even though they never drink, rarely talk to anyone new and always leave before midnight, thereby missing out on the reasons why people go to parties in the first place.'

Ashley looked embarrassed. 'Will you keep your voice down?' she whispered hoarsely. 'One of Miranda's friends might overhear.' She added, 'Look, I know they might not be the most exciting people in the world and, yes, some of them are a bit stuffy, but give them a break, Rob.'

'I *have*. I really have. Since I left you talking to Miranda I've had around eleven different conversations.'

'Well, that's good, isn't it?'

'Now ask me how many of those conversations were about house prices in Chorlton and Didsbury.'

'Six,' replied Ashley, laughing.

Rob shook his head. 'How about all of them?'

'All of them?' repeated Ashley, incredulously.

'Every single one. That's eleven different conversations with eleven different people about the price of bricks and mortar in south Manchester. It's unbelievable, Ash. Do people talk about nothing else round here?'

'It's an easy conversation starter,' explained Ashley. 'It can't offend anyone – apart from you. Anyway, stuff like houses, DIY and renovation, foreign holidays, jobs, kids and things we read in the weekend papers is important to people our age.'

'But it's not what I talk about with Phil and Woodsy,' said Rob.

'That's because all you guys ever talk about are those weird sort of nebulous bloke topics that you can never remember afterwards. I've lost count of the times when I've listened to your so-called conversations and haven't been any the wiser. As far as I can see, you all take it in turns to be the butt of each other's jokes, do a lot of blokey laughing and one of you tells a daft story about something that happened at work and you laugh some more. It's like watching one of those New Wave French films where nothing happens v-e-r-y s-l-o-w-l-y.'

Rob laughed. To a degree, Ashley was right. He could never remember what he and his friends had talked about after a night at the pub. But often a night at the pub wasn't so much about talking as it was about sharing each other's company. Some of the best nights he'd ever had with Phil and Woodsy had involved nothing more complicated than a four-pack of Carlsberg, a few packets of crisps and an evening of good telly.

'Well,' began Rob, trying a different line of attack, 'do you know what else the people I met tonight spoke about?'

'Enlighten me.'

'Their jobs.' Rob looked round the room. 'You see that guy in the glasses and the pale yellow golfing jumper?' Ashley nodded. 'He's a sales manager for a freight company in Stockport. And the guy with cropped hair in the blue shirt?' Ashley nodded again. 'The director of a regional radio-plugging firm.'

'And your point is?'

'Well, while I can tell you a dozen facts about any of these people – which I won't – do you know what they could tell you about me?'

'What?'

'Nothing,' said Rob. 'Not a single one asked me what I did for a living.'

'But you don't want to be asked what you do for a living, do you?'

'That's not the point,' said Rob. 'They weren't interested. I'm never going to make friends up here if everyone I meet is like this. I'm beginning to empathise with those *Sex and the City* girls, banging on about how there are no eligible men left in New York because all the good ones have been taken. That's how I feel. All the good male friends have been grabbed and all that's left are these boring, self-interested thirty-something zombies who can only talk about their jobs and house prices.'

'Come on,' said Ashley, 'don't give up yet. How about this? We give it one more hour, you mingle a bit more and then, if it's still not happening for you, I promise we'll go home.'

'One more hour?'

'Yes.'

'Okay. You're on.'

'Look,' said Ashley, waving at a post-pub influx of people, 'Chris, Bella and that lot have arrived. You've never really talked to them . . . and I'm pretty sure they won't go on about house prices. Maybe you should try them tonight.'

'In a bit,' replied Rob, despondently. 'But now I need to take a leak.'

Bathroom buddy

Rob was on the stairs waiting to go to the loo. There were at least six people ahead of him and although he had been standing in the queue for a few minutes it wasn't getting any shorter. As minutes passed by others became restless and a rumour circulated that a woman had locked herself into the bathroom in floods of tears. Rob was mildly amused by his companions' restrained indignation. At last, he thought, a tearful woman in a locked bathroom – no party's complete without one.

Gradually the queue diminished as another rumour spread of a loo somewhere on the ground floor. Soon only Rob and a tallish man in a blue shirt and cream chinos were still waiting.

'Hi,' said the man, turning to Rob. 'Pleased to meet you. I'm Jono Adams – I'm mates with Miranda's husband Carl.'

'Hi,' said Rob, and shook his hand. 'I'm Rob, Ashley McIntosh's partner – I think I met you briefly at Miranda and Carl's wedding.'

'Ah, yes,' said Jono. 'I thought I recognised you. You've just moved here from London. Miranda asked me a while ago if I'd go for a drink with you – introduce you to a few people up here. Can't remember why I didn't get in touch. Still, I expect you're settled now.'

'Yeah,' replied Rob. 'Absolutely.'

'What do you think's going on in there?' said Jono, jabbing a finger at the bathroom door.

Rob shrugged. 'Don't know. Do you think we should tell Miranda or somebody?'

Jono shook his head. 'Leave it to me,' he said, and proceeded to bang on the door so hard that Rob thought it would fly off its hinges.

'Hello?' bellowed Jono. 'Is anyone in there?'

There was no reply.

'Right,' said Jono, 'I'm going to find a screwdriver and do something about it.'

At that moment there was a metallic click from inside the bathroom. The handle turned and the door opened to reveal a pretty, dark-haired girl in a green top and jeans. She had dark brown eyes, and an open, almost innocent face. Even though she had done her best to tidy herself up it was clear that she had been crying.

'About time too,' said Jono. Then, without another word, he brushed past the girl into the bathroom and locked the door.

'Are you all right?' asked Rob. The girl was leaning on the wall as if she was trying to keep herself upright.

'I'm fine,' she replied, in a light Manchester accent.

'You don't look fine.'

'It's nothing. I've just had a bit too much to drink, that's all. I'll be fine.' She took a step forward but completely misjudged it and would have fallen over if Rob hadn't stepped forward to catch her.

'Listen,' he said, helping her to sit down on the stairs, 'just have a rest for a bit.'

She nodded and looked up at him. 'Don't suppose you've got a ciggie, have you?'

'I don't smoke, I'm afraid.'

She sighed heavily, stood up and started to go down the stairs.

'Where are you off to now?' asked Rob.

'I need a smoke. There's an all-night garage up the road. Sean and I drove past it in the taxi on the way here.'

Rob wondered who 'Sean' was and, more importantly, why he wasn't looking after this girl, who clearly needed it.

'Are you sure about walking there on your own at this time of night?'

'I'll be okay,' she replied. 'Thanks for asking, though.'

'Well, how about this?' said Rob, as they reached the bottom stair. ' You stay here and I'll nip out to get your fags for you.'

'You'd do that for me?' asked the girl.

'It's not a big deal. I don't want anything bad to happen to you.'

'Well, I need some fresh air. How about we both go?'

'Are you sure?' asked Rob. 'You don't know me.'

'Yeah, I do,' she replied. 'You're the bloke who's being nice to me. What more do I need to know?'

'Well, how about my name for starters?' Rob held out his hand. 'I'm Rob.'

'I'm Jo,' said the girl. 'Pleased to meet you.'

Down and out in Didsbury

'So,' said Rob, as they headed up the road towards the garage. It was cold now and their coats were buttoned to the chin. 'What do you do?'

'Oh, not that again.' Jo sighed. 'Why is everyone so obsessed with what people do for a living?'

Rob laughed. 'I only asked because I've been conditioned into it by everyone I've met tonight.'

Jo smiled. 'I'll forgive you. But why don't we have a conversation where we don't talk about what we do for a living, where we live, where we're from and, above all, why I locked myself in the bathroom?'

'I can't even ask that? Why not?'

'Because, believe me, the answer will bore you as much as it frustrates me.'

'So, what do you want me to do? Talk about myself?'

'Oh, no,' said Jo, quickly. 'At the minute I think you're an okay bloke but if I find out too much about you I might change my mind. Let's stick to general chit-chat.'

Rob found himself smiling at her. He couldn't help it. There was something about her that was instantly appealing. She was attractive, too, but he was sure she wasn't flirting with him, just being her slightly oddball, slightly depressed, slightly drunken self. 'What do you fancy talking about?' he asked.

'Anything.'

'Well, what interests you?'

'No, no, no, no,' said Jo, wagging a finger. 'I can see what you're doing and it won't work.'

Rob was confused. 'I wasn't doing anything.'

'If I'd answered your question I'd have given away something about myself – that I like flowers or Johnny Depp films before he went all rubbish. Things that would've revealed far too much about me. Anyway, there's no skill in talking about stuff like that. Whatever happened to real conversation?'

'It's alive and kicking . . . somewhere.' Rob grinned.

He stopped when they reached the end of the road. 'If this isn't too personal a question – right or left?'

'I thought it was right,' said Jo, 'but I might be mistaken. I'm rubbish with directions.'

'I think left.'

'Fair enough,' replied Jo. 'What do I know about anything?'

Walking and talking

'Okay,' said Jo. 'Here's a topic of conversation for you.'

'Go on,' said Rob.

'Us,' she replied. 'You. Me. Here. Right now. We're a topic of conversation.'

'We are?'

'I think so.'

'In what way?'

'In every way. For instance, you're a bloke and I'm not.'

Rob nodded. 'Well spotted.'

'Well, isn't that interesting?'

'In what way?'

'Well,' she began, pushing her hands deeper into her pockets, 'what do you think is happening here?'

'Is it a trick question?' asked Rob. 'Because as far as I'm aware we're looking for a garage so you can buy some fags.'

'But why?'

'Because you smoke.'

Jo laughed. 'But why are you here with me?'

Finally Rob caught on to what she was getting at. 'Do you think I'm here because I fancy you?'

'I doubt it. I'm guessing I'm not your type.'

Rob laughed. 'And my type would be?'

'That blonde girl I saw you talking to earlier. Girlfriend?'

'I thought we weren't doing personal information.'

'You're right,' said Jo. 'And I'm too nosy for my own good sometimes.'

'I bet you are,' replied Rob. 'But, yes, that was my girl-friend. Now back to the topic in hand.'

'Too late,' said Jo coming to a halt. She pointed across the road to the brightly lit forecourt of a Shell garage. 'We're here . . . Do you want anything?' she asked, as they reached the other side of the road. 'I mean from the garage,' she added. 'Some chocolate maybe?'

'No, thanks,' said Rob.

'How about chewing-gum?'

'No,' said Rob, as they approached the cashier's window where a lone bearded man was sitting. 'I'm fine.'

Jo seemed disappointed. 'I can't get you anything at all?' She laughed. 'I'm not your type, you've got a stunning girlfriend and I can't get you any chocolate – what a great night this is.' She walked up to the cashier's window. 'Hi,' she said to the man, 'I'd like some Golden Virginia, a packet of filters and some Rizlas.'

The man reached to the shelf behind him. 'Which papers do you want?' he asked. 'Red or blue?'

'Blue,' said Jo, smiling, 'like your eyes.'

The man, whose eyes were quite clearly dark brown, laughed raucously.

'Oh, and can I have some chocolate?' she asked, then mulled over what to choose. 'A Twix and – no,' she corrected herself, 'a Dairy Milk, one of the large bars, and a Caramel too.' She added, by way of explanation, 'I've had a bit of a rough night.' She dipped into her bag and pulled out a ten-pound note, which she slipped under the protective counter shield before the man had scanned in the items that were now piled up beside the till.

As he passed her her change and the purchases Jo peered through the Plexiglas at the name-tag on the man's jumper. 'Thank you, Barrington Farrelly,' she said, with a smile. 'Hope you have a good night.' Barrington Farrelly smiled and nodded at her.

'Do you mind if we sit over there while I roll myself a ciggie?' she asked Rob, indicating the low wall that enclosed the forecourt.

'Not at all,' he replied, and they walked across to it, then sat down. Rob watched as she opened the rolling tobacco, filters and papers, then began to construct a cigarette. She dropped two moderate pinches of tobacco on to a paper, then rolled it between her forefingers and thumbs until the contents were tight enough for her to add a filter. Once this was done she licked the gummed edge and sealed it. The whole process took less than a minute. She held up the cigarette and grinned.

'Perfect,' she said, admiring her handiwork.

'I wouldn't know,' said Rob. 'I've never smoked rollies – even when I did smoke. I could never be bothered with all that fiddling. How come you don't smoke proper cigarettes?'

'Does it bother you?' asked Jo.

'Not really,' said Rob. 'It's just that . . . well, I'm curious. Not just about you, but about people like you who smoke rollies. I mean, what's it all about? You can clearly afford to buy proper grown-up cigarettes, so why make out you're still a poverty-stricken student?'

'You're a right cheeky sod when you want to be.'

'Really?' replied Rob. 'That's news to me.'

'Why do I do this?' Jo examined her cigarette. 'Because it's creative. I made it. No one else, just me. A minute ago it didn't exist and now it does. And, right now, making rollies is the only creative pleasure I have.'

Rob laughed. 'Why don't you take up painting or pottery or something?'

'I once wrote a novel,' said Jo, casually. 'Does that count?'

'I'm impressed. Was it published?'

'If it was, do you think I'd be making roll-ups as a creative outlet?' Jo stood up and waved at an oncoming black cab. 'Listen,' she said, turning to Rob. 'It's been lovely – you've been lovely – but I'd better get off.'

'Of course.' Rob held out his hand and she shook it. 'It was nice to meet you, Jo.'

'And it was nice to meet you, too.' She kissed his cheek. 'Thanks for looking after me,' she whispered, 'and tell your girlfriend from me she's a lucky woman.'

Rob watched as she climbed into the cab and it began to move off. Just as he was about to turn away, though, it stopped abruptly. Jo wound down her window. 'I've got something for you,' she called, as Rob walked over to the cab. 'I'm keeping the chocolate but I want you to have all this.' She handed Rob the tobacco, filters and Rizla papers. 'What's this for?' asked Rob looking at the items in his hands.

'For you,' Jo replied. 'Because everybody needs a bit of creativity in their lives sometimes.'

The taxi pulled off again and Rob watched until it had disappeared.

When he got back to the party he found Ashley talking to the same group of friends she had been with when he left.

'How did you get on?' asked Ashley. 'Meet anyone new?'

'I did, actually,' replied Rob, almost wistfully, 'but I doubt I'll see them again.' He changed the subject. 'Are you ready to make a move, then?'

'That was the deal,' said Ashley, and kissed him. 'Let's go home.'

Desperado

'Hey, you,' said Rob, into his mobile.

'Hey, babe,' replied Ashley. 'Just calling to see what you're up to.'

'Nothing much. I'm about to go to the cinema.'

'On your own? Sorry . . . I shouldn't have said it like that. Do you want me to come with you? I can meet up with the girls another day.'

'You're fine,' said Rob. 'Anyway, I know how you ladies like your girl time together. I'll see you at home, okay?'

'Okay,' she said, reluctantly.

It was just after half past one on a relatively warm Saturday afternoon in May and Rob was sitting alone at a table in Bar 38 on Peter Street. He put his phone on the table in front of him and wondered why he had told Ashley he was at the cinema when she was sure to ask him about the film. He shook his head and looked down at the items on the table in front of him: an iPod (a happy-moving-in gift from Ashley, which gave him the illusion of not being alone), a pen and notebook (for noting down design ideas he was working on for clUNKEE mUNKEE) and a packet of cigarettes. Anyone who knew Rob well would have spotted which was the odd one out: he had given up smoking in his mid-twenties, yet a gold packet of B&H lay beside his Guinness.

Rob took a deep breath, tore off the Cellophane wrapper, screwed it into a ball, tore into the silver paper and plucked out a cigarette. He put it to his lips and bravely scanned the bar. This is it, he thought, my way in. A cigarette and nothing to light it with.

A slight interlude

Four months had now elapsed since the move to Manchester and Rob had still to make a friend. The day after the party in March, Rob had told Ashley, much to her surprise, that he was so desperate to make new friends in Manchester that he was prepared to accept the help from her that he'd previously declined – namely, to ask her female friends if they knew anyone who might fancy going for a drink with him. To this end, a week later Rob had met up with Peter Nicholls, the brother of Ashley's work friend, Lucy. He was thirty-nine and had been an army engineer since his early twenties but had recently left to work in his dad's haulage firm in Bolton. Ashley thought that because Peter had once seen the Rolling Stones at Wembley and Rob had their *Greatest Hits* in his CD collection they would have 'loads to talk about'.

When Peter had called Rob to arrange the date, however, they hadn't talked about the Rolling Stones. They'd talked about squash and Peter had insisted they play a game rather than go to the pub. Rob hadn't played squash since university but was willing to give it a go and the two men had played four consecutive games, all of which Peter had won without conceding a point. The humiliation didn't end there: in the bar of the sports hall Peter had sunk two pints of Fosters in the time it had taken Rob to get half-way through a single pint of Guinness. And at the end of the night – having continued at that pace all evening – Peter had been so drunk that Rob had had to bundle him into the back of a minicab and pay the driver an extra ten pounds to deliver him direct to his front door.

At the beginning of May Rob had gone for a drink with Stuart Farley, a Salford-based probation officer. Ashley had been getting her hair cut and telling Sian, her stylist, about Rob's predicament when Sian had told her that Stuart, her former lodger, had found it difficult to make friends too. At Stuart's suggestion they had met up at the Wellington Arms in the city centre. Stuart had been nice enough and the conversation was relatively okay until Stuart confessed he was a real-ale enthusiast. This wasn't Rob's thing but in an attempt to be more open-minded he had persuaded Stuart to tell him more about it and wished immediately that he hadn't. Out of a battered satchel Stuart had pulled out a black notebook in which he had listed every pub he had been to in the last ten years. Beside each one's name were a number of elaborate symbols representing 'essential categories', covering comfort, bar staff's knowledge of ale, the décor and service. Rob hadn't had the heart to tell Stuart that he only drank Carlsberg and Guinness. At the end of the evening Stuart had told him that he had enjoyed himself immensely and suggested they meet up again because the Black Horse in Salford was having a Special Beers of the World festival. A few days later Stuart had called and left a message on Rob's mobile but Rob hadn't called him back.

A week later Rob had met up with Russell, a twenty-seven-year-old junior doctor who was new to Manchester. Ashley had told Rob that she was sure they would get on because Russell liked 'good music and good films'. At Russell's insistence they had met up in a bar called Prague V. Rob hadn't been there before, and he liked Russell immediately. He was cool without being *too* cool. At the end of the night Russell had said he'd enjoyed himself and would call Rob to arrange another night out soon. But when no call had come by the beginning of the following week Rob had had his doubts. Finally, at Ashley's insistence, he had called Russell and left a message on his mobile. When a few more days had gone by with no word from him, Rob had contemplated leaving another message and had half dialled his number – *Maybe he's lost mine*, he thought, *or can't retrieve his voicemail. Maybe . . .* And that was when it had struck him: he'd been blown out and he hadn't even realised it. Rob had done the I-promise-I'll-call-you thing with women more times than he cared to remember, and now it had happened to him. Ashley had apologised on Russell's behalf, but Rob had told her not to worry. 'When you want to make friends with someone,' he'd explained, 'you've both got to get That Feeling. Because if you don't there's no point in trying to fake it.'

The following Saturday Rob had decided it was time he took control of his own destiny. Which was why he was now in Bar 38 with a cigarette and no lighter.

Desperado (part two)

To Rob's left there was a group of ridiculously good-looking Spaniards: two guys and two girls. One girl had dreadlocks; the other's nose was pierced. Although all four were smoking heavily, and therefore potential candidates for Rob's experiment, they were also wearing sunglasses indoors which, to Rob's mind, immediately disqualified them.

Behind the Spaniards he could see another table of smokers, this time a couple of student-looking guys talking animatedly. One had long hair tied back in a ponytail while the other wore a baseball cap and was cultivating his facial hair into something approaching a full-on beard. Rob strained to hear their conversation and having picked out words like 'rehearsals' and 'auditions' and 'the director' it became clear to him that they were actors. He shuddered as he recalled a conversation he had once had with an actor called Victor, whom he had met during a Christmas party a few years earlier. In the middle of a conversation about the difficulties of getting a black cab during the Christmas season Victor (for no good reason that Rob could see) had begun stripping off his clothes, until he was standing in the middle of the room wearing only his boxer shorts, fully aware that he had the attention of the room. In his best actorly voice he had announced to Rob and everyone else: 'Sometimes I can't help but express what I'm feeling inside.' That night Rob vowed that as long as he had breath in his body he would never again make the mistake of opening a conversation with anyone in the theatrical fraternity. Although these two men looked nothing like Victor he couldn't take the chance.

Finally, Rob's gaze locked on to a man of roughly his own age, sitting alone. Today Rob was in jeans, a black sweatshirt and green camouflage All Stars baseball boots and the other man was dressed similarly. On the table in front of him was an iPod, a pint of lager and a packet of Silk Cut. He'd got a lit cigarette in one hand and was engrossed in a novel.

Rob checked him out covertly. *He doesn't seem overly bothered about sitting in a bar on his own* thought Rob. *He's drinking a pint, which is always a good sign – although I don't know of what. And if he's got an iPod he must be into music, a bonus. All in all, he looks like my type of guy.*

Rob took a deep breath and stood up. His chair legs screeched on the floor loudly enough to gain the attention of the Spanish group and the actors. Fortunately the guy with the book didn't look up or Rob would have lost his nerve and abandoned his mission. He straightened the chair and, cigarette in hand, began the long walk to the man with the book. The closer Rob got to him the more detail he noticed: he was quite good-looking, with heavy eyebrows and a light scattering of faded freckles across the bridge of his nose. He had dark brown hair, and a slightly Mediterranean complexion. Right now, however, none of those details mattered to Rob: what mattered was that he didn't lose his nerve before he did what he had to do.

'Sorry to bother you, mate,' he said, on reaching the book guy's table. 'I was just wondering if I could have a light?' He waved his unlit cigarette in the air apologetically for emphasis.

''Fraid not, mate,' said the book guy, in an immediately

recognisable Manchester accent. 'I had to get one off those guys over there.' He pointed to the Spaniards. 'But you can bum a light off this, if you like,' he said, offering Rob his cigarette.

With a big smile Rob took it, held the lit end to his own and dragged deeply. The book guy then returned to his novel and Rob berated himself: *Come on, idiot! Say something! Anything! Don't just stand there staring like you're in love with him.*

The only topics that sprang to mind in the seconds available were:

1. The weather.
2. Why smoking is bad for you.
3. The real reason why he hadn't got a light of his own.

Rob didn't use them. Instead, once the tip of his cigarette was glowing, he said a very blokey 'Cheers, mate, nice one', and handed back the book guy's cigarette. He then returned to his table, plugged his iPod's headphones into his ears and pressed play. And although he stayed in the bar for a further half-hour finishing his pint and doodling on his notepad while he worked his way through an iPod playlist he had earlier entitled 'How Gay Is This?', he didn't attempt to speak to anyone else.

When Ashley arrived home around five, laden with carrier-bags from her afternoon's shopping, the first thing she asked was 'How was the film?' Without blinking an eyelid, Rob just shrugged and said it was so boring he'd fallen asleep. He felt bad about lying to Ashley, he really did, but the last thing he wanted was for her to think she was living with a man so desperate for male company that he hung around city-centre bars trying to make new friends.

Even if it was true.

Birthday

BlueBar on Chorlton's Wilbraham Road, just a bit down from Safeway, wasn't the sort of place Rob would normally have chosen to celebrate his birthday, but as he had now been in Manchester for a full six months he had no choice. In London he would have gone to one of the many old-men's pubs that he and his friends frequented, like their regular haunt the Queen's Head, with its desperately cheap beer promotions, or failing that, the Nag's Head in Balham, where Woodsy had once bought a TV for a tenner from a man hawking electrical goods from the back of a white mini-van, or the Bell and Basin in Clapham, which, when it came to licensing laws, was a law unto itself. They had certain characteristics in common that spoke volumes about the kind of people Rob's friends were: the absence of a jukebox (so that they could talk without yelling), a lack of interior design (because how a pub looked didn't matter to them) and no women under five foot five with all their own teeth (because no matter how much pleasure there was to be gained from observing attractive women, even they needed the odd night off).

But while Rob preferred pubs such as the Queen's Head, he didn't mind BlueBar. And as Ashley and her friends practically lived there he didn't have much choice. When-ever he went in with her there was always a good crowd of people there. People like Rob. Young men and women in their late twenties and early thirties with larger-than-average record collections, interesting haircuts and an attitude to fashion that said, 'I haven't given up quite yet.' He was going so often that he'd begun to recognise several faces even if he didn't know their owners to talk to. *What makes matters worse*, he thought, *is that they all look like the kind of people I could be friends with.*

The four guys at the bar.

The three guys smoking at a table near the window.

The two guys in suits finishing off their pints near the cigarette machine.

They all had the potential to be Rob's brand new Phil.

That evening Rob was surrounded by friends. They just weren't *his*. They were inherited friends, friends by proxy, Ashley's friends. Ashley had invited them to come out and celebrate his birthday: Christine and Joel, Luke and Lauren, Jason and Louise, Mia and Edwin and, of course, Neil.

'Happy birthday, mate!' said Christine, kissing Rob as she handed him a pint of lager.

'Cheers,' said Rob, eyeing the group of men at the bar. They were similarly dressed in jeans, T-shirts and trainers, and were laughing and joking among themselves. Why aren't I celebrating my birthday with you guys? he thought bitterly.

'You're only as old as the woman you feel,' joked Jason, as he sidled up to Rob with a grin.

Rob smiled at him uncomfortably.

'The woman he's feeling feels great to me,' replied Luke, squeezing Ashley's bottom. 'One hundred per cent peach.'

Rob's eyes flicked to Luke's hand, then to Ashley's bottom and back to Luke's face. Luke was always doing stuff like that to show Rob he'd known Ashley so much longer than Rob had that he could pinch her bottom secure in the knowledge that Rob couldn't say a word without seeming churlish.

'You can't do that to Rob's bird right in front of him – not on his birthday of all days,' chided Neil. 'Wait until tomorrow!'

Rob tried to laugh but his heart wasn't in it. Instead he smiled politely as if that was shorthand for genuine laughter and continued to scan the bar for more fantasy friends. He spotted some immediately – two guys at a table near the door. One was wearing a grey suit, the other faded bootcut cord trousers and a grey hooded top. Rob wondered whether they were talking about the latest series of *Alias*, which had just started on cable, because that was a conversation he was dying to have with someone who actually cared.

'Stop teasing him, you lot,' reprimanded Ashley, taking Rob's hand and giving it a squeeze of solidarity. 'It's his birthday. Give the man a break.'

Rob smiled his first genuine smile of the evening. No matter what situation he found himself in, Ashley could always make him feel all right – if only for a little while. He didn't doubt that he loved her or that he wanted to be with her. And right now, at this moment, he was sure that if there was anyone for whom he would have endured the torture of the last six months, it was Ashley. 'Do you know what?' he whispered in her ear.

'What?'

'I really love you.'

'Good,' said Ashley. 'Because I love you too.'

Rob took a long sip of the birthday pint Christine had bought him and gagged. He held up the glass and sighed heavily.

'It's the wrong beer, isn't it?' said Ashley, wincing.

He continued to stare at it as if it embodied the essence of his disappointment in life.

Ashley took the glass from him and sipped. 'It tastes fine to me – in as much as it tastes like lager.' She handed it back to him. 'I don't know why you're making such a fuss about it. How different can one make of beer be from all the others?'

'I'm not ungrateful,' explained Rob. 'In fact I really appreciate Christine's buying me a pint on my birthday. But I don't like whatever this is. Have you ever, in all the time I've known you, seen me drink any other beer apart from Carlsberg or Guinness?'

'No,' said Ashley.

'Exactly. I don't drink Grolsch, Stella Artois, Red Stripe, Löwenbraü, Leffe, Foster's, Castlemaine, Budweiser, Becks, Budvar, Staropramen, cheap no-name brewery lagers with fake-sounding German names, Miller or Tennent's. Yes technically they are all lagers, but they're not the lagers I like.'

'They all look the same to me.'

'The truth is, babe, while they might look the same they're not the same. Some I like. Some I don't. It's just a matter of taste.'

As he spoke, it struck Rob that the way he felt about lagers was the way he felt about friends. He'd always been particular about the kind of people he spent time with, which was why leaving his friends in London had hurt so much. It wasn't that he had always befriended the coolest, the most amusing or the most popular people – on the contrary, a number of his London friends were the most uncool, humourless and unpopular characters anyone could hope to meet. But the bottom line was that, just as with lager, there were some people in life he liked and others he couldn't stand.

'I'll get you another drink,' said Ashley.

'Nah,' he replied. 'I'll get you one, but first I ought to say an official thank-you.' He cleared his throat and raised his pint in the air, commanding Ashley's friends' attention.

'Quiet, everyone,' said Mia. 'Rob's going to make a birth-day speech.'

'I just wanted to thank you all for coming,' he said, looking at his glass philosophically. 'And . . . er, that's it, really.'

Everyone raised a glass, cheered, then immediately re-sumed the conversations they'd been having before he interrupted them.

'Thanks for doing this,' said Rob, turning to Ashley.

'Doing what?'

'Forcing your mates to come out on my birthday.'

'I didn't force them,' she said, squeezing his hand. 'They wanted to be here. They're your friends as well as mine.'

'You know as well as I do that I have no real friends here.'

Ashley opened her mouth as if to refute his claim, then closed it again.

'And I have to admit that having no friends is making me feel like a bit of a loser . . .' He trailed off.

Ashley squeezed his hand again. 'You're not a loser,' she reassured him, 'and you've got friends. It's just that they live in a different city.'

'I can't see how things are going to change,' said Rob. 'It's virtually impossible to make new friends when you get to your thirties. People my age don't want any more friends. They've got all the different kinds of friends they need for every eventuality. It's a closed shop. In fact, I think people at our age actively shed friends.'

'That's so not true.'

'Really? Then tell me this. When was the last time you made a new friend? And by "friend" I mean proper friend.

Not just someone you're on nodding terms with. I mean a going-for-a-drink-sharing-secrets-doing-each-other's-hair-remembering-their-birthday-asking-after-their-parents-not-worrying-if-it's-two-o'clock-in-the-morning-and-you-want-to-call-them-because-you're-having-a-crisis friend?'

Ashley thought about it. 'Hayley from work. A year ago.'

'Damn,' muttered Rob. 'I'd forgotten about her.' Hayley Legge was a locum who had come to work at Ashley's hospital for six months, then moved to Bath to marry her fiancé. She and Ashley had immediately become best friends.

'Women don't count,' he said defensively. 'Your lot are built differently from mine. I leave you alone in the queue at the supermarket for five seconds and come back to discover you telling the woman next to you your life story.'

Ashley laughed. 'It was just the once. And I could tell straight away that Sue was a really nice woman.'

'But what kind of person makes a brand new friend in the supermarket? I've never heard anything like it in my life.'

'But women share things. That's why we find it so easy to make new friends.'

'Exactly. And men are the opposite. We don't share things. We don't make small-talk if we can help it. We don't tell complete strangers the story of our lives in a supermarket queue.'

'Maybe you should.'

'Do you know who the last friend I made was?' asked Rob. Ashley shook her head.

'I don't either. But it was years ago. Do you see what I'm saying? The window of opportunity for making new friends has closed. I've missed the boat. I'm too old to make real friends now. Not like the ones I've left behind anyway. It's an impossible task.' He paused. 'I know how I made friends in my twenties – by living in crap house shares and hanging out in the pub – but how I'm supposed to make friends in my thirties is a mystery to me. How do you do it when the people you want to befriend are settling down and getting on with their lives?'

'Are you saying you want to go back to London?' asked Ashley, nervously.

'Of course not,' replied Rob. 'I said I'd give it a year and I meant it. I just don't know how it's going to work for us, though, if I can't make my own friends.' He gazed enviously across the bar at a group of guys in their thirties who had just come in. 'I don't know . . . Maybe I should just lower my standards. I'm never going to find a bunch of mates like the ones I've left behind. I doubt I'll ever find someone I get on with as well as I do with Phil . . . But do you know what? Right here, right now, I'd settle for being able to go for a drink once a week with someone – anyone – I could be myself with for a little while.'

'You're right,' said Ashley, as though a thought had occurred to her. 'You do need your own friends. And I'm determined to help you do something to sort out this problem once and for all. In fact, I'm going to find you a brand new friend if it kills me.'

'But how?'

'Well, I've got an idea and it's going to take me a while to sort it out. But you have to promise me that, whatever happens, you'll give it a go.'

Rob looked around BlueBar once more at the groups of friends sitting together, drinking, talking, having fun. 'Fine,' he said. 'Whatever it is you've got in mind, I'll give it a go.'

PART THREE

(Principally concerning obstacles)

City life

It was six thirty on a Friday night, roughly a month after his birthday, and Rob was sitting in front of the TV waiting for Ashley to get home from a meeting. Since he had finished for the day an hour earlier he had put the dishwasher on, tidied the kitchen and prepared the ingredients for their evening meal. After that he watched the tail end of *Neighbours* and the beginning of the *Six o'Clock News*. He only moved from the sofa when he saw Ashley's convertible pull up outside. When he opened the door to greet her, he was met with a firm kiss on the lips and a smile. 'I've got some good news for you,' she said, grinning.

'What is it?' asked Rob.

'First things first,' she replied, kicking off her shoes and going into the living room. 'Highlights, lowlights.'

'My lowlight,' began Rob, as he flopped on to the sofa again, 'was waking up this morning. As for my highlight . . .' He let the silence do the talking. 'There wasn't one today. Just one very long lowlight. How about yourself?'

'Well, my lowlight is pretty bad news,' said Ashley. 'As of today I'm moving from Geriatrics to the orthopaedics team covering A and E, which means more hours, more weekends and, worst of all, regular night shifts – beginning tonight.'

'Tonight? Oh, that's great. I was looking forward to spending some time with you. I'll never see you now. We'll be

91

working completely different hours.' He paused, then said the one thing he knew they were both thinking: 'I might as well have stayed in London for all the good being here is doing.'

'Don't,' said Ashley. 'Look, it's just until they get a few staffing problems sorted. And . . . well, it's not that bad, really. I'll be on for four days and off for four days, so we'll have time together.'

'You'll be catching up on your sleep for most of it.'

'You're right, it's not great, but I don't have a choice.'

Suddenly Rob felt guilty for giving her such a hard time. 'So, what was your highlight?'

'As usual,' she said, cheering up considerably, 'coming home to you.'

'Even when I'm like this?'

Ashley nodded. 'You could be in the worst mood ever and it would still be the highlight of my day because you're here . . . But go on, ask me what my second highlight of the day was.'

'What was the second highlight of your day?'

'I've done it,' she replied. 'I think I've got a way to find you a new friend.'

She hadn't mentioned finding Rob a mate since his birthday and he'd assumed (or rather hoped) she'd forgotten about it. While it was kind of her to offer to sort out his life, there was little dignity in knowing, at the age of thirty-three, that his girlfriend was trying to find him a playmate.

'What have you done?' he asked suspiciously.

'Nothing bad.'

'So why do I feel nervous?'

'Well, after we talked about finding you a friend I started thinking about ways to do it and realised you were right. It *is* difficult. Most people at our age make their new friends through work and, of course, that's not an option for you. Then I had another thought. Why not place a personal ad in a What's On type magazine like *City List*?'

'A personal ad?' echoed Rob.

'I know what you're thinking,' began Ashley. 'Personal ads are for the lonely, the desperate and the just plain weird.'

'I wasn't going to say that exactly but thanks for spelling it out.'

'I didn't mean that – but I knew you'd see it like that. But the truth is a lot of cool people use personal ads these days.'

'Like who?'

'Jenny at work. She put one in *City List* last year and look at her now.'

'Isn't Jenny the one who was single for ages and is now engaged to . . . what's his name? The guy with the pale skin and beady eyes who looks like he'd crumble into dust if he ever went out in the sun?'

'His name's Stephen,' said Ashley, tersely, 'and there's no need to be so mean. They're very much in love.'

'Well, that's as may be. But her ads were in the Love Wanted section, weren't they?'

'Yes, but they have one for friends too—'

'Let me stop you there,' interrupted Rob. 'First, no matter what you say, anyone who wears Mickey Mouse socks over the age of ten is *not* cool. Second, finding a bloke in the personals is not the same as finding new friends – there's something too weird about it. In this age of speed dating and suchlike it might be socially acceptable to try to find a new partner through a magazine ad – but a friend? You might as well get "loser" tattooed on your forehead. How can anyone admit in black and white that they're so socially inadequate that they can't make a friend without advertising?' He paused to let Ashley answer the question, and realised that *he* was *precisely* the type of loser who was so socially inadequate that he couldn't make new friends without advertising for them.

'How did this happen?' he asked himself.

'For the last time you're *not* a loser,' Ashley told him. 'But the way I see it you've got two options. You can either sit and sulk in the house or get up and do something about it.'

'I'll sit and sulk,' said Rob, sullenly. 'There's no way I'm putting an ad in *City List* asking for people to be my friends.'

'But—'

'No way.'

'You *promised*.'

'I know. But I didn't promise to do this.'

'Yes, you did. You promised to go along with whatever plan I came up with . . . and, anyway, it's sort of too late.'

Rob looked at her and she glanced away guiltily. The penny dropped. 'You've done it already, haven't you?' he accused her.

'I did it the day after your birthday,' she said, delving into her handbag and taking out a rolled-up copy of *City List*. She opened it and read aloud: '*Chorlton based thirty-three-year-old male new to the north-west wishes to meet up with like-minded souls for drinking and carousing. Likes: music, literature, cinema and sitting in pubs. Dislikes: soap operas, hazelnuts, peanuts and people who own Anastacia albums. If this sounds like you then drop me a line and we can set the world to rights.*'

'Is this some sort of practical joke?' asked Rob, standing up to study the magazine for himself.

'No,' snapped Ashley. 'It may seem far-fetched but this is

me doing something to help you out. If you don't want any help, fine – I'll leave you alone.' With that, she sat down on the sofa, changed the TV channel with the remote and folded her arms across her chest.

'Look,' said Rob, sitting down next to her, 'I'm really sorry. You're right, I did say I'd try to be open-minded about this. It's just that—'

'What?'

'You're asking me to go on a date with a bloke.'

'And?'

'Well, it's a bit gay, isn't it? I mean surely a bloke going on a date with another bloke is pretty much the definition of gayness. And as I'm completely heterosexual I think I'd just feel a bit uncomfortable doing it.'

'Making friends through personals ads is not "a bit gay".'

'You're right,' replied Rob. 'It's not a bit gay. It's actually *very* gay. Two men who don't know each other meeting up in a bar or a restaurant for the sole purpose of getting to know each other better is completely and utterly gay. There's no way round it.'

'But, Rob,' said Ashley, 'you're *not* gay. You have a girlfriend – *me*. You're not suddenly going to swap which team you bat for just because you've gone for a drink with a bloke.' Rob shrugged, unconvinced. 'Anyway,' she continued, 'other than it being "a bit gay", what did you think of the ad? It took me ages to write.'

'It was . . . okay.'

'Only okay? Didn't you hear me say it took ages?'

'Well . . . just out of curiosity,' began Rob, 'why did you use the word "carousing"?'

'I thought it was funny,' explained Ashley. 'I did wonder whether people do still carouse, but I decided to go with it anyway. Why do you ask?' She looked at Rob and frowned. 'No, Rob, "carousing" isn't shorthand for being gay.'

'You've still got to admit it's pretty gay, though,' said Rob. 'Think about it. Do straight people carouse? I don't think so. Straight people are terrible at having a good time. Terrible. Gay people invented Disco. You can't get better good-time music than Disco.'

Ashley sighed in disbelief. 'You do realise that you're employing an embarrassing level of stereotype?'

'Of course.' Rob nodded. 'All I'm saying is that since I'm not gay there's not a lot of point in writing an ad that makes me sound like a latterday Liberace.'

'Was there anything you liked about it?'

Rob paused for a moment. 'I liked the "likes" you've put down but I'm not sure about the "dislikes".'

'But they're all true and they're not gay. You're always telling me how disgusting hazelnuts and peanuts are. And you said you knew straight away that you weren't going to get on with Mia's boyfriend Edwin because you saw he had an Anastacia album in his car.'

'All that screeching,' said Rob. 'Surely no normal person can like that stuff.' He sighed heavily and studied the ad again. 'It's quite sobering having your personality reduced to three sentences. Puts everything into perspective. This is me: a slightly camp bloke with an intense hatred of caterwauling songstresses and hazelnuts. Anyway, thank you very much for doing all this for me, babe, but I can't see it working somehow.'

'You don't even want to hear your replies, then?'

'What?'

'Don't get too excited. You've only had four.'

'Four?'

'Yes, four.'

'You're telling me that out of all the thousands of people that read *City List* every week only four wanted to befriend me? I thought you said people were more friendly "up north".'

'They are usually,' replied Ashley, 'but I think you're looking at it all wrong. If the ad had read, "Handsome and witty man working in the creative industries wishes to widen his social circle in the north-west" you'd have been inundated with people wanting to be your friend. But I thought you'd prefer to play it down a little. You know, make friends with people who like you for being you.'

'It all sounds more than a little desperate,' he said, then paused. 'So, the four people who are interested in my ad, what are they like?'

'Well, the idea is that when people see an ad they like they ring and leave a message for you. Call them up and have a listen.'

Rob dialled the number Ashley gave him, and entered the pin number that enabled him to access the messages.

Message 1: 'Has this thing started? Oh, right . . . okay . . . My name's Veejay . . . People call me . . . er . . . Veejay. I like music . . . a lot and I'm looking for someone to go to gigs with and the pub . . . and, er . . .' Laughs '. . . someone to go chasing birds with because . . . I've tried it on my own and it's no fun without a mate to back you up. So, if this sounds like you, give me a call. Cheers.'

Message 2: 'Hi, my name's Andy Ward. I've just started working at my brother's software sales company out in Hale Barns. At the minute, though, I'm living with my sister in Chorlton. I just think it would be nice to make some new mates out this way as I've been living in Spain for the last few years and don't know many people around here. Anyway, that's me. Give us a ring if you're interested.'

Message 3: 'Hi . . . er . . . I'm Nigel Wilshire. I'm thirty – hang on, make that thirty-one – and I'm looking to expand my circle of friends. I work in IT for an insurance firm but in my spare time I like to play the acoustic guitar. I like cinema too, and going to the pub. I don't mind peanuts, though. Hope this all sounds up your street.'

Message 4: 'Hi there . . . I'm Patrick Metcalfe. I'm thirty-nine, just coming out of a five-year marriage, and I've moved jobs up here. I liked your ad and I'm trying to broaden my social horizons. That's pretty much it. Give me a ring.'

'So, what do you think?' asked Ashley, as Rob put down the phone.

'What do I think?' repeated Rob. 'That this whole exercise has just become more gay than even I dreamed possible.'

'Besides that,' said Ashley, laughing, 'which one did you like?'

'None of them sounded like someone I could be mates with.'

'You can't tell anything from a call,' said Ashley. 'Although, that said, my gut feeling is that the first guy, Veejay, sounded a bit laddy for my liking. The second however, Andy, sounded really nice. And well that guy Nigel seemed a bit needy if you ask me, and I wasn't sure about the last guy, Patrick, at all. But you should see them all, then make your decision. What have you got to lose?'

'Oh, I don't know,' replied Rob. 'How about my dignity, self-respect and sense of self-worth?'

'But you'll do it?'

'No,' said Rob. 'Absolutely not.'

'Then what *are* you going to do? I don't want you carrying on feeling the way you've been feeling.'

'Well, I won't,' began Rob. 'At least, not any more. Because, bizarrely, your extremely gay plan has helped me come to a decision and it's this: I've been thinking about it in the wrong way. I don't need friends up here. I've got you, the boys are only a train ride away and I've more than enough work to do. Why would I need anyone else? No, from now on, I'll be fine with my own company.'

'That'll never work,' said Ashley. 'It's what you've had since January and it's made you miserable.'

'Yeah, I know. But this time round it'll be different. I'm choosing to be happy about it. I'm going to celebrate my no-mates status. Before I came to this conclusion I felt like I had a flashing neon sign over my head with "loser" spelt out on it. But you can only lose *if you take part*.'

'So you're refusing to take part?'

'Yup.'

'But what are you refusing to take part *in*?'

'The belief that humans need friends,' said Rob. 'I'm refusing to believe that I need anyone in my life apart from you and the boys in London. The truth is, I've always liked my own company. I don't know why I've been torturing myself trying to make new mates when I'm the best mate I'm ever going to have.'

Ashley looked confused. 'You're planning to become a hermit?'

'Yeah,' said Rob, suddenly finding the word 'hermit' amusing. 'A hermit with a girlfriend. And before you say anything, this doesn't mean I'll start begging you to listen to bands you won't like or go and see films you'll hate or anything like that. No, there has to be no pretence. From now on I'm going to be a pint-and-crossword man.'

'A pint-and-crossword man?'

'Yes,' said Rob, standing up and putting on his coat. 'A pint-and-crossword man. And do you know what else?'

'What?'

'As you're going back to work in a bit I'm going to take myself off right now and have my first northern pint-and-crossword session. I'll see you in the morning.'

Pint-and-crossword man drinketh

It was fast approaching nine thirty and Rob was sitting in the Lazy Fox on Barlow Moor Road contemplating the *Guardian* quick crossword over his second pint of Guinness. He had selected this pub because, unlike BlueBar with its crowd of cool young drinkers, the Lazy Fox was a scruffy pub popu-lated mainly by old men, with the odd scattering of late-thirty-somethings and early-forty-somethings. And as a solitary bloke doing a crossword and sipping a pint, Rob was almost invisible. He looked around and saw plenty of other pint-and-crossword men besides himself: a middle-aged guy with a beard, a pint of mild and the *Manchester Evening News*; a tallish guy in his late thirties with a pint of lager and a folded copy of *The Times*; and a small, wizened, elderly man with half a bitter, who was spending more time staring into space than tackling the *Daily Telegraph*'s cryptic crossword. Pint-and-crossword men were everywhere.

Rob had first come across the pint-and-crossword man phenomenon when his first boss at Ogilvy-Hunter had sent him to Norwich to attend a three-day software training course. It had finished at five thirty every evening and, as Rob didn't know anyone in Norwich and had no one to do nothing with, he decided to go to the pub on his own. He sat down with his pint in the lounge of the Crown and Spire, possibly the dingiest pub in Norwich town centre, picked up an abandoned newspaper and did the crossword. Three hours and four pints of Guinness later, having spoken to no one but the barman he had completed the *Daily Mail* crossword. When he told Phil the story on his return to London, his friend had pointed out that Rob had now joined an elite band of males known as pint-and-crossword men. 'They're all over the place,' Phil explained. 'In every pub across the land there's at least one solitary bloke sitting with a pint, doing the crossword.' Soon Rob found it difficult to go into a pub without making sure first that there was a pint-and-crossword man in attendance. Without exception there were always one or two – men happy to be out of the house, challenging their minds while sipping a pint. It was clever, really: a manoeuvre that gave the impression you were socialising without any of the inconvenience of real people. These men proved that John Donne was wrong: any man could be an island, entire of himself, if he had a drink in his hand and something to occupy his mind.

Live theatre

Having been a pint-and-crossword man for half an hour, Rob was pondering the answer to five down, six letters, 'A tasty time if only once a year', when his concentration was disturbed by a couple entering the otherwise empty rear room in which he had lodged himself for the evening. They sat down at a table a little way from him. He could only see the back of the man's head, which was obscuring the woman, but from their clothes and demeanour Rob guessed they were of a similar age to himself. He couldn't fathom why they were in the Lazy Fox rather than somewhere more happening on a Friday night.

He returned to his crossword and his pint, but occasional snippets of their conversation kept filtering through. He abandoned the crossword and listened, fascinated, to what was going on. The man didn't speak much, but the woman had enough to say for both of them. At one point Rob overheard her demand, 'Why aren't you saying anything?' and had to bite his tongue to stop himself rejoining, 'Because you won't let him get a word in edgewise.' He could see that the guy was as tense as a cornered animal. As Rob continued covertly to observe them, their untouched drinks and constant whispering all began to add up. This wasn't a young couple on a date. This was a young couple in the process of splitting up.

Now Rob could barely take his eyes off them. Watching a couple split up in public was one of the best forms of free entertainment ever devised. It was theatre at its purest, in which the actors and the situations were chillingly real and reassuringly familiar. He knew that it was rather ghoulish to enjoy a couple's misery but it was such a rare, delicate pleasure – the French truffle of overheard conversations – that it was impossible not to indulge in it for just a few moments.

Over his newspaper Rob could see that the boyfriend's hand gestures seemed defensive, as though the woman might attack him at any second. As their argument became more heated they both found it difficult to control their voices – the woman especially. Soon, every time the man tried to open his mouth she spoke over him and eventually he faded away without a fight. Rob knew his body language all too well from his own failed relationships: the man was in the wrong and didn't have a single argument with which to defend himself. And, sitting across from him, the woman was in the right but was never going to get what she wanted, the way she was going about it.

Rob looked at his watch and tried to guess how long it would be before the argument reached a conclusion. The woman had made the key mistake all women make in arguments: she didn't know when to stop. Yes, she was right. Yes, her boyfriend understood he was in the wrong. But once those two facts had been established what else was there to say? By dragging out the argument and meta-phorically kicking him when he was on the ground she was undoing all her good work. With each word that left her mouth Rob could see that the man was caring just a little bit less about her and their relationship. In a few moments he'd explode. Another minute and a half, Rob guessed. Seven seconds later he realised he'd been wrong.

'I've had enough of this,' barked the man, standing up. 'I'm sick of this and I'm sick of you. It's over between us and there's nothing you can do about it.'

'Just go,' shrieked the woman, her face still obscured, 'like you did before. I'm getting used to you walking away from me now – and while you're at it take this with you!' She picked up her now ex-boyfriend's pint glass and threw the contents into his face.

Without saying a word, or for that matter wiping the beer off his face, the man stormed out of the room, staring at Rob with a mixture of anger and acute embarrassment. Rob shrugged: *Well, where was I supposed to look?* The woman slumped on to the padded seat that he had just vacated and said to herself, 'I feel so stupid.' It was at this point that Rob realised he had encountered her before. It was Jo, the girl he had met at the party and, once again, she was in tears.

Four key scenes in the life of Jo Richards from the six weeks before she burst into tears in front of Rob

One

'If you're going to be like this,' said Sean, 'I'm going upstairs.'

'Go!' yelled Jo. 'Just don't slam the door.'

It was one o'clock in the morning and thirty-two-year-old Jo Richards fumed silently as her boyfriend stormed into the hallway, pausing only to slam the door behind him. Jo sank into the sofa and wanted to cry so much that the effort involved in holding back the tears was almost a good enough excuse to give in to them. As far as she was concerned, she wasn't being 'like' anything. What did it mean anyway? What was she being 'like'? The only thing she was being was a nice, proper girlfriend. She wasn't – and never had been while they had been together – the type of girlfriend to nag (more than moderately), whine (more than the basic amount needed when she was talking about her problems) or be clingy (she'd not once moaned about him spending more time with his friends than with her).

All she'd asked Sean was whether he would be around the following weekend because she was thinking of booking somewhere for them to go. They were both quite broke and although she would have preferred to stay in a hotel or a bed-and-breakfast in the countryside, she had been considering Wales under canvas. That was how much she wanted to spend quality time with Sean: she was prepared to go camping. Jo hated camping. She'd never seen the point of exchanging a perfectly good bed for a tent, some plastic sheeting and the hard, damp ground.

When Sean had replied that he didn't know what he was up to that weekend, Jo had pointed out that therefore he lacked an excuse not to spend it with her. He had lost his temper and told her that this was 'typical' of the way things had been between them recently. Then Jo had said, as forcefully as she could, that spending the weekend away with your partner was not meant to be a form of punishment.

Under normal circumstances she would have gone after him and made him talk to her. She'd never understood the male propensity to yell when they were winning an argument, then shut down when they were losing (or, in this case, remove themselves from the scene). Left to his own devices, she was sure, he would stay upstairs sulking under the guise of listening to music or playing on the computer without wondering how she was feeling. How could he just leave the room in the middle of an argument? If it had been Jo who had stormed out she wouldn't have been able to settle in a million years. She couldn't sulk to save her life. She could brood, but that was different. She could sit and dissect the argument until she arrived at the usual conclusion that everything was her fault. This time, however, she didn't. Who was at fault wasn't the point any more. The point was this: was Sean being deliberately vile to her in the hope that she would get sick of him and kick him out? No one could get as irate about nothing as Sean had without having an ulterior motive. Things hadn't been right between them since they had had that argument at the party and she'd locked herself into the bathroom for more than half an hour.

It was obvious he had a plan: he'd been staying out late with his friends, drinking too much, smoking too much and generally being a slob for weeks. Suddenly it all fell into place: he was trying to goad her into ending their relationship because he was too much of a coward to do it himself. What he'd failed to factor into his plan was that when Jo had agreed to let him move in with her, it had not been a casual arrangement. It was Commitment. She had not spent the last five years investing in their relationship to give up on it just like that. She was determined to make him stay. So, no matter what he did in his continuing strategy to make her stop loving him, he would lose. She wasn't going to abandon herself to a life of loneliness without a fight.

With a heavy heart, Jo headed upstairs. She could hear music coming from behind the door to the spare room so she rapped on it twice – even though this was her house and Sean had contributed nothing to the mortgage payments: it was her way of signalling that she was sorry. She opened the door and peered in. Sean was lying on the bed with his hands folded behind his head. He didn't look at her when she entered the room.

'I'm sorry,' said Jo. 'You're right. I should stop hassling you.'

She waited eagerly, but Sean said nothing, just lay there, lips pursed, and stared at the ceiling.

Two

'Look,' spat Mr Clarkson, menacingly, 'I'm only going to say this one more time. Are you going to replace the broken toilet in my bathroom or am I going to have to take matters into my own hands?'

It was Monday afternoon, a month after Jo's argument

with Sean. She was at her place of work, the Cresta Community Housing Association (South Manchester), being shouted at by one of her tenants.

It was without doubt her greatest regret that she had ever accepted the temporary post as housing officer ten years ago when she had been a new graduate – greater than having allowed her brother to 'shoot' an apple off her head with a dart when she was twelve, greater than walking out of the exam room ten minutes into her second A-level history paper because it was too hard, thereby ensuring that she got a U, greater than selling half of her record collection for a hundred pounds to raise funds when she was a student for a week in Turkey with her mates.

As she gazed at Mr Clarkson it dawned on her how much she hated this job. She hated it with a passion – with everything she had to give and a little more. The only thing that stopped her getting up and walking out was that she had nowhere else to go.

'Mr Clarkson—' said Jo, patiently.

'What?' he snapped.

'I don't understand why you're telling me this again because, as I said to you when you arrived this morning and the last eleven times that you've called, I can't send anyone out to repair your broken toilet until the requisite paperwork has been filled in. Since you refuse to tell me how your toilet was damaged, my hands are tied.'

'What does it matter how it got broken?'

'It matters to the paperwork.'

'It's your paperwork,' he said, 'you fill it out. But let me warn you, if someone from Housing doesn't get themselves round to my place and fix my toilet soon there's going to be trouble.'

Jo didn't doubt this for a second. Nine months ago when the Benefits Agency had threatened to stop Mr Clarkson's income support, on the grounds that he'd been spotted working on a market stall in the city centre, he had come to the conclusion that someone at the housing-association office had 'grassed' him up and come into the office screaming about how he was going to 'get' everyone. Three days later a masked man, who was clearly Mr Clarkson in a bright orange balaclava, had thrown a large chunk of masonry through the association's office window, then hurled a barrage of expletives at the staff before making his escape. The police couldn't do anything because Mr Clarkson persuaded a few of his friends to give him a watertight alibi. With no forensic evidence to tie him to the scene, and only association staff's eye-witness reports that the man responsible 'looked, acted, dressed and sounded like Mr Clarkson in a ski mask', it was depressingly inevitable that he would get away with it.

'This is pathetic!' snarled Mr Clarkson.

Jo stared at him blankly. She knew that Mr Clarkson had smashed his own toilet on purpose because it had happened several times before. No one could break toilets quite like Mr Clarkson, who had had two new ones in the last year alone. She was aware that he knew that she knew he'd smashed up his own toilet. She couldn't understand why he insisted on continuing this charade. Perhaps it gave him something to do.

'Is that all, Mr Clarkson?' she asked.

'You'll be hearing from my solicitor,' he barked, then kicked one of the grey plastic waiting-room chairs against the wall. He picked it up by the back rest as if he was going to throw it at the security screens, but snorted and let it go. It tumbled across the floor and came to rest under Jo's window. When he left the office Jo, and the queue of people waiting to see her, breathed a sigh of relief.

Today can't get any worse, she thought.

Then the phone rang.

'Cresta Community Housing Association,' said Jo, robotically.

'It's me,' said a voice she recognised as Sean's. 'You ought to know that I've sort of moved out.'

Jo couldn't believe what she was hearing. How could somebody 'sort of' move out? When she'd gone to work that morning she'd been cohabiting with her boyfriend and now he was telling her that some time during the day he had taken it upon himself to de-habit or un-habit, or whatever the word was for a boyfriend moving his stuff out without telling his significant other. What was worse was that he hadn't even cleared his throat before he made the announcement. He'd just said it.

'Did you hear me?' asked Sean, when Jo didn't reply. 'I said I've moved out.'

'What do you mean? I don't understand.'

'I mean exactly what I've said. I've moved my things out of the house.'

'You're leaving me?'

'Things aren't working between us, are they? We need to take time out from the relationship to find out what we really want from life, don't you think? Surely you must see that.'

Jo knew that Sean was trying to persuade her to agree that their relationship was over. But she didn't want it to be over.

'I don't see it like that,' she countered. 'Not at all. I can't believe that after all the time we've been together you've got so little respect for me that you're telling me our relationship is finished over the *phone* . . . when you've *already moved your stuff out*.' Tears welled in her eyes. 'This is so typical of you.'

'I didn't want a scene.'

'You wouldn't, would you?' she snapped. 'You'd like everything to be clean and clinical. Well, you can't just slip out of my life like that. You can't do it to me!'

'It might not be permanent. I just think we need to get our heads round what's going on between us. We need to get some perspective because if we don't we're dead in the water.'

'Where will you go?'

'Davey's going to put me up.'

'I hope the two of you will be very happy together.'

'There's no need to be like that,' said Sean. 'It's for the best.'

'If it's for the best,' she said, 'then why am *I* so upset and why are *you* so relieved?'

Sean remained silent.

'Don't move out,' said Jo, desperately, as tears rolled down her cheeks. 'Please don't. I know things haven't been very good for a while and it's all my fault, but I promise you I'll change. I really will. But don't move out! Not even for a night!' She was clutching at straws now. 'You'll hate it at Davey's. He's never got any food in and his place is a pig-sty. Stay with me and we'll work everything out, okay?'

'No,' said Sean. 'It's not okay. I'll speak to you in a few weeks.'

And then he put down the phone.

Three

Jo had spent the last two days crying and was now scrolling through the numbers in her mobile phone's address book, looking for a friend in whom she might confide. Forty-seven numbers were stored on the memory. When she had discounted those relating to parents or relatives (seven), she did the same for those relating to Sean (four), his friends (five) and his friends' girlfriends, with whom she spent most of her time (three), friends from school she hadn't seen in years (three), people from work (eight), Domino's Pizza (one), and Rail Enquiries (one). The remaining fifteen (home, work, and the occasional mobile) belonged to Liza, Vicky, Sonia, Karen, Gina and Kerry – friends from Jo's days at what had been Manchester Polytechnic. The six had been the centre of her social life for a long time but once she had got together with Sean they had faded away. Jo hadn't been in touch with five of them for nearly a year, and when she removed them that left her with just one friend in the world: Kerry Morrison. And Jo wasn't sure that Kerry even liked her any more.

'Hello?' said Kerry, croakily. 'Who is it?'

'Kerry, it's me,' said Jo.

'Oh, don't tell me,' said Kerry, abruptly, 'let me guess. This is about you and Sean, isn't it?'

'Yes, but—'

'You've split up, haven't you?'

'You're right. I'm that predictable, aren't I? I don't call you for weeks on end –'

'More like months.'

'– and now that Sean's gone the first person I call is you. I know I've been the worst friend in the world over the past few months—'

'More like years.'

'Okay, years—'

'In fact you've been the worst friend ever since you started going out with Sean.'

113

'I know—'

'No,' snapped Kerry, 'you don't know at all. And you certainly don't know anything about me. Were you aware that Sammy had died?'

'No,' said Jo, recalling the tortoiseshell cat that Kerry had owned for as long as Jo had known her.

'I'm really sorry to hear that, but—'

'Or that I'm an auntie now?' interrupted Kerry.

'No, I—'

'Or that I got promoted at work?'

'You're right,' said Jo. 'I don't know anything about your life, do I?'

'You haven't returned a single one of my calls in the last six months,' said Kerry. 'Not one.'

'I know I—'

'Well, I'm sorry, Jo,' said Kerry, 'but now is not a good time to talk.' And with that she hung up.

With tears in her eyes and the dialling tone in her ear Jo looked around her bedroom as if she was seeing it for the first time. It was like a crime scene. Everything was as she had found it when she got home on the day Sean had moved out. Both wardrobe doors were open, revealing a gaping hole among her clothes where Sean's had hung. Next to the wardrobe, the bottom two drawers in the chest from the same IKEA range were half open and empty. The table on Sean's side of the bed had nothing on it but dust marking the outlines of his clock-radio, the pile of paperbacks he'd been reading and the bedside lamp they had bought two summers ago during a sale at the Pier in the Trafford Centre. She was just about to begin crying again when the phone rang. 'Hello,' she said, hoping it was Sean.

'It's me,' said a female voice. 'I'm sorry,' said Kerry. 'I shouldn't have hung up on you like that.'

'I should be apologising to you,' said Jo. 'I've been the worst friend in the world.'

'Some of the girls are getting together next Thursday night at BlueBar in Chorlton,' said Kerry, briskly. 'I'm sure you'd be welcome to come.'

'Really?'

'Yeah, of course. They're always asking after you.'

'I'd love to.'

'I'll come by yours and pick you up. How does eight sound?'

'Great. I'll see you then.'

Four

It was just after nine o'clock and Jo was sitting at the table in BlueBar surrounded by her old college friends. Over the last hour she had heard everyone's news: Liza and her boyfriend Craig were engaged and getting married the following summer; Vicky and her long-term partner, Roger, were three months pregnant; Sonia and her husband, Ivan, had just bought a four-bedroom house in Didsbury that needed extensive renovation; Gina and her boyfriend, Dimitri, were planning to sell their house, buy a new one in Bradford near her parents and then go travelling for a year; and Karen was applying for the deputy-headship of her primary school and, with her partner, John, was planning to buy a three-bedroom house in Fallowfield. Jo was the only one at the table who was single.

'So what's new with you, Jo?' asked Karen, having reached the end of her job-promotion/house-buying saga.

'Nothing really,' said Jo.

'And how are things with Sean?'

'Not too good,' said Jo, looking at Kerry and wondering why she hadn't primed them not to ask. Kerry looked back at her apologetically and winced as she mouthed, 'Sorry.'

'You haven't split up, have you?' asked Vicky.

'Not officially,' said Jo, avoiding all eye-contact, 'but he has sort of moved out.'

'You poor thing,' sympathised Liza.

'He says he needs time,' added Jo.

'Why do men always think they need time?' asked Sonia. 'They're supposed to be great decision-makers and leaders, yet when it comes to relationships they can't make up their minds about anything.'

'How long were the two of you together?' asked Gina.

'Five years,' said Jo, and her friends blanched.

'Does anyone want another drink?' asked Kerry, diverting their attention. Everyone nodded, so she took their orders and looked at Jo expectantly.

'I'll give you a hand,' said Jo, and stood up.

'Thanks.'

By the time they had returned with two gin-and-tonics and a bottle of red wine the others were suggesting names for Vicky's baby. Kerry slipped into the conversation, offering up her favourites: Leon for a boy and Clarissa for a girl. Jo couldn't think of any names she liked and, to make matters worse, couldn't imagine ever having children. She had felt out of the loop all evening and now she felt invisible too.

The conversation soon moved off in a different direction (house prices in Chorlton and Didsbury) but instead of joining in, Jo sat back to observe the table. These women weren't the people she remembered. They were strangers. And it was all her fault.

She hadn't meant to stop being friends with any of them. It had just happened. It was a weakness in her that she had known of since she was at school. She had always been desperate to be liked by the right people. When she was seven, they had been the pretty, popular girls, like Harriet Jones, Serena Gill and Stephanie Mills. The wrong people were her best friends, Lizzy Furnish, with her lazy eye, and Chloe Woodall, who was constantly afflicted with bad haircuts. Later on, at secondary school, the right people were the beautiful and popular Tina Osbourne, Tracey Matthews and Josie Barton; the wrong ones were Chloe Woodall, who still had bad haircuts, and Diane Miller, who was so extraordinarily tall for a fourteen-year-old that she was often mistaken by younger kids for a teacher.

It hadn't been until sixth-form college that the right people had changed sex. Ten weeks before her eighteenth birthday Jo had met and fallen in love with Adrian Boateng. He was her first proper boyfriend, and the happiness she felt from the sense of completeness he gave her was so overwhelming that, within a month, she had stopped seeing her friends. The wrong people – her new sixth-form college friends: Vivien McCarthy, Sarah Coe and Shelagh Prideaux – all tried to tell her that what she was doing was wrong but Jo wouldn't listen. At first she justified it with the idea that if they had fallen in love with boys as good-looking as Adrian they, too, would be spending every second of the day either with him or thinking about him. It didn't matter to her that half the time she was with Adrian his friends, Jamie, Rich and Dom, were there too. When, one by one, they too acquired girlfriends and when Adrian did boy things – like playing football, reading music magazines or listening to his Walkman – she had other girls to talk to. They formed a separate friendship of their own – which Jo's old friend Vivien McCarthy labelled 'The Girlfriends of Ade, Jamie, Rich and Dom' and Shelagh Prideaux referred to, more pithily, as 'The Four Stooges'. Jo and Adrian split up a month before he went to university in London because they didn't want to do the Long-distance Thing. Jo's friendship with Adrian's friends' girlfriends had long been on the wane as members came and went, and as she gradually came to realise that they weren't really her friends anyway – convenient though they might be. She spent the month before her degree course began pining for Adrian but mostly for the friends she had abandoned at the sixth-form college who no longer returned her calls.

All that time, she thought now, *and all those friends, but I still haven't learned a single lesson*.

Jo excused herself from the table, took her bag and went outside to call Sean on her mobile.

'Hello?'

'It's me,' said Jo.

'I was going to call you,' he said coolly.

'Well, I've saved you the effort. It's nearly two weeks since you moved out and that's more than enough time for you to sort out your head. We need to meet up and talk through this mess once and for all.'

'Fine,' he said. 'Tomorrow – say, nine o'clock in the Lazy Fox in Chorlton? It's quiet in there.'

'Okay,' said Jo. 'The Lazy Fox tomorrow at nine.'

Rob talks

Rob didn't know what to do for the best. Through no fault of his own he was now sitting in a small room in a quiet pub, attempting to have a pint and do the crossword, while a woman he'd met only once before was sitting not far from him crying her eyes out. What exactly was the etiquette here? Was he supposed to walk over and comfort her – maybe tell her there were plenty more fish in the sea? Pretend to do his crossword to save her from embarrassment? Everything he came up with made him feel so uncomfortable that he decided that the best he could do was nothing. After all, she hadn't addressed him directly when she'd said, 'I feel so stupid.' She'd said it in a general way. Rob was pretty sure that, had the room been empty, she would still have said it. He tried to feel relieved at this but failed. The fact was the room wasn't empty. He was there. And even though he didn't know the woman in tears very well, he still knew her, so doing nothing wasn't an option.

Rob took a deep breath. 'Are you all right?' he asked.

The woman looked up, apparently bewildered that the room's only other occupant was addressing her.

'It's you,' she said unevenly.

'I'm Rob . . . and you're Jo, aren't you? And, well I don't mean to bother you – I'll leave you alone, if you'd rather – if you want to be left with your thoughts and all that.' He held up his paper to show her that he could amuse himself. 'I was doing the crossword and having a pint and I can go back to doing that. I can even sit next door if you like – just tell me what to do and I'll do it.'

Jo cleared her throat and blew her nose on a tissue. 'It's just . . . I feel *really* stupid.'

'Why?'

'Because I threw Sean's pint over him.'

'I take it Sean's your boyfriend?'

'Ex-boyfriend now.'

'And what did he do to deserve having a pint thrown over him?'

'He moved out.'

'I see. Who paid for the pint?'

'I did,' she replied.

'Well, then,' Rob grinned, 'technically speaking it was yours so you could do what you liked with it.'

For a few moments Rob thought she might smile but then she blew her nose again and wiped her eyes with the heels of her palms.

'Are you on your own?' she asked eventually.

Rob nodded.

'Why?'

'What do you mean? Why am I in the pub on my own?'

'I mean, what are you doing on your own in *this* dingy place on a Friday night? I'm here because my selfish boyfriend chose it. It's round the corner from where he's living and it's such a rubbish pub that there was no chance he'd bump into any of his mates. But why aren't you out somewhere like BlueBar?'

'Because I've got no mates and I didn't think anyone would notice in here,' replied Rob, matter-of-factly.

Jo half cracked a smile, as if she thought Rob was joking, but when he didn't return it hers faded. 'You've got no friends at all?'

'Well, none in Manchester.'

'But you *do* have friends?'

'In London, yes. Loads.'

'You've moved here recently then?' asked Jo, sounding marginally relieved.

'At the beginning of the year.'

'For work?'

'For love. My girlfriend lives here.'

'The one I saw you with at the party?'

'The very same.'

'And you haven't made any friends at work?'

'I work from home.'

'What about her friends' boyfriends?'

'They're not my kind of people – but, to be fair to them, I'm not theirs either.'

'But, like you said, you have friends somewhere?'

'Of course,' replied Rob, wondering where she was going with this line of questioning. 'I lived in London for just under ten years.'

'You're wondering why I'm asking all of these questions, aren't you?' Jo said. 'It's because I'm nosy. And because a few moments ago I was in tears over Sean and now I'm not. And that's the second time that you've had that effect on me.'

'But I didn't do anything,' said Rob. 'I only asked if you were all right.'

'I know,' said Jo, 'but sometimes that's all you need.' She glanced at Rob's pint of Guinness. 'Well, Rob, as you've been very nice to me on two separate occasions, can I buy you a drink as a thank-you?'

Rob looked at his half-drunk Guinness, then at Jo, then at the crossword and then at Jo. He knew there was something odd about accepting a pint from a woman he barely knew but he couldn't put his finger on what it was.

'Another Guinness would be lovely, thanks, but only on one condition,' he said.

'What's that?' she asked.

'The next round is on me.'

The comfort of strange girls

When Jo returned from the bar with two pints of Guinness she seemed to have forgotten that she had just split up with her boyfriend. And, as before, Rob was at ease in her company. By the time he'd finished his previous pint she'd made him laugh at least half a dozen times. And before he'd taken a single sip of the pint she'd bought him the total was in double figures.

That evening Rob and Jo covered such random topics as politics (she felt sorry for the Prime Minister because he had aged so much while he'd been in power), the Internet (she dismissed it as 'CB radio for computer nerds'), and the Apollo moon landings (she'd seen a documentary on Channel Five that claimed they had never happened and firmly believed that it was all a big fake). Rob laughed so hard that he could hardly breathe. Then, finally, they exchanged life stories.

Ten random facts Rob learned about Jo
1. Jo was younger than Rob.
2. She was born in Oldham.
3. She owned a two-bedroom terraced house in Levenshulme.
4. Her birthday was on 21 February and she was now thirty-two.

123

5. She had been born Katie Joanne Richards but three months after the birth was registered her mum had decided there were too many Katies in their road and had started calling her Jo.

6. She sometimes liked to imagine that her alter ego Katie Richards was in fact her evil twin sister. 'When I'm tired and I feel really irritable and bitchy, it's Katie coming out,' she revealed. 'When I'm all sweetness and light, it's Jo.' When Rob asked, 'Who am I speaking to right now?' a big grin spread across her face and she said, 'A bit of both. Although I'm pretty sure it was Katie who threw the pint over Sean.'

7. She had seen the film *Dirty Dancing* a staggering 526 times, owned four copies of the video (three were still in their shrink wrapping) and two copies on DVD.

8. She was afraid of heights.

9. As a teenager, her favourite member of Bros was Matt.

10. She had missed her university graduation ceremony and ball because on the day she had been taken to hospital with acute appendicitis.

Last orders

'So,' said Jo, as the barman called last orders, 'how am I doing?'

'What do you mean?' asked Rob, confused by her question and the numerous pints of Guinness he had drunk.

'You told me earlier that you didn't have any friends, right? Well, I'd like to apply for the position.'

'As what?' asked Rob.

'Your friend. I'm doing a great job, aren't I?'

Rob laughed. 'You're doing . . . okay, I suppose.'

'Only okay?' she exclaimed.

'Okay, you've done well,' said Rob, and stared into the bottom of his glass. 'But, come on, you must know we can't be mates, surely.'

'Why not?' protested Jo.

'Because we can't,' said Rob, uncomfortably.

'*Because we can't,*' repeated Jo. 'That's no reason, is it? That's just you using a whiny voice to say nothing. Give me a proper reason.'

'I can't believe you're making me spell it out.' Rob laughed. 'The reason I can't be mates with you is because . . . well, because you're a bird.'

'And that's it?' said Jo. 'I'm a *girl* therefore we can't be mates? I don't fancy you, if that's what you think.'

'I'm not saying you do fancy me. I just—'

Mike Gayle

'You just what?'

'I don't think my *partner* would be too happy about it,' said Rob, eventually.

Jo sighed theatrically. 'I think you'll find that we established last time when we met that your girlfriend is a bit of a hottie so it's not like you're going to swap her for me. And, anyway, even if I *did* want to jump your bones – which I don't – I couldn't. At least, not tonight.'

Rob's curiosity was piqued. 'Why?'

'Because I haven't shaved my legs.'

'I haven't shaved mine either,' joked Rob.

'You don't understand,' she said, then lowered her voice so that Rob had to lean closer to her. 'I haven't shaved my legs tonight and I didn't shave them last night or the night before that. In fact, I haven't shaved them since I first split up with Sean – a couple of weeks ago. It's like some sort of world record of disgustingness.'

'Is that all?' responded Rob. 'I'm not even moderately rattled by that revelation.'

'You would be if you saw them,' said Jo. 'I'm a bit sickened every time I catch sight of them. I get out of the bath looking like I'm wearing skin-tight mohair trousers. I've never gone so long without shaving my legs. Not even when I went backpacking in Thailand.'

'Why have you stopped?' asked Rob.

'At first because I was in mourning for my now deceased relationship but now it's more as a safety device.'

It was as if she was speaking in a strange language. 'A safety device?' he echoed.

'To stop me rebounding into some random bloke in a moment of desperation,' she explained, elbowing Rob in the ribs. 'Believe me, no matter how much I drink tonight or

126

any other night I'm not going to take my clothes off in front of anyone – *and I do mean anyone* – with legs like mine.' She laughed and squeezed Rob's arm. 'Admit it, you're revolted, aren't you?'

'Not at all.'

'Not even a little bit?'

Rob shook his head. 'Not even a little bit.'

'Anyway,' said Jo, 'it's not just you who needs friends right now. I do too.'

'You've lived in Manchester for well over a decade,' said Rob. 'You must have friends here.'

'Are you trying to make me sound inadequate?' Jo rolled her eyes. 'I was just about to open my heart to you but I don't think I will now.'

'I didn't mean it like that,' said Rob. 'It's just that, well, I'd have thought someone like you would make friends easily.'

'I used to have the best bunch of friends in the world,' she explained. 'They were great but – well, then I met Sean and I did that thing girls do sometimes.'

'What's that?'

'Make their boyfriends the centre of their world. His friends became my friends. His friends' girlfriends were the people I spent my time with. But now it's all over I'm out of the loop. No one likes an ex-girlfriend hanging about making the place look untidy, do they?'

'I'm sorry to hear that,' said Rob. 'Friends can be hard to come by – especially when you're our age.'

'Tell me about it,' said Jo. 'I went out with my old friends last night for the first time in ages and it was . . . well, it was . . .'

'Like going out with a bunch of old-age pensioners who

can only talk about careers, weddings, babies and house prices in South Manchester?'

Jo laughed. 'You know them too, then.'

'Yeah,' said Rob, grinning. 'And plenty of people like them.'

Post-pub problems

'Here we are,' said Jo as the minicab pulled up outside her house. 'Welcome to Casa Richards.'

It was now close to midnight as Jo and Rob peeled themselves out of the cab, paid the driver and stood staring at the entrance to her house on Birdhall Grove. Half an hour earlier, when they had been ejected from the Lazy Fox, Rob had suggested that they get something to eat from Panico's on Barlow Moor Road, but Jo had said Abdul's on Stockport Road did the best post-pub doner kebabs in the north of England: they could get a minicab over to Levenshulme to get one. Without a second's thought Rob had said, 'Why not?' and they made their way to the Buzzy Bee office on Keppel Road and ordered a car to take them to Jo's via Abdul's. Five minutes later the two were in the back of a maroon Vauxhall Nova.

If Rob had been single and this had happened in any other context he would have been rather pleased with himself. It was late at night and an attractive girl was practically begging him to go back to her place for 'coffee'. But Rob didn't want to have 'coffee' with Jo. Or 'tea'. Or even 'tap water'. Part of him was afraid that if he went back to her place, his resolve to eat his takeaway, hang out with her for a while, then go home would fade fast. If he was open to temptation for long enough he knew that, even if her legs were as hairy as she claimed, there could come a moment when he might think it was a good idea – metaphorically speaking – to get out the Nescafé. Which would only end in disaster.

But Jo hadn't mentioned coffee. In fact, he was sure that 'coffee' was the furthest thing from Jo's mind. All she had indicated to him on their journey to Abdul's was that she was having a nice time hanging out with him and didn't want it to stop. And Rob felt that way too.

It had been a long time since Rob had had as good a night out as this one had been. And that it was all thanks to a woman who wasn't his girlfriend didn't seem relevant. But once he was standing in front of her white uPVC front door he wondered if he had been fooling himself. Was this entirely innocent? Had they been flirting? Or were they just two people who got on well? Then, of course, there was Ashley: what would she think if she saw him right now? How would she react if he told her how his evening had unfolded? Would he ever tell her the truth? But the really big question was, what was he going to do next?

Jo opened her front door and stepped inside. Rob followed – ninety-nine per cent sure that he doing the right thing and one per cent wondering if he was making the biggest mistake of his life.

PART FOUR

(Principally concerning being 'just good friends')

Morning has broken

A soft foot on Rob's left calf triggered his journey from sleep to semi-consciousness. He cracked open an eyelid. The left side of his face was buried in a pillow so he scanned the room with his right eye. He could see an unfamiliar wardrobe with a pine frame and dark blue doors, both ajar, and an alarm clock that told him it was 06.08 a.m. He closed his eye and rested it while he took a few slow, deep breaths and tried to recall why he felt so rough. *Am I ill? Or . . . have I been drinking? That's it. I knew I'd get it eventually.*

His stomach gurgled vociferously.

Next Rob asked himself, *Can I move my tongue? Lack of tongue mobility is always a good indicator of alcohol abuse.*

Just as he'd feared, his tongue was so dry that it was stuck to the roof of his mouth. He was forced to call for help. With considerable effort he sent a signal from his brain through his arms to his hands and his fingertips. But before they made their way to his mouth they had to let go of whatever they were holding. He brought up his hand to his face and stared at a small card: 'Carlton Minicabs'. Confused, he put it down and proceeded to separate his tongue from the roof of his mouth.

Now he did not doubt that he had been drinking – a lot.

The foot nudged his leg.

Of course, he said to himself, *I can ask Ashley to tell me what happened last night . . . Ashley . . . Why doesn't that sound right? Ashley . . . is . . . Ashley's what? Okay, let's start with the basics. Ashley is . . . my girlfriend! Correct! Ashley is . . . a doctor! Correct again! Ashley works . . . in a hospital . . . and last night . . . she was doing a night shift . . . And what time does Ashley normally get back from a night shift? Just after nine in the morning . . . So? What do you mean 'so'? If it's just past six and Ashley doesn't get home until nine . . .*

As the message reached his brain that something was very wrong indeed, he clenched his eyes tight shut and screamed at the top of his lungs without emitting a single decibel: *Please don't let there be a naked housing officer lying next to me!*

An arm draped itself across his chest. He opened his eyes and looked at Ashley's side of the bed . . . only it wasn't Ashley's side of the bed because he wasn't at home. It was a bed he'd never seen before.

The bad news was that the person with their arm draped across his chest wasn't Ashley.

The good news was that she wasn't naked.

And neither was Rob.

About last night

It all came back to him. Some time after he had finished his kebab, Jo had opened the first of several bottles of wine. Then around one o'clock he had worked his way through her CD collection. At about one forty-five he vaguely recalled the two of them getting on to her mountain bike (Rob pedalling, Jo hanging on for dear life) and cycling from her front door along the hallway to the kitchen. At two he had been watching cable TV on the sofa. And then, around three fifteen, he had asked her if he could call a minicab.

The minicab card! thought Rob. *I must have gone upstairs to find the number and fallen asleep on the bed. Nothing happened between us! Nothing!*

Rob had never before been this pleased to have been so resolutely unsuccessful with an attractive woman. It was like getting a last-minute reprieve from a death sentence. As he climbed gingerly out of bed – discovering that he even had on his trainers – he went over the previous night again. They'd talked and laughed, and it had felt completely natural. Being with Jo had felt like being with Phil and the boys – in one evening she had become someone who knew him well enough to make jokes at his expense yet showed that she cared about how he felt. He'd never thought it could happen with a woman, but Jo had the potential to be not just a stop-gap drinking buddy between

135

visits to London but the real thing: a one hundred per cent, full-time friend. But there was one thing wrong with her and he couldn't think of a way to solve it.

Rob went down the stairs, picked up his jacket from Jo's sofa, and headed for the front door. He stepped out into the early morning and fumbled for his mobile phone. When he found it he called the one person he trusted to come up with a solution to the situation he'd got himself into.

Advice

'So what's the problem, Bobman?' asked Phil.

'Who said there was a problem?' replied Rob, as he passed a milk float trundling up Jo's road. 'Can't a man just call his business partner every once in a while for a chat?'

'Yeah, he can,' replied Phil. 'But not at half past six in the morning, mate. So, let's get to the point. What's going on? Something happen to you last night?'

'How did you—'

'Use your brain, mate. You're calling me at six thirty a.m. and you're not at home because I can hear traffic. Have you been out on a bender with your new Manchester mates?'

'Not exactly,' said Rob, who had hidden from Phil his lack of social activity since the move. 'Nothing like that, it's just, well . . . I need your advice as an impartial observer.'

Phil perked up immediately. 'Bring it on.'

'Well, there's something I haven't been telling you about life up here,' began Rob. 'It's like this. All the time I've been here I haven't . . . well, I haven't made any new mates. I've been trying but it hasn't worked out the way I wanted it to.'

'In what way?'

'I haven't made any friends.'

'None at all? But—'

'Anyway,' continued Rob, in a bid to move things on, 'to cut a long story short, things came to a head on my birthday and, well . . . Ashley came up with this awful plan to find me someone to hang out with and—'

'What was it?' asked Phil.

'What was what?'

'The plan. Ashley's big idea.'

'Mate,' replied Rob, sorrowfully, 'believe me, you *don't* want to know.'

'Yeah, I do,' said Phil, unhelpfully.

'Fine,' said Rob. 'There's a magazine up here called *City List*—it's a bit like *Time Out*—and she placed an ad in it for me.'

'Saying what?'

'Bloke new to the area wishes to make new friends,' mumbled Rob.

'Oh, mate,' said Phil unable to hide his amusement. 'That is *so* gay.'

'I know,' said Rob, 'but—'

'No buts, mate,' Phil chuckled, 'that really is *incredibly* gay. It's like supergay. It's like gay plus. So how would it have worked? Some guy you've never met before calls and tells you he likes the sound of your ad, you call him back and then you arrange to go out on a sort of date?'

Rob swallowed hard. 'Yeah. That's the long and short of it.'

Phil exploded with laughter. 'That is *so* gay it's almost beyond gay. It's like a whole new level of gayness.'

'Anyway,' continued Rob, refusing to dignify Phil's comments with a response, 'I said no and went to a local pub on my own to do the *Guardian* crossword and have a pint. There I was, minding my own business, pondering six down or whatever, when I got talking to a girl called Jo.'

'Hang on,' Phil broke in, 'what do you mean you "got talking" to her? You didn't chat her up, did you?'

'*No*,' said Rob, defensively. 'I'd met her briefly at a party a while back and basically she'd come to the pub with her boyfriend and they ended up having a row and she was crying and—'

'Let me guess,' said Phil. 'You *consoled* her.'

'Not like that! We just got talking, that's all, and we had a few drinks and I went back to hers . . . and, well . . . I spent the night there.'

'You spent the night with another woman?' Phil sounded genuinely shocked.

'Not like *that*.'

'Like what, then?'

'Like mates.'

'Where did you sleep?'

'On top of her bed – *fully clothed*.'

'And where did she sleep?'

'On the bed next to me – *fully clothed*. Look, I'd had a bit to drink – I must have been trying to phone a taxi to get back to mine when I fell asleep on the bed.'

'Bobman,' began Phil, clearly entertained by Rob's plight, 'only you could get yourself into a mess like this.'

'It sounds ludicrous, doesn't it? But there's something about Jo that – we just clicked.'

'As mates?'

'Absolutely one hundred per cent as mates. Is that ridiculous?'

'You've had female friends before, haven't you?'

'Yeah,' said Rob, 'but this is different somehow. For starters I haven't made any new female friends since I've been with Ash. And most of the ones I had have sort of faded away over the last few years. You know how it is – you start seeing someone, they start seeing someone and then you drift apart.'

'I wouldn't know, mate,' said Phil. 'I've never had any female friends.'

'What about Adele from the ad agency? You were pretty close to her for a while. And there was that girl who worked in the press office at EMI.'

'I wouldn't call them mates exactly,' clarified Phil. 'Truth is, they were more like ongoing projects, if you know what I mean. They responded better when my obvious charms were on slow release rather than fuel-injected. I don't think I've ever had a female friend who wasn't an ongoing project.'

'Not one?'

'Nope.' Phil paused. 'Are you trying to tell me you don't fancy this girl?'

'Don't get me wrong,' said Rob. 'She's definitely attractive. And I'll admit that when I pictured myself finding a new drinking buddy I never saw them with breasts. But this is the twenty-first century and that stuff doesn't matter, does it? Because when you're making friends with people all that matters is that you click with them – that you get . . . I don't know . . . that *feeling* about them. That's what counts and that's what I got last night.'

'What about Ashley in all this?' asked Phil. 'Come on, mate, think it through, will you? What do you think she's going to say if she discovers that your new bosom buddy is a girl you find attractive? She's not going to get it, is she?'

'First off,' said Rob, 'I didn't say I *found* her attractive. I said she *was* attractive – it's a simple observation of fact. And what's the big deal? Loads of people have friends of the opposite sex.'

'Only on the telly,' said Phil. 'Not in the real world, when you're thirty-three and have a long-term girlfriend. How would you feel if Ash was suddenly best mates with some hunky doctor?'

'She already is,' replied Rob, 'and his name's Neil.'

'And you're fine with it?'

'Well, I've got no choice, have I? She was friends with him before I met her. Anyway, Ashley's not going to run off with Neil now I've moved up here, is she? Defeats the object, doesn't it?'

'I suppose,' conceded Phil. 'But I know *I* wouldn't like it. And I don't think Ash will either.'

'But that's not even fair,' countered Rob. 'It's hypocritical *and* sexist. If Jo was a bloke, Ashley wouldn't get a say in whether he could be my mate.'

'Good point,' said Phil. 'But if Jo *was* a bloke and you'd just spent the night at his house you wouldn't be calling me up at this time in the morning to ask my advice, would you? Bob-man, what you've got to remember is that the way things are in life is the natural order. After all, you wouldn't keep a fox in a chicken run and not expect him to make himself a snack.'

'Did you just make that up?' asked Rob.

'No. I nicked it from a film.'

'I can't see her again, can I?' said Rob. 'You're right. Ashley's never going to get it, is she?'

'My guess is no, but then again I'm not her boyfriend. You know her best. How do *you* think she'll react?'

'I don't know,' replied Rob. 'But I don't think I can risk it. The last thing I need is for her to get cold feet about us because I'm hanging out with some bird. I've got to face it. I'm just going to have to forget about seeing Jo again.'

'It's the only conclusion,' said Phil. 'And then what you need to do is find yourself a nice, straightforward, uncomplicated bloke.'

Mirror mirror

'What do you think?' asked Rob, turning round 360 degrees.

'I liked what you had on before,' replied Ashley.

'Really?' asked Rob, studying himself from behind in the bedroom mirror. Ashley nodded.

'But don't you think the V neck is a bit . . . *trying too hard*?'

Ashley rolled her eyes. 'Is "trying too hard" your new shorthand for "is this a bit gay"?'

It was a quarter to six on a Thursday night in July, a week after Rob's conversation with Phil, and he was standing in front of Ashley, showing her the clothes he had chosen for his first ever bloke-date. He had decided to take Phil's advice and find himself "a nice, straightforward, uncomplicated bloke" and knew he had to contact one of the respondents to his *City List* ad in the hope that at least one might be normal. He was meeting Veejay first, purely on the basis of chronology. *This*, he had thought, as he put down the phone having arranged to meet him in BlueBar at eight, *is going to be the longest night of my life.*

'How about I go with what I had on before,' continued Rob, 'but maybe swap the V neck for that T-shirt I bought in Aspecto last Saturday?'

Ashley shook her head – more in sorrow than sympathy, Rob suspected – and he began to change again. Over the following half-hour she helped him whittle down his wardrobe to two 'dressed-down-look' contenders: Levi's, green Carhartt T-shirt, trainers, army jacket ensemble, or old G-star jeans, a grey V-neck jumper and a beige jacket he'd bought from Duffer of St George in Covent Garden. Ashley told him both outfits worked well – neither was 'trying too hard' but both displayed enough fashion sense to show that he wasn't a complete idiot. 'The best way to decide what to wear,' she told him, 'is to work out what you want to say with your clothes.'

Rob thought about it. 'I think mostly it's "Hi, I'm Rob, this situation is making me feel uncomfortable. I'm not gay but please like me."'

'And you think the clothes you're wearing will tell someone that?' said Ashley, grinning. 'Anyone would think you were wearing a Technicolor dreamcoat the way you're going on about this.'

'You don't get it, do you?' said Rob. 'First impressions are everything. If I was going out with a girl tonight I'd know exactly what to wear.'

'Which would be?'

'What I'm wearing now. The jeans, trainers and V neck.'

'Why?'

'The jeans and trainers say "casual" and women like us to be dressed casually on first dates because most can't stand vain men. The V neck says, "Come and have a look at my neck," because women like their sexual messages subtle – and my neck is one of my best features.'

Ashley looked puzzled. 'So, if your V-neck jumper is so devastating to womankind, why are you wearing it for your date with Veejay?'

'First, it's not a date,' said Rob, 'just two blokes going for a

143

drink. Second, with heterosexual men there's no subtext in clothing. He'll take one look at me and think, ''Here's a bloke wearing clothes that aren't rubbish.'' The only way he'd notice anything more than that would be if I turned up naked, in which case he'd think, ''Here's a bloke not wearing any clothes. I'm off.'' Most men are straightforward like that.'

'You can call it a meeting of minds,' teased Ashley. She kissed him, then began to get ready for work. 'You can call it two roustabout young bucks drinking at the same waterhole – you can call it what you like – but it's still a date. And you know it.' She smiled. 'Wear the V neck. You'll look great.'

Small town boy

It was five to eight when Rob entered BlueBar, holding a rolled-up copy of *City List*. It was packed with after-work drinkers and early weekenders, and the air was buzzing with conversation. Although Rob wasn't usually the kind of person to worry about whether or not his breath was fresh, he'd been popping mint Tic Tacs into his mouth at the rate of two or three a minute since he'd left the house.

He spotted a couple leaving a table near the window – and several other drinkers with designs on it. He was in need of a drink but even more in need of a table: he'd made up his mind that talking to a complete stranger standing up was less heterosexual than sitting down so he therefore had no choice but to battle for the table. Fortunately the male half of the couple leaving the table made eye contact with him and did the 'Oh, do you want this table?' mime, involving hand gestures and raised eyebrows, to which Rob replied with his own 'Well, if you don't mind I would actually' semaphore in reply. The other drinkers had watched this exchange and, in accordance with the rules of social etiquette in bars, reluctantly relinquished their claim. Rob smiled at the couple as he squeezed past them and sat down. He could feel the eyes of the tableless drinkers boring into his back as they tried to work out why a man on his own would need an entire table to himself.

Just as Rob was settling into his seat, a man wearing a dark grey pin-striped suit, a white shirt with the top button undone and a blue tie – just as he'd described – came into the bar. The look said, 'I've just finished work and I'm dying for a pint.'

This was it.

Veejay.

Rob's date with a bloke was about to begin.

'Hi,' said Veejay, waving his rolled-up *City List*. 'Are you Rob Brooks by any chance?'

'No,' said Rob, adopting a Yorkshire accent, 'I'm afraid not, mate. You must have mixed me up with someone else.'

Veejay apologised profusely for disturbing him and, unable to hide his embarrassment, scuttled off to get himself a drink. Barely able to breathe Rob waited at his table until Veejay was being served, then slipped out of his chair and made his way to the door. Outside, he leaned against the wall, breathing so heavily that he thought he might faint. Did he feel bad about what he had just done to Veejay? Yes. Was he going to return to the bar and explain that he had lost his nerve? No. He'd walk home and feel sorry for himself instead. But then a silver Peugeot, with an Express Star Radio Cars sticker on the door, pulled up at the side of the road and beeped its horn.

'Taxi for Mr Moloney?' asked the driver, as Rob approached.

'Yeah,' said Rob climbing in.

'Where are you going, mate?' asked the driver, as Rob put on his seatbelt.

'A friend's house,' he replied. 'Birdhall Avenue, Levenshulme.'

Twenty minutes later Rob was in Jo's road, scanning the

front doors and trying to remember which was hers. Then he recognised one – white uPVC with orange and white leaded lights. He took a deep breath and rang the doorbell. The light came on and a figure moved along the hall.

'Rob!' exclaimed Jo, as she opened the door. 'What are you doing here?'

'I was in the area,' he said, 'and I was wondering if your offer's still open. You know, the one about you and me –'

'– being friends?' said Jo, grinning as if she'd just won the national lottery. 'Absolutely.'

Something to talk about

It was now just after midnight and Rob was still on a high after his second best night out in Manchester. He and Jo had stayed in drinking, laughing, playing music from their youth and talking about the meaning of life. There was no doubt in his mind that he had finally found the friend he was looking for. Rob liked the way Jo 'got' him. She was on his wavelength and he was on hers. He had lost count of the times when she had voiced an opinion that matched his.

She, too, thought that *Scarface* was the world's most overrated film.

She, too, thought that Radiohead hadn't done a decent album since *OK Computer*.

And she, too, couldn't understand why people were so down on reality television when it was clearly the greatest art form of the last hundred years.

It was constant validation in stereo.

At the end of the evening when Rob's minicab arrived, he had kissed Jo's cheek, then spent the journey home trying to work out how he was going to break the news to Ashley, without making it into a big deal, that he was going to hang out with a funny, attractive, single girl.

He shuddered as he imagined the words leaving his lips.

He shuddered as he imagined the silence that would fall as Ashley contemplated his revelation.

And he shuddered again as he imagined the torture she might inflict on him in reaction to his news.

The silent treatment?

The immediate withdrawal of all conjugal relations?

A lot of furious yelling and slamming of doors?

Or some terrifying combination of all three?

The idea that he might set off a potential megatonne bomb's worth of feminine fury with one conversation made him wary of broaching the subject without assistance, so the moment he was through the door at home he was on the phone to Phil.

'Mate,' said Rob. 'I need your help and I need it now.'

He told Phil about his evening and what he intended to do next.

'So, let me get this right,' said Phil. 'Despite our previous conversation on this subject it's your intention . . .' he cleared his throat ' . . . to inform your girlfriend that you're going to be getting drunk regularly with some woman you met in a pub.'

'I know it sounds bad when you put it like that but, honestly, it's like hanging out with you and Woodsy only she smells better.'

'It sounds like suicide,' said Phil.

'But what about Ashley being friends with Neil? Surely that gives me some ammunition.'

'Nope,' said Phil. 'Ash still won't get it. Neil was there before you so he's not part of the couple equation. Whatever deal they had about working this friends-versus-fancying-each-other thing has been worked out – as evidenced by the fact that they're not together. Jo on the other hand has arrived after you and Ashley got together so she *is* part of your couple equation. You and Jo won't have worked out a

deal on the friends-versus-fancying-each-other thing and
therefore have no evidence that you won't end up together.
Ashley will feel threatened and within her rights to exercise
her right of veto.'

'But she hasn't got a right of veto.'

'Oh, yes, she has,' said Phil. 'You might not have talked
about it but it's in the small print at the bottom of the contract
when you do the long-term thing. It says that once you're a
couple everything you do affects her and everything she does
affects you. She will tell you about a million and one things
that you don't care about – like she might be getting her hair
coloured or that she bought a different brand of shower gel or
that she's going to visit her mum at the weekend – because
she thinks they will impinge on your life in some way. That's
how women's minds work, mate, believe me. Ash definitely
gets a say about Jo, and as long as Neil doesn't try anything
on he gets life-long immunity.'

'But it's not fair, is it?' said Rob. 'I really do get on well with
Jo. And I don't fancy her at all. We're mates and nothing
else.'

'So you keep telling me,' replied Phil. He paused for a
moment. 'Look,' he began carefully, 'there *might* be a way
round this but it's a long shot.'

'Go on.'

'You see, the problem you've got is that you've made
being friends with Jo into an issue. Even having this conversation with me is fanning the flames.'

'Good point but—'

'So, this is what you do. You tell yourself that seeing Jo
isn't a big deal. In fact, you don't even do that. You tell
yourself it's an ordinary, completely and utterly common-
place thing.'

Rob laughed uncomfortably. 'But it *is* a big deal – I'm hanging out on my own with a woman I met at a party.'

'That's one way of looking at it,' said Phil. 'Another is that you're hanging out with a human being who just *happens* to be a woman you met at a party. You see? It's all about your point of view.'

'Ashley's never going to go for this,' said Rob. 'When I tell her I'm going out with Jo and I use the words "she" or "her" she's going to have me under the bright lights with a gun at my head. It'll never work.'

'So don't use the personal pronouns. It's perfect when you think about it. You talk about "my friend Jo". Think about it. After years of social conditioning Ashley will assume that "Jo" is a "Joe". Which is the sort of outrageously sexist assumption she ought to be ashamed of.'

'So you think I should lie to her?'

'No,' said Phil. 'You're not lying because that, my friend, will get you into big trouble. What you're doing is challenging her preconceived notions about the social construction of gender politics.'

Rob sighed. 'Sod it,' he said. 'It doesn't look like I've got much choice. I'll call her right now at work and get it over and done with.'

The call

'Hey, babe,' said Rob, when Ashley answered her phone. 'How are you?'

'Fine,' said Ashley. 'Pretty good, actually. It's been a quiet shift. A few emergencies came in just after ten but we dealt with them fairly quickly . . .' She yawned. 'Excuse me. I must be more tired than I thought.' She yawned again, then added, 'All in all it hasn't been too bad.'

'Great,' said Rob, bracing himself for what he was about to do. This was his moment. 'I know we haven't seen each other for a while—'

'You're telling me,' said Ashley, attempting to stifle another yawn. 'I can barely remember what you look like. How did your bloke-date with Veejay go? Was he nice?'

'Put it this way,' said Rob. 'We didn't click.'

'Poor baby,' sympathised Ashley. 'Don't give up just yet, will you? I know it's tough but just hang in there. The other guys who called sounded like they had more potential anyway. One will be right, I know it.'

'Maybe,' began Rob, 'but I don't think I need them now. I've finally met someone. I bumped into them the first night I went to the pub on my own. I didn't tell you because I wasn't sure I wanted to . . . take things further, but after tonight's fiasco I've decided to give it a go. Anyway, they're really nice, and I think you'll like them.'

'That's brilliant news,' said Ashley, 'the best ever. I'm so pleased for you.'

'Cheers,' said Rob.

'What's this new friend of yours called?' asked Ashley.

'Jo,' said Rob. 'Jo Richards.'

That was it. It was out there. Rob held his breath as he waited for her reaction.

'Well, tell Joe from me that I'm really pleased you've managed to find someone you think you might be friends with,' replied Ashley. 'Honestly, babe, I just want you to be happy.'

Part of Rob felt so guilty about deceiving her that even now that he had technically told her about Jo he still felt the need for further clarification.

'So, you're cool with it?' he asked.

'Of course,' said Ashley. 'Really, sweetheart, you don't need my permission to make new friends.'

'I know,' said Rob. 'I just wanted to make sure you were cool with it, though.'

'I feel terrible hearing you say that,' said Ashley. 'I feel like I've castrated you or something. You'd have never asked my permission to make new friends in London. You'd have just got on with it and I would've had to learn to like their colourful personality quirks. Listen, babe, you're your own man. I know how much your independence means to you. Just do what makes you happy.'

Rob was well aware that he was employing the worst kind of Homer Simpsonesque reasoning to deceive her, but she had made a more than convincing case for why he shouldn't feel guilty. She was right. This wasn't about Rob making friends with a woman: it was about Rob needing to be an independent being. Since he had moved from London, he had felt as though nothing in his life was his own any more. And Ashley was right, too, about him feeling emasculated: in Tooting he had been king of his castle, but in Chorlton he felt like the biggest eunuch on the block. When they went out locally with friends he wasn't Rob Brooks any more, he was 'Ashley's boyfriend'. His own sense of self was gradually being eroded. Who *was* Rob Brooks if he wasn't having meaningless conversations about television, music or film? Who was he if the only people he socialised with didn't understand his outlook on life? Who was Rob Brooks if his girlfriend had the right to veto his choice of friends? To Rob, the answer was simple: Rob Brooks was no longer Rob Brooks. He was becoming someone else and that, more than anything, convinced him he was doing the right thing. 'After all,' he said to Phil the following day, when he had finally come to terms with his decision, 'if a man can't even choose his friends without his girlfriend getting involved there's a strong possibility that he isn't much of a man in the first place.' And so over the following weeks, as Rob began to see Jo more regularly, he did not feel guilty about what he was doing because, in his mind, it was the right thing.

Platonic dating

(1a) An evening round at Jo's watching Dirty Dancing

It was just after ten p.m. the following Wednesday, and as Ashley was working yet another night shift Rob was round at Jo's house, sitting on the battered seventies-style tan leather sofa having just watched *Dirty Dancing* on DVD for the first time in his life.

'Isn't it just the best film ever?' asked Jo, turning off the DVD player. 'When I was a kid my parents used to take me on holiday to Woolacombe Bay every summer and I used to dream of being taught some basic moves by the hotel's dancing instructor. But they never had one at the places we stayed at and even if they did I knew they wouldn't be as sexy as Johnny Castle.'

'So that was *Dirty Dancing*?' said Rob. 'That was the life-changing film you've been going on about all this time?'

'Are you kidding me?' Jo wiped away a tear. 'Didn't you think it was brilliant?'

'Can't say I did. It didn't get me at all.'

'How can it not have got you?' asked Jo, incredulously. 'Have you no heart? She's a seventeen-year-old girl, she's holidayed in the Catskills, learned lots of things about life and the mambo, and fallen in love for the first time. How can you not feel all warm inside after that?'

'Easily,' said Rob. 'Well for starters, it's called *Dirty Dancing*, right? So how come the dancing wasn't that dirty then? It wasn't even risqué. Some greasy-haired bloke rubbing himself up against a scrawny seventeen-year-old girl to some old-time music is hardly the raunchiest dancing, is it?'

'It was risqué for 1963 when the film's set.' Jo sighed in exasperation. 'In 1963 that was probably as dirty as dancing got.'

'I think it's because I'm not a fourteen-year-old girl,' said Rob, 'but a thirty-three-year-old bloke. It wasn't aimed at me.'

Jo looked scandalised. 'I'm not a fourteen-year-old girl.'

'Technically, no. But I think – with the exception of Ashley – there's a fourteen-year-old girl in every woman.'

'Why with the exception of Ashley?'

'Because she once told me that when she first saw *Dirty Dancing* with her schoolfriends she was the only one who didn't like it. She said it was – I quote – "stupid".'

'Each to their own,' said Jo, with a shrug, but Rob could see that she really wanted to say, 'How can anyone call themselves a woman and not like *Dirty Dancing*?'

(1b) The conversation with Ashley afterwards

Ashley: So what did you get up to last night?

Rob: I went round to Jo's and watched a movie.

Ashley: Oh, yeah? Which one?

Rob: I dunno . . . wasn't my choice . . . Some film about dancing.

Ashley: Was it any good?

Rob: Not really. (Pauses.) Fancy going out for dinner next week? Somewhere posh?

Ashley: That sounds great. What have I done to deserve it?

Rob: Nothing. I just fancied treating you as you're not on nights.

(2a) A gig at Matt and Phred's Jazz Club

It was a Friday night and Rob and Jo were at packed-out Matt and Phred's Jazz Club on Tibb Street to see some live music. When Rob had booked the tickets a few weeks earlier Ashley had agreed to come with him but her work rota got in the way so Rob had brought Jo instead.

'Who's this guy we're seeing tonight?' asked Jo, looking at the empty stage in front of her.

'Josh Rouse.'

'And he's British?'

'No, he's American.'

'And this tour is to promote his début album?'

'No, he's made three – *Dressed like Nebraska* and *Home* and this one, which he's promoting now, *Under Cold Blue Stars*.'

'Right,' said Jo. 'Is he famous?'

'He's not in the charts, if that's what you're asking.'

'So what does he sound like?'

Rob shrugged. He hated putting labels on music but he knew he'd have to for Jo or she'd stand there perplexed for the next few hours. 'It's sort of an alt-country – grown-up-pop sort of thing.'

'I have no idea what you're talking about,' said Jo. 'What's alt-country?'

'Alt-country is . . .' He didn't finish the sentence. Instead he laughed and said, 'Trust me, you'll like him.'

(2b) The conversation with Ashley afterwards

Ashley: How was the gig?

Rob: Great. He played a lot of stuff off the new album, which sounds really cool.

Ashley: And what did Joe think?

Rob (pauses): Jo thought it was great too.

(3a) An evening in the Lazy Fox

It was ten to ten on the following Thursday evening. Once again, Ashley was working a night shift, which was why Rob and Jo were sitting in what they now considered to be 'their' spot in the Lazy Fox. They had arrived at the pub at just after eight and the conversation had included a long list of weird and wonderful websites Rob had discovered, the highlights and lowlights of Denzel Washington's acting career (Rob's highlight: *Training Day* – 'I love it when good cops go bad'; Jo's lowlight: *The Bone Collector* – 'The silliest film I've ever seen'), and the news that Jo's cousin Jenny was pregnant ('Yet another thing for my mother to be disappointed in me about').

'Can I ask you a question?' said Rob.

'Fire away.'

'Ever since the night I met you at that party, you've never said any more about the novel you told me you'd written.'

'Yeah,' said Jo. 'I know.'

'But why?'

'Because there's nothing to say. I wrote a novel. It wasn't very good and it didn't get published.'

'But you sent it to a publisher?'

'No,' said Jo. 'It was too rubbish. There was no point.'

'But how do you know it was rubbish?'

'Because I read it and it was.'

'Did anyone else read it?'

Jo paused. 'Well, my brother Ryan took a look at it but . . .'

'What did he think?'

Jo smiled. 'He told me it was the best thing he'd ever read.'

'Maybe it really is good.'

Jo shook her head. 'Ryan only said it was because that's what big brothers do – the nice ones, anyway.'

'Maybe he wasn't just saying it to be nice,' said Rob. 'Maybe he really thinks it's good.'

'Maybe.'

'When do I get to read it?' asked Rob.

'Look,' said Jo, 'I know you're trying to be nice and I don't want to be rude but that's not going to happen, okay?'

'But—'

'No buts,' said Jo, firmly, then stood up, making it clear that the discussion was over. 'I'm going to the bar to get another drink. Do you want one?'

'Yeah,' replied Rob, wondering why her book was such a sore subject. 'I'll have another Guinness.'

'One Guinness coming up. And when I get back can we talk about something else?'

'Yes,' said Rob, confused by her mood change. 'Of course.'

When Jo returned to their table, with a packet of prawn-cocktail crisps between her teeth and a pint of Guinness in each hand she was back to normal. She put down the drinks, tore open the crisps and immediately ploughed into an in-depth discussion of the film director Ken Loach: she'd cried virtually non-stop for two days after seeing *Ladybird Ladybird*. 'I haven't watched a Ken Loach film since,' she confessed, grinning, 'and he's one of my favourite directors.'

At the end of the evening Rob walked Jo to the Buzzy Bee minicab office and while they waited for a car to arrive for her they talked about work, their plans for the coming weekend and when they might meet up next. Soon, she was in the back of a silver Ford Orion, and Rob was walking home in the rain, wondering why their exchange about her book had upset her so much.

(3b) The conversation with Ashley afterwards

Ashley: Good night out?

Rob: Yeah, it was.

Ashley: And how are things with Joe? Is he up to anything new?

Rob (pauses): Nah, *Jo's* not up to anything new.

Ashley: Hmmm. (Pauses.) What did you say Joe does for a living?

Rob (pauses): *Jo* works for a housing association in Moss Side.

Ashley: That sounds interesting. What does he do?

Rob (pauses): Did you hear that?

Ashley: What?

Rob: Oh, I thought I heard a noise outside. Probably the nextie's cat.

Ashley: I didn't hear anything.

Rob: No? Oh, well. Must be me. (Pauses.) How's your mum?

Ashley: Fine. Nothing much to report. (Pauses.) Has he got a girlfriend?

Rob (pauses): Who?

Ashley: Joe.

Rob: No, Jo has not got a girlfriend.

Ashley: That's a shame. Does he mind being single?

Rob (pauses): Does Jo mind being single? Not as far as I know.

Ashley: You should invite him round here and I could invite Bryony too – she's single at the moment and definitely on the lookout for some new talent.

Rob (quickly): Believe me, it wouldn't work.

Ashley: Why? Don't you think she's attractive enough for Joe?

Rob: Trust me. As lovely as Bryony is, I guarantee she is definitely not Jo's type.

Mates

During all of these occasions, Rob was pleased to note that there hadn't been the slightest hint of sexual tension between him and Jo.

Nothing.

It was as if he was blind to the fact that she was a woman and as if she was blind to the fact that he was a man. They were no more and no less than just good friends.

Plans

As childish as Rob's plan had been, there was no doubt that its chief success had been in avoiding confrontation, thereby ensuring a peaceful home life. Thanks to his failure to correct Ashley when she used 'he', 'him' or 'his' in relation to Jo, and that he never referred to her with a personal pronoun, Rob could go about his business with her as he pleased. And while it didn't make him feel good about himself, he no longer felt like a friendless loser. He had a friend and he was happy with her.

Rob was now seeing Jo twice a week, depending on Ashley's work and social timetable. When Ashley went out with her friends, Rob went out with Jo. If Ashley was working nights and he fancied a bit of company he phoned Jo. As far as Rob was concerned, it made Ashley, Jo and himself happy. Ashley benefited from having a considerably less grumpy boyfriend, Jo benefited from feeling less lonely, and Rob had his little piece of independence.

The knock-on effect of Rob now being in possession of a social life was that he felt more inclined to make the time he spent with Ashley seem special: he was more attentive, talkative and romantic than he had been in months. It wasn't guilt that had brought about the change: it was Jo. Now that he no longer obsessed about his lack of friends he could see that he had neglected Ashley and, like any good

163

boyfriend, he reasoned that he should make amends for it. He took her away on her weekend off, left notes around the house for her to discover when he was in London on business, and generally behaved like top-grade boyfriend material.

Inevitably, though, with a plan as flawed as Rob's, it was only a matter of time before something came along to threaten it. One Saturday in August, just a few weeks into his covert friendship with Jo, Ashley's friends had been round for a barbecue after a scorching summer's day. Rob had enjoyed the evening far more than he had expected to: Mia wasn't as irritating as usual; Luke wasn't as boorish; Lauren's braying-hyena snort of a laugh, though still unattractive, didn't make him want to scream. And even Neil, seemed slightly less . . . well, like Neil. None of it, however, had anything to do with Rob coming round to liking Ashley's friends. It was all down to one thing: that he now had a friend of his own. With Jo in his life, he was not only becoming a nicer person to be around but also seeing other people in a better light.

'Well, that was good,' said Ashley, entering the kitchen with three empty bottles of Sancerre, a plastic carrier-bag containing empty beer cans and a couple of empty bottles of vodka. 'Everyone seemed to have a good time.' She made eye contact with Rob. 'Even you.'

'I did actually,' said Rob. 'I don't know how that happened.'

'I do,' said Ashley. 'You've been so much happier and more positive about life since you started hanging out with Joe. Don't you think?'

Rob shrugged. 'Who knows?'

'I do,' said Ashley. 'Believe me, I can see the change in you. It's almost like you've been given a new lease on life.'

Suddenly Rob felt uncomfortable. 'Do you fancy going out to dinner somewhere nice next week?'

Ashley scrutinised him. 'Why do you always do that?'

'Do what?'

'I've noticed recently that every now and again when we're talking about one thing you change the subject for no good reason.'

'I don't, do I?'

'Yes,' said Ashley, 'you do. Is something wrong?'

'No,' said Rob. 'I just want to take you out. Is it a crime to want to spend some quality time with your girlfriend when she's been working so hard?'

'Not yet,' said Ashley, only half joking. 'But how about this? Instead of you taking me out for dinner next week why don't we invite Joe round for the evening? I'm dying to meet him. It's weird that you've said so little about him. I've got a picture in my head of him being a cross between Phil and Woodsy. Is that what he's like?'

'You want Jo to come round for dinner?' spluttered Rob.

'Nothing too flashy. A simple supper, really. It would be nice to meet him. After all, we've spent tonight with my friends so it's only fair I do the same with yours. Plus I'd like the opportunity to get to know him.' She laughed and added, 'Y'know, make sure he's not leading you astray.'

'Jo's *really* busy next week,' said Rob. 'A lot on at work, apparently.'

'Does that mean you won't be seeing him for a drink then?' said Ashley. 'You'll be miserable if you don't.'

Rob cursed himself inwardly. Through her unfailing niceness Ashley had got him well and truly boxed in. If he gave her the impression that Jo was too busy to come to dinner he wouldn't be able to see her, but if he told her Jo was free she wouldn't rest until he had agreed to proffer the invitation.

'I'll tell you what,' said Rob, 'how about this? I'll give Jo a call, find out how next week's looking and arrange a date. How does that sound?'

'Excellent.'

With his brain working overtime as he tried to think of a way out of the situation Rob headed into the hallway to get his mobile phone from the table where he'd left it. He scrolled through the numbers until he found Jo's, which rather than being located under her Christian name 'Jo' was under her surname 'Richards'.

'It's me,' said Rob, when she answered.

'Hey, you,' she said. 'What are you up to?'

Rob laughed nervously. 'I was just wondering how you're fixed next week.'

'What do you mean?'

'Well, are you busy?'

'If you mean had I planned to spend every night next week rewatching my small but perfectly formed DVD collection, the answer is yes. Although I'd planned to see you – oh, and Kerry's invited me to hers next Friday, but other than that it's just me and the DVDs. Why?'

'Because Ashley wants to invite you round for dinner.'

'She wants me to come to yours?'

'Yeah.'

'For dinner?'

'Yeah.'

'How did she sound when she asked you?'

'What do you mean, "How did she sound?" She sounded like Ashley.'

'The thing is, Rob, you've never really told me how Ashley

is about you hanging out with me. I never liked to ask because I thought it wasn't my business. But . . . I don't know . . . I'm pretty sure that if Sean had started hanging out with some girl he'd met down the pub I'd want to invite her round for dinner so that I could get close enough to her to scratch her eyes out.' Jo laughed. 'I'm only joking but you know what I mean. You and I know that there's nothing going on between us but I just want to know that Ashley's cool with us being friends because . . . well because I don't want *my* eyes scratched out – I sort of need them for seeing and stuff.'

'Oh, she's fine about it,' said Rob, preparing to stretch the truth right to its elastic limits. 'That's why she wants you to come round. She was just saying that hanging out with you has made me a much less miserable bugger to live with.'

'Really?' said Jo, evidently impressed. 'Well, in that case I'd love to come.'

'How does Thursday night sound?' asked Rob.

'Great,' said Jo. 'Tell Ashley I'm really looking forward to it.'

Rob pressed the end-call button and sat down on the bottom stair to contemplate his situation. Jo had been right: he had never told her how Ashley felt about them being friends because many women, unlike men, lived by a weird honour-based belief system that meant empathy was obligatory with the sufferings of womankind in general. It was why Rob's mother was obsessed with the books of Catherine Cookson, and why Ashley was more affected by the medical problems of women her own age than anyone else's. And it was why Jo had imagined herself in Ashley's shoes even though they had never met. And Rob had reasoned that if he told Jo the truth, it might have resulted

in Jo empathising so much with Ashley that she might have
come to the conclusion that their friendship would be impossible to maintain, and that was something he didn't want
to happen if he could help it.

Now, of course, he was in an impossible position. Ashley
was going to meet Jo and World War Three would break
out. Of this he had no doubt. In his life, Rob had only
ever witnessed women at war in disputes over men. From
long-ago hair-pulling scream-a-thons in Bedford's Shangri-
la wine bar to hard stares and the occasional 'If-I-see-
that-bitch-talking-to-my-boyfriend-again-there'll-be-trouble'
at London venues in his twenties, the cause was always the
same: men.

Girlfriend meets girl friend

It was five to eight and Rob was in the kitchen with Ashley, helping her put the finishing touches to the starter they would soon be eating: grilled goat's cheese with a lemon and pepper dressing. Since she'd got home from the supermarket Ashley had already prepared the main course (swordfish steaks in a Japanese marinade with new potatoes and broad beans) and had asked him make sure the house was tidy.

Today was D-day. And, as far as Rob was concerned, the end of life as he knew it. Perhaps even the end of life itself. Rob couldn't help but feel short-changed that instead of the usual fourscore and twenty he was getting a measly thirty-three years, even though, on the whole, they had been quite good ones. Ashley would detonate the moment she found out that Joe was Jo. He could see no way round it. Several times during the week he had wondered whether it might be safer to confess all before the dinner took place but each time he had concluded that a better option would be to bury his head a bit deeper in the sand and hope for a miracle.

'Can you pass me the pepper?' asked Ashley.

He handed her the peppermill. 'Anything else I can do?'

'The table's set?'

'Yes.'

'The merlot's open?'

'Yes.'

'The chardonnay's in the fridge with the mineral water?'

'Yes.'

'You've put some music on in the living room?'

'Yes.'

'Then that's it,' she said. 'We're ready – apart from one thing.'

'What?'

'You need to kiss me.'

He kissed her so intensely that she dropped the pepper-mill.

'I'll have more of that later,' she said.

Now was the moment to tell her everything. 'Listen, babe,' Rob began, 'there's something I need to—'

The doorbell rang.

'There's something you need to what?' asked Ashley, straightening her clothes.

'Nothing.' He was all out of time. 'I'll tell you later.'

'Okay, sweetie,' replied Ashley. She twirled in front of Rob. 'How do I look?'

She was wearing jeans and a grey-patterned floaty top that showed off her bare shoulders. Rob thought she was more beautiful than he had ever seen her. 'You look amazing, babe. Absolutely amazing.'

'Thanks. You look great too. You'd better go and let Joe in.'

'Yeah,' said Rob. 'Of course.'

He got as far as the kitchen door before he was compelled to stop and turn around. As this was what he imagined would be one of his last moments on earth he thought he should say some poignant final words by which Ashley might remember him. 'Listen,' he began, 'I just want you to know that this means a lot to me. You've been really cool about it.'

'It's no big deal,' said Ashley. 'Honestly. I've got a really good feeling about tonight.'

'Me too,' lied Rob. He crossed the room, kissed her lips again, then headed back into the hallway. At the door he paused in front of the mirror to check himself, and wondered if he had chosen the correct attire for the first meeting between his platonic female friend and his girlfriend. What was the etiquette? Smart? Casual? Ever one to hedge his bets, Rob had gone for smart-casual and was wearing jeans and a short-sleeved shirt. He wiped a smudge of Ashley's pink lipstick off his lips, took a deep breath and opened the front door.

A grinning Jo was standing on the doorstep in a linen jacket and jeans, holding a bottle of wine. She looked prettier than ever. She had done something different to her hair, and her skin was glowing. And for the first time (albeit briefly) the thought popped into his head: *If I was single I could actually really fancy her*.

'I think I'm a bit early,' she said, apologetically, as she offered him the bottle of wine. 'This is for you and Ashley.'

'Cheers,' said Rob, taking it as she stepped into the house. 'That's really kind.' He kissed her cheek.

'How have you been today?' she asked, as she unbuttoned her jacket.

'Fine,' said Rob. 'No worries. How about you?'

'I've been feeling a bit jittery all day,' said Jo. 'Are you sure Ashley's okay with this?'

'It's fine,' Rob reassured her.

'And she's not just saying that?'

'No,' said Rob. 'She's not.'

'And she's not going to suddenly reach for a steak knife and stab me to death for hanging out with her boyfriend?'

'I've told you a million times,' said Rob, 'she's been the coolest girlfriend in the world. She's just pleased that I'm feeling a bit more settled.'

'I'm so glad,' said Jo, and breathed a sigh of relief, 'because if she wasn't this could be a long, painful evening—' She stopped and stared at Rob. 'What's wrong?'

Rob was staring intently at her top – a floaty grey-patterned thing that showed off her bare shoulders.

'What's wrong?' asked Jo, nervously. 'Do you think it's horrible?'

'No.' Rob found his voice. 'It's not that. It's just that . . . It's nothing,' he said. 'It'll be fine.'

And that was the moment when Ashley stepped out of the kitchen to meet 'Joe'.

Girlfriend versus girl friend

The second Jo saw Ashley and Ashley saw Jo everything – for Rob – went into slow motion.

On seeing Jo, Ashley looked momentarily confused.

On seeing Ashley's top, Jo looked momentarily crestfallen.

But in keeping with the ability of their sex to cope in a crisis both women recovered their composure in an instant. With a beaming smile Ashley held out her hand. 'Hi,' she said, as Jo took it. 'I'm so pleased to meet you. You must be Joe's girlfriend. Rob didn't tell me his new best friend was bringing a guest,' she glared at Rob, 'but I always cook more than I need to so I'm sure it'll stretch.'

Had it been possible to view the inside of Rob's head at that moment, one would have seen what is known technically as 'total brain meltdown'. For a few seconds he was convinced he couldn't hear and that his vision was blurred. His knees were weak and he had an overwhelming urge to use the toilet. At the same time, his mind was chanting in time to his rapidly accelerating heartbeat, *How could I have been so stupid? How could I have been so stupid? How could I have been so stupid?* Which after a while was modified: *Two women wearing the same top. Two women wearing the same top. Two women wearing the same top.* And then, seconds later, became: *I am going to die. I am going to die. I am going to die.*

173

As his panic subsided Rob opened his eyes to see that the two women wearing the same top were staring at him, one for explanation, the other for leadership, and then at each other.

'Er, Ash,' said Rob, throatily, 'can I see you in the kitchen?'

'What's up?' asked Ashley. 'Where's Joe?'

Rob looked at Jo, who was now looking only marginally less worried than he was, and said, 'Erm . . . do you mind taking a seat in the living room while I have a quick chat to Ash?'

Jo obediently left them, and they headed for the kitchen.

'What's going on, Rob?' asked Ashley, when they were out of earshot. 'Is this about Joe's girlfriend wearing the same top as me? I don't know which of us was more embarrassed. She looked horrified. I can go and change mine if it's going to be a problem.' Ashley laughed. 'Still, it's one way to break the ice. She's very pretty, don't you think?'

'She's – she's – she's all right,' stuttered Rob.

'What's wrong with you?' asked Ashley, impatiently. 'It's only dinner with another couple.'

'There's something you haven't quite . . . *understood*,' began Rob. 'It's like this . . . There's a little bit of a problem to do with Jo.'

'What is it?'

'Well, the problem is . . . Jo is not exactly . . . I don't know how to put it . . .'

'Just come out with it.'

Rob took a deep breath. 'Well, you know the woman sitting in the living room wearing the same top as you?'

Ashley nodded.

'That's Jo.'

'I don't understand. Are you saying your friend Joe has got a girlfriend called Jo?'

'No. I'm saying that the person in the living room *is* Jo. She's who I've been hanging out with all this time.'

Ashley looked confused. 'But Joe's a man, isn't he?'

'No,' said Rob. 'Jo is a woman.'

'A woman?'

'I met her at that party Miranda threw for Carl and then I bumped into her in the Lazy Fox the night I decided to become a pint-and-crossword man. We got talking and, well . . . we got on. At the time I wondered if you'd mind me hanging out with her and I decided you would so I didn't see her again. But then I had that bloke-date with Veejay and . . . well, my resolve crumbled. I told myself I was making a big deal out of nothing – after all, you and Neil are mates and nothing's going on there – and I decided . . . why not? I've been hanging out with her ever since.'

Rob could see from Ashley's face that his explanation was far from adequate.

'You're telling me that all the time you've been talking about Jo, spelt J-O, you let me think you were talking about a J-O-E?' she asked, teeth gritted.

'Look,' said Rob, defensively, 'I didn't—'

'That explains everything,' said Ashley. 'I could never understand why your sentence construction went all weird whenever you spoke about *your friend* Jo. It was because you didn't want to use the words "she" and "her", wasn't it? You must think I'm really stupid.'

'No,' said Rob. 'And I can explain. You know as well as I do that I've tried a million and one ways to make new friends up here and nothing's worked. It's not your fault or mine. It's just the way things are. We want to be together, and I moved here so that we could. But I haven't found it easy to make friends and, well, Jo was the first person in

Manchester I met whom I can hang out with and just be me.'

'Well, I'm very pleased for *you*,' snapped Ashley, 'but you've made a right fool of *me*.'

'I didn't mean to,' said Rob. 'You said yourself I didn't need your permission to do anything.'

'I can't believe you're saying this to me,' said Ashley. 'Do you think that after the underhand way you've been skulking around behind my back I'm going to be okay about you being friends with a woman?'

'I don't know,' said Rob. 'All I know is that everybody needs friends. And no matter how much I love you, you can't be everything to me, can you?'

'Well, that's tough,' said Ashley, 'because now you've got no choice. It's up to you. Her or me.'

'You're not really trying to tell me who I can and can't be friends with?' said Rob, part dismayed and part indignant. 'Are you really issuing me with an ultimatum?'

'It is what it is,' said Ashley, coolly.

He knew she wasn't bluffing, just as she hadn't been when she'd told him it was all over unless he moved to Manchester. When it came to brinkmanship she was a master and Rob a mere amateur. He didn't want to lose Jo – but there was no way he could afford to lose Ashley: she was The One.

'So, what's it to be?' asked Ashley, after a few moments.

'Doesn't look like I've got much choice, does it?' replied Rob, despondently. 'I'll tell her to go.'

He had got as far as the kitchen door when Ashley said, 'Stop.'

'What now?' He turned to face her. 'Do you want to start telling me what clothes I should be wearing?'

'Forget it,' snapped Ashley. 'Just make sure she's out of my house right now.'

Rob slammed the door after him and stormed into the living room, where Jo was sitting, clearly pretending not to have overheard the heated conversation coming from the kitchen.

'I'm really sorry about this,' said Rob, 'but you'll have to go.'

Jo stood up. 'I knew this was a bad idea,' she said.

'It's got nothing to do with you. This is about me and Ash. I can't believe she's being such a hypocrite. I mean, she's been close mates with a guy called Neil for as long as I've known her and I've never even raised an eyebrow.' He exhaled angrily. 'What does she think's going to happen? That you and I are going to have an affair? If we were going to do that why would I introduce you to her in the first place? She's not thinking straight.'

'Take a deep breath and calm down,' said Jo. 'Getting worked up isn't going to help anyone.'

Rob sat down on the edge of the sofa. 'Will this do?' he snapped.

'There's no point in biting my head off just because you didn't go about things the right way,' said Jo, as she sat down too. 'It's not me you should be angry with, it's yourself. What did you think would happen, Rob? You've been practically lying to Ashley all these weeks. Did you think she was going to forgive you just like that and open her arms to me?' Rob didn't answer. 'That's exactly what you thought, isn't it?' said Jo, incredulous. 'You thought you were in the right, so Ashley would just forgive your deception *and* accept me. Honestly, Rob, I thought you were better than that. It could be that Ashley isn't angry with the situation as much as she's angry with you for not being upfront with her.'

'You're right,' said Rob, 'and I'm sorry. This is all my fault. What do we do now?'

'You have to sort it out with Ashley,' said Jo. 'I'm not interested in coming between you and her.'

Rob sighed. 'Do you want me to call you a cab?'

'No,' said Jo, and stood up. 'It's still early. I'll get the bus.'

'I'll get your jacket for you,' said Rob, standing up. They went into the hallway where Rob took Jo's jacket from the coat rack by the front door and helped her on with it.

'Look,' he said, as they stood by the open front door, 'I don't know if—'

'I know,' said Jo, 'but you have to think of Ashley first. And that's fine. That's how things should be.' She looked away, and Rob thought she was crying. 'It's such a shame,' she continued, 'because we could've been really good friends.' Without looking back, she stepped outside, walked along the path, opened and closed the front gate, then turned towards the main road and disappeared from sight.

PART FIVE

**(Principally concerning
a certain amount of confusion)**

Talking and thinking it over

It was one o'clock on Saturday afternoon, two days after Ashley and Rob's failed dinner with Jo. Ashley was having lunch at Wagamama on Corporation Street with her friends Mia and Christine. She had told them about meeting Jo and how she and Rob were now barely on speaking terms.

'I can completely understand you not talking to Rob,' said Mia, once Ashley had finished telling the story, 'but where does he get off on not talking to you when he's just turned up with another woman he's been seeing behind your back and expects you to like it?'

'But she's just a friend,' said Ashley.

'But how do you know she's just a friend?' asked Christine.

'Because Rob said so and—'

'But he's a man,' interrupted Mia. 'And don't get me wrong I like Rob but in this case he's being more than a bit naïve. It's highly likely that he believes this woman wants to be friends with him – he's that kind of bloke, an absolute sweetie who doesn't realise how scheming some women can be – but, come on, we're women. We know better. There's only one reason why a woman hangs out with someone else's boyfriend.'

'I agree,' said Christine. 'She's definitely up to something. I mean, you just don't go befriending someone else's boy-

181

friend, do you? It's not the done thing and she must know that. In my entire life I've never intentionally made friends with someone else's boyfriend unless their girlfriend was a close friend of mine.'

'And that is the only exception to the rule as far as I'm aware,' added Mia. 'Even then you have to be careful.'

'But you're friends with male doctors at the hospital,' said Ashley, 'and some are married or have girlfriends.'

'Yes, but that's different,' said Mia. 'The guys at work are colleagues as well as friends. I didn't go out and meet them in some bar.'

'But that's just it,' said Ashley. 'Rob works from home on his own. He could never have met someone like Jo in that context. What does it matter where they met? And to be truthful she didn't seem scheming to me,' added Ashley. 'She was as shocked as I was when she realised Rob had kept me in the dark about her.'

'I'm not convinced,' said Christine. 'She's just a good actress.'

'Anyway,' added Mia, 'I can't believe you're taking the trouble to see things from Rob's point of view when he's so clearly in the wrong. Surely you can't be contemplating letting them be friends even if it is all innocent.'

'Why not?'

'Because even if it is innocent the one thing we do know is that Rob gets on with her so well that he risked telling you he wants to be friends with her.'

'Mia's right,' said Christine. 'That means he really likes her already.'

'As a friend,' corrected Ashley. 'He likes her *as a friend*. Men and women can be just good friends – look at Neil and me. We've been friends since university. In fact, you were really good friends with a lot of the guys at medical school as I recall – Charlie Ingham, Sam Cottrell, Rupesh Uppal. Don't you remember?'

'The operative word there is "*were*",' responded Christine. 'We *were* good friends with those guys back then. But when you're young it's easy to be friends with boys because real life hasn't begun. You're living in this weird student bubble where you can sleep in the same bed as a boy without it meaning anything. I lost count of the times I crashed out in one of the guys' beds overnight. And they were all perfect gentlemen the next morning.'

'There was something gloriously asexual about those times,' added Mia. 'I suppose it's because when you're at university and you're meeting this huge body of people – some male, some female – you can't possibly fancy all of the men because of the sheer number of them so out of necessity some of them naturally become friends. By the time you've left university to go into the real world you know so much about each other and have such a shared history that any potential sexual attraction has worn off.

'And if it hasn't,' continued Mia, 'like with me and Rupesh—'

Ashley laughed. 'I'd forgotten you two had a bit of a will-they-won't-they thing going on for quite a while after we graduated, even while you were seeing other people.'

'And do you remember what stopped it?' asked Mia.

'Rupesh marrying that trainee barrister he met when he was travelling in Japan didn't help.'

'Exactly,' said Mia. 'Rupesh and his wife live two roads away from me in Didsbury and the last time I spoke to him for longer than five minutes was at his wedding two years ago. Why? Because his wife has got him on lock-down. I don't doubt for a second that she's told him in no uncertain terms he's not allowed to see me any more. And I don't blame her – not that I'd go after him now that he's married. But I definitely understand the idea of a woman trying to protect her investment.'

'Investment?' echoed Ashley, incredulously. 'Rob's not an investment, he's my boyfriend.'

'You've been with him for three years,' said Christine. 'He's living in your house and one day you want him to be the father of your children. Of course he's an investment.'

'Have to agree there, I'm afraid,' chipped in Mia. 'And in the same way that you wouldn't leave your savings in the hands of a convicted embezzler there's no way you should be letting Rob hang out with another woman. You have to put your foot down.'

'And how do I do that without losing him? I already feel terrible for the way I behaved on Thursday. I can't stand him not talking to me. And it feels wrong. Why should I be able to say who he can and can't be friends with? He's a grown man.'

'It's easy,' said Christine. 'I do it all the time with Joel. When he first met me he was friends with all of these beery rugby-playing types whose idea of a good time was drinking until they fell over. I told him if he wanted to carry on seeing me he'd have to stop seeing them. And he did. Now he's got much nicer friends.'

'You have to put your foot down,' said Mia firmly. 'No two ways about it.'

'It's not even that clear cut,' said Ashley, with a sigh. 'You're forgetting that Rob doesn't have any real friends in Manchester. He's tried really hard and nothing's happened. He's left London, his life *and* his friends for me.

184

And if he hasn't got his own friends and a bit of independence from me there's no way that us living together will work.'

'Well, if you let him see this woman,' said Mia, 'you'll regret it.'

'Regret it or not,' said Ashley, quietly, 'if I want Rob and me to work I haven't got a choice.'

Two people

Later that night as Rob and Ashley were lying in bed after an evening spent apart at opposite ends of the house, Ashley finally spoke: 'Babe?'

'Yeah?' said Rob.

'Can we talk?'

'Of course,' said Rob. 'But before you begin can I just say one thing? I'm really sorry for not telling you Jo was a girl. It was so stupid of me. I put you in a really awkward position.'

'It did take me by surprise, and I reacted badly to it. But I've thought about nothing else over the last few days and now I know why you didn't tell me and . . . I'm partly to blame.'

'Why?'

'For not letting you know that I trust you.'

'You trust me?' replied Rob, with such bewilderment in his voice that he almost sounded as if she was mad to entertain the idea.

'Of course,' she replied, 'and I should've told you sooner.'

'Sooner?' echoed Rob.

'Yes. In all the time we've been together you've never once commented on my friendship with Neil. Not once. And believe me, that hasn't gone unnoticed.'

'I didn't want to make a big deal of it,' said Rob. 'One of your close mates happens to be a bloke – so what? If you wanted to be with Neil you'd be with him now instead of with me.'

'I'm with you because it's you I love. It's you I want to spend the rest of my life with. And being friends with someone of the opposite sex doesn't have to be an issue. It doesn't have to be – as you always say – "a thing". It can just be what it is – two people being mates.'

'Yeah,' said Rob. 'Of course it can.'

'All I want is for you to be happy. Don't think for a second that I don't appreciate all you've done for us. I know how much you still miss the boys and London, how much you miss being where you feel you belong. I know this year has been tough for you. You've been working on your own in the office all day every day with no one to talk to and I've been doing nights. I'm sure there must have been times when you asked yourself, "What am I doing here?" and wanted to pack your bags. But you didn't. You stuck it out for us. So part of me thinks, female or not, how could I begrudge you a new friend when it's the one thing you most need?'

'But?'

Ashley smiled softly. 'You're right. There is a but . . . I know it's not logical or, given my friendship with Neil, fair . . . But I can't help wishing that J-O really was a J-O-E – it would be so much simpler if she was.'

'But it's not,' said Rob.

'I know,' said Ashley. 'And you have to admit that even though you get on with her really well you'd prefer it, too, if you were friends with someone more like Phil or Woodsy.'

Rob nodded. Given a choice between hanging out with a guy he liked and a girl, he would take the guy every time. It would be a simpler friendship, with no room for confusion, it would feel more natural – it would be *easier*.

'Well,' said Ashley, 'how about you give this making-friends thing one last try? We've still got the phone numbers of the guys who responded to the ad in *City List* and one might even be better friend material than Jo. Of course it's up to you, but what if you give it a month? Work your way through them and see what happens.'

'And what about Jo?'

'You can see her too and I won't say a word – I promise. If you get to the end of the month and you haven't found someone you like you can invite Jo here again and I'll make us a lovely dinner and that will be my last word on the subject. How does that sound?'

'If it makes you happy I'll do it,' said Rob. 'And I'll sort out my second meeting first thing in the morning.'

Two men on a date

It was a quarter past seven when Rob entered BlueBar for his seven thirty "bloke-date" with Andy Ward, a thirty-two-year-old mail-order software supplier who was new to the area having spent the last few years in Spain. Rob had originally planned to arrive half an hour earlier in order to knock back enough alcohol to prevent him running away, but on his first attempt to leave the house he had only got as far as High Lane before he lost his nerve and went home to tell Ashley it would never work. But before she could try to persuade him to go, Rob remembered that he wasn't meeting Andy for himself but for Ashley and felt better. Without a word he had kissed her goodbye and headed for the bar.

As usual BlueBar was busy but this time there were plenty of seats so Rob bought himself a Carlsberg and sat down near the window that looked out on to Wilbraham Road. Just as he was reaching the half-way point on his pint, a guy with round glasses, jeans, a black Ramones T-shirt and a tan leather jacket – just as he'd described on the phone – came in and scanned the room. This was it. Rob's second date with a bloke was about to begin. And he was staying put, no matter what.

'Hi,' said the man, offering Rob his hand, 'I'm Andy.'

'Hi, Andy,' replied Rob, standing up and shaking it in as

manly a fashion as he could muster. 'I didn't see you come in. I'm Rob.'

'That's really good to hear,' said Andy, and laughed, 'because there's another guy sitting on his own – over there – and I was really hoping it wasn't him.' He pointed across the room to where a fragile-looking octogenarian, sporting a loud checked suit, was sitting smoking a pipe. 'What are you drinking?'

'I'll get this,' offered Rob.

'You can get the next round,' Andy replied, grinning widely. 'I've got a feeling we're in for a good night.'

Talking the talk

It was Andy who took the lead in their conversational début. They exchanged biographies, and it turned out that Andy had gone to a further-education college in Luton. As Rob had spent a lot of his youth drinking in Luton because it was close to Bedford they had plenty to talk about in terms of the pubs and bars they had frequented.

Andy explained to Rob how, after leaving college, he had worked in marketing for a number of small companies in the north-west but had grown bored with his job and moved to Madrid where he had taught English as a foreign language. A few months ago his Chorlton-based older brother had invited him to become co-director of the mail-order-software company he had set up, which was now going well. The downside of moving back to the UK, however, was his reliance on his brother and sister-in-law for a social life, which was why he'd answered the ad.

Following the basic biographical information, the conversation widened into interests. Andy talked about recent albums he'd bought and films he'd seen, and all the time Rob could see that his brain was ticking over just like his own was as they wondered, *is this the right thing to say?* At one point Andy revealed that *LA Confidential* was one of his top five all-time-favourite films. Without thinking, Rob said he thought it was one of the worst films in celluloid history, only surpassed in awfulness by *1492 – Conquest of Paradise, Jay and Silent Bob Strike Back* and *Scarface*.

'You don't like *Scarface* either?' marvelled Andy. 'It's a classic. One of De Palma's best films.'

'Granted I've never been to Cuba,' said Rob, 'but I'm pretty sure not everyone who lives there speaks like they've got a mouth full of golf balls.'

Had Rob been talking to Phil or Woodsy this outburst might have jerked a few laughs, and an extended harangue until he shut up and got another round of drinks in, but unfortunately, Rob's '*Scarface* is crap' riff was met by stony silence, swiftly followed by the announcement that Andy was going to the loo.

Rob hadn't meant to be so forthright so early in the conversation but he'd felt so relaxed with Andy that for a few moments he had forgotten he wasn't talking to one of his London friends. But Andy wasn't an old friend he had known for over ten years: they had met through an advert and until an hour and a half ago had been complete strangers.

Round two

Neither man returned to films for the rest of the evening.
Instead they talked about their favourite albums (Andy's,
Radiohead's *The Bends*; Rob's, Prince's *Purple Rain*). Wary
of insulting Andy any further Rob praised the Radiohead
album, but reserved a modicum of scorn for their later
output, which Andy agreed was at best 'not up to much'.
In turn he admitted that while he liked a number of singles
from *Purple Rain*, he had been put off buying the album
because, like the *White Album* and *What's Going On*, it
always appeared in those 'Hundred Best Albums Ever'
charts published in music magazines. This amused Rob
and he confessed he'd used exactly the same logic for never
purchasing *Blue Lines*, *Exile On Main Street* or any of the
music of Bob Dylan.

'It's the rebel in us.' Andy chuckled. 'We're obviously both
big on nonconformity.'

'Yeah,' replied Rob. 'We're really sticking it to the Man.'

At around ten, having discussed everything from football
and Formula One to their schooldays, and what they had
thought they would be doing when they were thirty, they left
the bar and went to Azad Manzil, an Indian restaurant on
Barlow Moor Road. Over chicken Jalfrezi, Rogan Josh and
four pints of Carlsberg they talked about family, friends and
ex-girlfriends. Just after midnight they called for the bill and

paid up. As they were putting on their jackets Rob realised he felt great. While his evening with Andy had been no better than an average night out with his London friends, he could see that there was scope for improvement. The important thing was that he and Andy had had men's conversation. They'd explored the stuff that mattered to them in a way that no kind-hearted girlfriend, family member or even platonic female friend could. Rob was overjoyed to have spent time talking bloke stuff with a real live bloke.

'Thank you for your custom,' said the waiter, opening the door. 'Please come again.'

'Cheers,' replied Andy, standing still.

'Nice one,' replied Rob. He wondered why neither of them had moved, then realised it was because they didn't want to break the spell. They knew that once they were outside the restaurant everything would go weird. They would cease being two men who had had an enjoyable evening of drinking and conversation, and would become again the bumbling heterosexual idiots who had arranged a date with another man because they had no friends.

What was more, things might be worse now: at the beginning of the evening they hadn't known each other and therefore couldn't like or dislike each other. Now they weren't strangers: they were two guys who liked each other – with added tension.

Rob had enjoyed himself. He was pretty sure Andy had too. *But what happened next?*

If Andy *had* been a girl and this *had* been a date Rob knew exactly what he would have done next – he would've tried to have kissed her. After all, following an evening that began as shakily as theirs which then managed to pull itself round into an all round top night, a kiss would not only have been inevitable but practically obligatory. And, more importantly, it would've had the desired effect of sealing the deal. Would she (the female Andy) have kissed him back? Rob didn't doubt it for a second. Would she have wanted to see him again? Rob was absolutely convinced on that one too. *Yes*, thought Rob, *I'd kiss her. She'd kiss me back. We'd talk a bit. And then I'd promise to call her later in the week. That's what would be happening now if Andy had been a girl.*

But Andy was a bloke. And despite Rob's gay-o-meter being in the red all evening, neither of them were that way inclined. So the big question in his mind was: How do two heterosexual men make the first step towards friendship?

'So,' said Andy, as he stepped out on to the pavement.

'Hmm,' replied Rob. 'That was a great meal.'

'You're not wrong,' said Andy. 'I've had a lot of Indian meals in my time but that was probably in my top ten.'

'Really?' asked Rob.

'Absolutely,' replied Andy. 'Straight in at number five.'

There was a long silence while Andy surreptitiously glanced at his watch and Rob pretended to do up his shoe-laces. As Rob stood up his heart was racing – the last thing he wanted. He did not want anything to happen that made this situation any more gay than it was already. Now his masculinity wasn't feeling merely threatened, it was posi-tively menaced. Suddenly Rob saw that he and Andy had been doomed before they met because men in their thirties *did not* make new friends like this. They kept hold of their old friends, forgot about having friends altogether or relied on men-only establishments, like golf clubs, five-a-side foot-ball leagues or the smoking lounges of spit-and-sawdust pubs to find like-minded individuals.

'Right,' said Andy, uncomfortably, 'I'd . . . er, better be off.'

'Cool.' Rob offered his hand for Andy to shake. 'Well, it was good to meet you.'

And that was that. There was no talk of seeing each other again, of calling or exchanging emails, just a brief but firm handshake, a warm smile and a sort of half-nod in acknowledgement that, great as the evening had been, they weren't going to see each other again.

Men: a user's guide

'Let me get this right,' said an astonished Ashley as Rob climbed into bed next to her. 'Tonight was about you finding a new mate and you've met a guy you like but you're not going to see him again.'

'That's about the long, short and tall of it,' replied Rob.

'I'm not getting it,' said Ashley. 'I'm trying to but I'm not. None of what you're saying makes sense to me.'

'It's easy,' said Rob. 'At the end of the night he didn't suggest meeting up so therefore I won't be seeing him again.'

'But you didn't say anything either.'

'I know.'

'Doesn't that mean you're as bad as he is?'

'I suppose,' replied Rob. 'But if he wanted to see me again he would've said, wouldn't he?'

'But *you* wanted to see *him* again and you didn't say, did you?'

'No,' acknowledged Rob, 'which is why we're not going to see each other again.'

'But do you want to see him again?'

'Put it this way,' said Rob. 'If he called and asked me if I wanted to go for a drink next week I'd say yes.'

Rob could tell from Ashley's stunned silence that she didn't understand what was going on here. And who could blame her? He wasn't sure he understood either. She was right: he and Andy were as bad as each other. But Rob didn't make the rules and neither did Andy. They received them at birth with their DNA and chromosomes.

'You should phone him,' said Ashley. 'You've got his number. Just bite the bullet and call him.' She paused. 'Is this because you're afraid of looking like a girl?'

'That's exactly what I'm afraid of. Andy and I had a good time tonight, but who knows if we would next week? And if we did have a good time next week what about the week after that? There are too many questions and not enough answers so it's safer to let it go. We had a good time but I won't call him and I know he won't call me.'

'But why not?' asked Ashley.

'For the same reason I never called Kate Newton the day after I got off with her at her eighteenth birthday party, even though I'd been madly in love with her for a whole year, that Nicola Freeland, who sat next to me at Ogilvy-Hunter, didn't talk to me after the night we got together at the office Christmas party, and that most people don't do the things they really want to do. It's shyness, combined with acute embarrassment, self-loathing and the fear of looking stupid.'

'You and Andy had a one-night stand, then?'

'Pretty much. Only without any awkwardness the morning after.'

'Men are just too weird,' said Ashley.

'Tell me about it,' said Rob. 'Still, at least there are only two more to go.'

'You're going to do it again?' asked Ashley.

'I promised you I would and I'm nothing if not a man of my

word,' replied Rob. 'Anyway, if tonight with Andy taught me anything it was that I do miss hanging out with guys and talking bloke stuff. All I need to do is find someone a bit more like me and things should be sorted.'

Opinions matter

It was eleven o'clock on the following Saturday morning and Rob and Jo were sitting in the Lead Station Café on Beech Road having just consumed an English breakfast. Ashley was shopping with Christine and Mia and this was the first time Rob had seen Jo since she'd come to his house. When he'd called her to arrange their date he explained that he and Ashley had made up and that it was fine for them to be friends. He left out the part about agreeing to continue his bloke-dates, mostly because he didn't want Jo to feel as if she were second-best. All Rob wanted to do was the right thing for everybody concerned, but he no longer knew what it was.

Initially Jo had been unsure about seeing him and he'd had to reassure her several times that their date had Ashley's blessing. Even when she turned up at the café conversation had been stiff and awkward as if she was holding back. Half-way through breakfast, though, they got into their old conversational rhythm and Rob realised how much he'd missed her.

Over the last hour they had discussed the TV they'd watched, new films they wanted to see, books they had read, new restaurants and CDs without once resorting to rising house prices. But it was only now, as the waitress cleared away their plates, that Rob asked the big question.

'So,' he began, 'disastrous dinner dates aside, what did you think of Ashley?'

'Men are so rubbish sometimes,' said Jo. 'If you were a woman, that would've been the first question you asked me. Men can't stand confrontation, can they?'

'Well, it was a weird night,' replied Rob. 'I wasn't sure how comfortable you'd be talking about it.'

'But everything's turned out okay,' said Jo, 'and that's the important thing, isn't it?'

'I suppose,' said Rob. 'And your opinion?'

'Of Ashley?' Rob nodded. 'Well, before we get to that, what did she think of me?'

'She said that from the little she could gather in the short time you were in the house you seemed like a really nice person,' replied Rob. 'And from what I've told her about you she said you sounded funny and charming.'

'Am I funny and charming?'

Rob laughed. 'Well, I would've said you were more amusing than funny, and entertaining than charming, but that's me.'

'Cheeky sod,' laughed Jo. 'I am funny and charming, I'll have you know. Ashley is obviously very good at sussing out people of quality stock.'

'Anyway,' said Rob, 'she's now very positive about you.'

'Didn't she say anything negative about me at all?'

'Nothing,' said Rob. 'Anyway, now we've settled all that, what did you think of her?'

'She seemed really nice,' said Jo, 'from the little I saw of her . . . and she's stunning to look at. She's got that whole cool, calm and collected *über*-babe thing going. *And* she's a doctor. You're a lucky man.'

'Everyone says that about us,' said Rob, 'even Phil. As

soon as new people meet Ashley they always tell me how lucky I am – as if I've just won the lottery or something.'

'Do I detect a note of jealousy?' asked Jo. 'Look, no one's saying you're not a bit of a catch too, it's just that . . . well . . . she's a babe *and* a doctor. Looks and intelligence in one package. Really, she ought to be going out with either a self-made millionaire businessman or George Clooney but she's going out with *you*.'

'I thought you were supposed to be my mate?'

'You haven't let me finish my point—'

'Which is?'

'That the qualities you've got that make her lucky to be going out with you – none of which I'm going to name for fear of swelling your head – aren't so obvious but they *are* worthwhile.'

'Cheers,' said Rob. 'I wasn't fishing for compliments but sometimes it's hard going out with the perfect woman.'

Jo laughed. 'I know what you mean now that I've seen her in the same top I was wearing.'

'But you both looked fine to me,' said Rob.

'That's very sweet of you, Rob, but we certainly didn't look the same. She was an elegant gazelle and I was a hippo. I can't tell you how horrified I was to be wearing the same top as her. *And* gutted.'

'But you looked the same,' said Rob. 'I couldn't tell the difference.'

Jo rolled her eyes. '*And* she's got great taste.'

'What do you mean? In the house?'

'I could tell from the hallway and the living room that she spent ages choosing the right colours and fabrics. That sofa of yours is gorgeous, and the chair by the fireplace. The whole house was just like her – *together* – not like my place, which has a thrown-together this-is-going-cheap-in-IKEA-so-I'll-have-it look.'

'Did you find her intimidating?' asked Rob.

Jo nodded. 'I'd be lying if I said I didn't.'

'I only ask because in the past when she's met Phil's girlfriends for the first time they've all confessed to feeling in awe of her. I put that down to her being a doctor and the confidence that goes with knowing that what you're doing could save life but maybe she *is* just intimidating.' Rob shrugged. 'Could you ever see yourself being friends with her one day?'

'Probably not,' she admitted. 'Not that she isn't lovely but I just don't think there's enough . . .' she searched for the right word '. . . *crossover* between us.'

'Fair enough,' said Rob. 'And, anyway, it's done now. You've got the official seal of approval so we can be mates.'

'That's a bit self-centred, isn't it?' said Jo, indignantly.

'What do you mean?'

'You're so clueless sometimes. Why does everything have to be about you?'

'You're losing me,' said Rob.

'Well, what if there's somebody I need you to meet?'

'You've split up with Sean and I can't imagine you'd want me to meet your parents. Who else is there?' said Rob blankly.

'Grab your coat,' said Jo. 'We're going for a ride.'

Philios

It was ten past twelve when Jo pulled up in the car park at Oldham's Greenacres Cemetery. The car park was nearly full but Jo found a space between a metallic blue Vauxhall Astra and black Fiat Punto.

'What are we doing here?' asked Rob, as she turned off the engine. 'This is a cemetery.'

'I know,' said Jo, quietly, and peered up at the sky through the windscreen. 'There's someone I want you to meet.'

Jo climbed out of the car and waited for Rob to join her.

'Are you okay?' he asked.

'I know this all seems a bit over-dramatic, and maybe it is, but I want you to indulge me. Is that okay?'

'No problem. Which way are we going?'

'This way,' said Jo, pointing to the nearest gravestones. 'Follow me.'

She led Rob through the graves, treading carefully. Occasionally as Rob passed a stone he found his eyes automatically absorbing the name and wondering briefly about its owner's life. What had Joseph Hallen (husband and father) been like? Had Valerie Chambers (daughter and friend) been a good woman? How might the world have been different if Charles Edgar Morrison (grandfather) hadn't suddenly been 'taken' on 12 August 1977?

After a few minutes Jo stopped in front of a grey marble

headstone. In gold lettering it read: 'Ryan Lewis Richards, 4 January 1968 – 11 March 1995', and underneath 'in loving memory'. Rob looked at her. 'I didn't know,' he said.

'There's no reason why you should have,' said Jo.

'But the way you've always talked about him . . .' began Rob, thinking of when Jo had told him that her brother had described her unpublished novel as the best thing he had ever read, and had become agitated when he had asked to see it.

'Like he was alive?' Jo finished his sentence.

Rob nodded.

'I still talk to him sometimes when I'm on my own. I even write him letters.'

'About what?'

'Life in general, how much I miss him. Why I hate my job. Everything, really. I was twenty-four when it happened. I had to go and see a bereavement counsellor because my family thought I was going to lose it completely.'

'And were you?'

Jo shrugged. 'Who knows? I couldn't come to terms with him not being there any more.'

'It's understandable,' said Rob. 'I don't know how I'd be if I lost one of my family.'

'The counsellor told me to write the letters,' continued Jo. 'She said it would be a good way to get to grips with what had happened. After I stopped seeing her I carried on writing them because it made me feel better.'

'You should do whatever makes you happy,' said Rob.

'Thanks,' said Jo, and looped her arm through Rob's. 'I knew you'd understand.'

'What happened to your brother?' asked Rob.

'He'd been made redundant from his sales job in London

and decided to go travelling with his redundancy money. He met up with some old university friends in Cambodia and a group of them had gone to a party. Afterwards Ryan talked some of his mates into going swimming in a nearby river and they all agreed, even though they'd had quite a lot to drink. They'd only been in the water ten minutes when Ryan's friends noticed he was missing. They searched the river but it was too late. His body was found two days later.'

'I don't know what to say,' said Rob. 'It must have been terrible.'

'It was the worst thing I've ever experienced,' she said. 'Even now it doesn't seem quite real. For years I tried to make sense of it but I couldn't. It just seemed so *senseless*. Such a waste. He would've done much more with his life than I have. He wouldn't have stayed in a crappy job he hated. His life would've had meaning.'

Back in the car, as Jo started the engine she said quietly, 'Sean was Ryan's best friend.'

'*Really?*'

'No need to sound so shocked,' said Jo, smiling. 'Originally I never understood what Ryan liked about him either. They'd been friends since secondary school but I always thought Sean was a bit of an idiot. He wasn't there when Ryan died. He'd stayed in Manchester because he had quite a good job in ad sales at the *Evening News*. He was really cut up about losing Ryan. For a long time he couldn't do enough to help out Mum and Dad. He was always round at ours and . . . Well, from that he and I became friends. I used him as a way of holding on to my brother. He understood – in part – what I was going through, and when I found myself wanting to talk about Ryan years later he was the only person who would listen. My parents stopped talking about

Ryan after the first anniversary of his death – as if the pain was too much for them – and then we stopped being a family. My parents split up the year after and moved out of Oldham to make new homes with new partners. That's why I never spend Christmas Day with either of them because if I do I feel like a reminder of a past they want to forget . . . Anyway, all this time I was still just friends with Sean and then somehow we became a couple. At the time I knew I was making a mistake but I went along with it because it was easier than making the decision not to.' Jo laughed. 'How messed up is that? I go out with my brother's best friend because I don't know how else to keep his memory alive.'

'You did what you thought was right at the time,' said Rob. 'I don't think anyone would blame you for that.'

Jo smiled. 'He would've liked you, you know.'

'Who?'

'Ryan.'

'Why?'

'I can't explain it – except that you see the world a lot like he did. Maybe if he was still alive he would've become your new friend, not me.' She shrugged. 'Then again maybe not. You can never tell anything with men, can you?'

Rob smiled. 'No,' he said. 'I don't suppose you can.'

Hello, Nigel

It was a week later, and Rob was back in BlueBar for his bloke-date with Nigel Wilshire, the third man who had responded to his personal ad in *City List*. This time he hadn't worried about his clothes, just went out in what he would have worn if he'd been going for drink with Jo. Deep down, his mind was made up – Jo was the one for him. Still, he got himself a drink, found a table by the window and waited.

'Rob Brooks?' said a male voice, rousing him from his thoughts.

Rob looked up – and was ashamed to feel disappointed. There was no way that this man was new-friend material. He had a beard, and underneath his denim jacket he was wearing a T-shirt that stated, 'IT consultants do IT better'.

Rob considered denying once again that he was Rob Brooks but his conscience wouldn't let him.

'Er . . . yeah,' he replied reluctantly. 'I'm Rob. And you must be Nigel.'

Nigel put his drink on the table and they shook hands.

'I've never done anything like this before,' said Nigel, as he settled himself into his chair.

'Me either,' lied Rob.

'Normally I like to chat to people on-line. In fact, even though I say it myself, I have loads of friends on the web. Have you ever been to www.uk.sci-fi-fans-united.org?'

'No,' said Rob.

'Oh,' said Nigel. 'I'm very popular there anyway.'

'Cool,' replied Rob, but this was getting too weird for him. He decided to inject some normality into the proceedings. 'Have you come far tonight?'

'Whalley Range,' he replied, 'North Road.'

'Oh, not too bad,' said Rob, and Nigel nodded thoughtfully. A hulking pause grew and Rob took a sip of his pint. 'This weather's a bit rubbish, isn't it?' he said.

'Apparently tomorrow's going to be like this too,' said Nigel.

'Oh,' replied Rob.

There was another long pause.

'Well,' said Nigel, abruptly, when he, too, could take no more of the silence, 'why don't I tell you a bit about myself?'

'Yeah,' said Rob, 'why don't you?' He took another sip of his pint and thought, *This is going to be a long night.*

Seven of Nine and one of the other

'Do you like *Star Trek*?' asked Nigel, taking Rob by surprise. For the past half an hour he had listened to Nigel's extensive biography and was begining to feel there was nothing he didn't know about the man sitting opposite him – but this question revealed that there was one topic on which Nigel had held back.

'I suppose the original series was okay,' said Rob, thoughtfully, then added, 'I always liked the way that the women on the *Enterprise* had to wear those short dresses. Who would've thought the future would focus so much on getting a better look at women's legs?'

'I didn't like the original series,' said Nigel. 'It was kids' stuff. But I'm a huge fan of *The Next Generation*, *Enterprise*, *Deep Space Nine* and *Voyager*. Far more cerebral.' He paused, then added, 'Seven of Nine is my favourite character.'

'Who or what is Seven of Nine?'

'She was originally part of the Borg.'

'Who or what are the Borg?'

Nigel's face lit up. 'Actually,' he said, 'your question should have been, "What are the Borg?" because they're a cybernetic life form that's thousands of years old, part organic and part artificial life. Even better, they're a collective life form.'

'A what?' asked Rob.

'A collective life form,' repeated Nigel. 'They are simultaneously one form but made up of multiple forms that are collectively aware but not conscious of themselves as individuals. Which is why they don't use singular pronouns but refer to themselves as, for example, "Seven of Nine".'

'Hmm.' Rob nodded. 'Interesting.'

If it had been up to Rob this would have been the point at which he thanked Nigel for his time, stood up and left, but there was no way of extricating himself without embarrassing both of them. For the rest of the evening he let Sci-fi Nigel talk solidly about his *Space 1999* DVD boxed set, the letters column in *SFX* magazine, Terry Pratchett's *Discworld* series, George Lucas's beard (and a whole host of *Star Wars* rumours), the first season of *Stargate SG1* versus the second season and, finally, how his perfect woman would be a combination of Faith from *Buffy the Vampire Slayer*, Seven of Nine from *Star Trek Voyager* and the original Kochanski from *Red Dwarf*.

At the end of the evening Rob looked at the pint of Guinness in front of him as if it were the only drug in the world that might numb the pain, but could barely find the will to lift it to his lips. He couldn't believe that twenty-four hours earlier he had been sitting in the Lazy Fox with Jo having a different type of evening. A good evening. A fun evening. The kind of evening that didn't feel like a slow death. Now and then, as Nigel droned on, he would imagine he'd seen Jo out of the corner of his eye, laughing at something or returning from the bar with two pints in her hand and a packet of crisps between her teeth, and he'd feel happy. When he realised she wasn't there everything around him turned grey.

'So, what do you think?' said Sci-fi Nigel.

'Sorry?' replied Rob, who hadn't been listening. 'My concentration lapsed. What did you say?'

'I was just checking that you're free for those dates I was talking about.'

'Which ones?'

'For the Science Fiction, Nostalgia and Fantasy Convention at the NEC in Birmingham next month.'

'No,' replied Rob, firmly.

'I don't understand,' said Sci-fi Nigel, looking confused.

'I'm really sorry, Nigel,' he said, 'but this has all been a hideous mistake.'

'What has?'

'You. Me. Sitting in this pub trying to be friends. It's not working, is it?'

'But I thought—'

'Look,' said Rob, 'it's not you, it's me. I'm not right for you. You need someone who is . . .' he struggled '. . . more like you.'

'But you are like me,' replied Nigel, sadly. 'I thought you said you liked *The X-Files*.'

'I'm afraid I only watched the first series, then got bored.'

'But didn't you say you liked *The Matrix* too?'

'Don't get me wrong,' said Rob, 'it was a great film, but the best thing about it was Carrie-Anne Moss in that black latex catsuit.'

'And you're not interested in learning Klingon?'

'It's not my thing, Nigel,' said Rob. 'I'm much more of a pint-and-a-nice-talk-about-life kind of bloke.'

Nigel nodded thoughtfully. 'It was good to meet you anyway,' he said philosophically, and gave Rob a four-fingered Vulcan salute. 'Live long and prosper.'

Overcome by the need to relieve his bladder, Rob headed for the loo. While he was standing at a urinal, keeping his eyes resolutely in front of him, he listened carefully as groups of men came in, laughing, joking and chatting. As they stood at either side of him, and continued their conversations it occurred to him how ridiculous it was that they could be standing next to him with their flies open, yet if he attempted to talk to them he would have been on the receiving end of some very strange looks. Making friends with men is so hard it might as well be impossible, he thought.

With a heavy heart he made his way back to the bar. He looked towards the table where he had sat and saw that Sci-fi Nigel had gone. He walked across the crowded room and stepped outside, breathing in the fresh late-night air. As if from nowhere he felt the urge to jog, and then he was running. In less than a minute he was outside the Buzzy Bee minicab office, and moments later he was in a run-down red Mercedes C-class on his way to Levenshulme and Jo.

Pillow talk

A few nights later, Rob climbed into bed next to Ashley, having came to a conclusion. 'Listen,' he said, 'I know I've still got that Patrick guy to meet up with but I think it's the end of the line for me and these bloke-dates.'

'Why?'

'Because I've found what I was looking for and there's no point in pretending I haven't. I honestly did give it my best shot – you know I did – but it hasn't worked and it never will. So, from now on I'm going to be hanging out with Jo, okay? And I promise you there's nothing to worry about because it's you I love and no one else.'

'I know you've done your best,' said Ashley, 'and I trust you completely. I've been selfish, that's all, and I'm sorry I didn't tell you this sooner. I want you to invite Jo round again next Thursday, and I promise I'll be on my best behaviour. Then, hopefully, we can put all this rubbish behind us. Is that a deal?'

'Yeah,' said Rob, leaning forward to kiss her. 'It's a deal.'

Girlfriend versus girl friend – the return match

Although Ashley had reassured him several times beforehand that everything would go well, it was still an excruciating evening, from the moment Jo arrived (having called him from home to check what Ashley was wearing) until she left at just after midnight.

Rob was almost trembling when the two women met for the second time. As Ashley approached Jo to greet her he half expected it to turn into a hair-pulling, nail-slashing extravaganza. But Ashley was the perfect hostess: from pouring drinks and passing round pre-dinner nibbles, she did her best to put Jo at ease. She sat next to Jo on the sofa and began chatting to her in what Rob could only describe as a 'friendly fashion'. Her opening conversational salvo was a joke about the Clash of the Tops, which, under normal circumstances, would have been a great ice-breaker but terrified Rob. He couldn't help imagining Ashley as a land-mine so sensitive to pressure that even bad vibes might detonate it. So while Jo relaxed, Rob became more tense – to the extent that at one point he stopped breathing for so long that when he finally remembered he was panting like a man crossing the finishing line of the London Marathon. Ashley and Jo stared at him, equally bewildered, and Rob faked a coughing fit to cover his breathlessness.

During dinner the conversation was amiable. Questions

(mainly from Ashley) about Jo's history were the order of the day and tended to begin 'How long?' and regularly featured '. . . and what were you doing before that?' but they weren't issued in a digging-for-information-that-can-and-will-be-used-as-evidence-against-you way.

Later, Ashley talked about the meal – which cookery book she had got the idea from and where she had bought the key ingredients – and Jo used every opportunity to let Ashley know that she was a wonderful cook.

Soon they were on to their favourite recipes and Jo mentioned a coconut, chick pea and ginger soup she had made after reading about it in the *Observer*. Ashley nodded enthusiastically and told her she had made the same soup a few weeks ago when a group of friends had come round for supper. From there they discussed the cookbooks of Jamie Oliver, Rick Stein and Sophie Grigson, then concluded with an in-depth Nigella Lawson lovefest that covered the cookbooks, the TV programme and the woman herself.

After dinner they all retired to the living room for coffee, which Rob volunteered to make. Such was the state of his nerves that he now felt he understood nothing about women and didn't want to be left alone with either Jo or Ashley for fear of saying the wrong thing.

Eventually Jo announced it was time she was going. Ashley called a minicab for her and until it arrived they chatted about a recent exhibition of impressionist paintings at Manchester art gallery and how they wished that they had more time to do cultural things.

Rob watched in amazement as Ashley kissed Jo goodbye, but when Jo tried to kiss him he extricated himself expertly and gave her an obviously platonic hug. Perplexed, she climbed into the cab, which sped off into the night.

As Ashley closed the door Rob became aware suddenly that they were alone. This is it, he thought, I'm about to feel the full force of a woman scorned. 'So?' he said.

Ashley yawned and stretched her arms above her head. 'Well,' she was clearly trying to fight off sleep, 'that was nice, wasn't it?'

Rob knew full well that women could mean many things when they said, 'That's nice,' and he had worked out most of them. He ran Ashley's sentence past his internal sarcasm-scanner but failed to pick up a single reading. He could only conclude that when Ashley had said, 'Well, that was nice,' she had meant, 'Well, that was nice.'

'Hmmm,' he said. 'I suppose it was.'

He turned on the burglar alarm and they went upstairs to bed. Soon they were lying in each other's arms, under the duvet.

'Rob,' said Ashley, and pulled his arms tighter round her.

'Yeah?'

'Promise me one thing about Jo?'

'Of course,' he said. 'Anything.'

'Promise me that, whatever happens, you won't fall in love with her. That's all. Don't fall in love.'

PART SIX

**(Principally concerning
two people not falling in love)**

Popcorn and explosions (part one):
Mr Cuong's ceiling

'But when will this be done?' asked Mr Cuong. 'You said last time it would only take a week and now it's five weeks later.'

It was ten o'clock on the first Tuesday in October and Jo was already wishing she had stayed in bed feeling sorry for herself rather than venturing out to work. Mr Cuong, whose case she was now dealing with, had been forced to take time off work to come into the housing office to complain about a damp patch on his bedroom ceiling that was getting bigger by the day. In the time that had elapsed since he'd first reported it, it had grown from a circumference of about an inch to more than three feet and had turned pale brown. Her heart went out to him. He only wanted someone to come and look at it and she couldn't even manage that.

'I don't know, Mr Cuong,' she replied. 'I've called our maintenance contractors countless times and no one ever gets back to me. I understand this must be very frustrating for you.'

'So what shall I do?' he asked.

'I really don't know. As soon as I've finished talking to you I'll call them again and hopefully scare some life into them.'

'Do you really think that will help?'

Jo thought carefully about her reply. There was no point in sugar-coating things. 'No,' she replied. 'Not really. This housing association is possibly the most disorganised organisation in the whole of the United Kingdom. Do you know how many forms I have to fill in to request a new batch of plastic pens from supplies? Three. And the only reason I'm requesting plastic pens is so that I can fill out the forms to request the plastic pens. It's ridiculous, Mr Cuong, and petty. Really petty.'

Mr Cuong looked at her blankly. She suspected that her little diatribe had gone straight over his head.

'I'll call them, Mr Cuong,' she added. 'In fact, I'll make it my mission to call them every hour on the hour until someone rings back and promises to come to your house and fix that damp patch.'

Mr Cuong nodded. He seemed happier now, which Jo thought bizarre: she'd said the same thing to him the last time he had come into the office. She looked at her watch. Time for her mid-morning break. As she pulled down the 'position closed' blind she began silently to scream her 'I hate my job' mantra. Eventually she ran out of steam, reached into her bag, pulled out her phone and dialled her favourite number.

'Rob, it's me,' she said, when he answered the phone. 'What are you up to?'

'Working. What did you think I'd be up to?'

'I don't know,' said Jo. 'Taking one of your many tea breaks or bidding for stuff on eBay?'

'Nope,' said Rob. 'I haven't got time for any of that these days. Phil's been talking up our company to an important art director at Ogilvy-Hunter who's looking to outsource some of his work to us. I'm supposed to be coming up with some revolutionary design ideas that will change the way they think about marketing and make them spend their budgets with us.'

'What have you done so far?' asked Jo.

'Nothing,' said Rob.

'Well, that's not very good, is it?'

'No,' said Rob. 'I've been over-analysing and deconstructing things too far. I need to feed my brain with new ideas.'

'Excellent,' said Jo. 'I'm having one of the worst days of my entire working life and I don't know how much longer I can stand being here. I've been thinking of ways to cheer myself up all morning and a trip to the cinema might do the trick, especially as in all the time we've been friends we've never seen a film together.'

'Really?' replied Rob. 'Can't say I've noticed. I suppose it's because we always talk so much that it makes more sense to go to the pub than somewhere where we have to be quiet.'

'Can you make it?'

'Yeah, I suppose,' said Rob. 'Ash is on shift tonight and I was going to stay in and do some work but . . . yeah, why not? What do you want to see? Not some chick flick, I hope.'

'There you are with that cheeky sod thing again.' Jo laughed. 'I don't know what's on at the cinema because I haven't looked. And I don't care – I just fancy seeing a film – any film.'

'How can you not care what you see?' asked Rob.

'It's very easy,' replied Jo. 'You just take a deep breath and not care.'

'Now who's being sarcastic?' said Rob.

'Look,' said Jo, 'just be ready for half seven, okay? I'll pick you up and we'll go to the Odeon in town.'

'I don't like it there. It's always full of students being studenty.'

'How about the Trafford Centre?'

'No,' said Rob. 'I can't do cinemas in shopping centres.

They're normally full of spotty teenagers sucking the faces off each other.'

'Right,' said Jo, patiently. 'What about UGC Didsbury? It's modern, it's got big screens and I doubt there'll be many kids.'

'Sounds perfect.'

'Are you always so picky when you go to the cinema?'

'If you think that's picky watch me tonight when I work out where we should sit.'

Rob and Jo and the month of September

It had been four weeks since Rob and Jo had entered the new phase of their friendship. During this time Rob had thought of Jo as a stray cat in need of looking after and as no one else appeared to be doing the job (her ex-boyfriend, her parents and least of all Jo herself) he willingly stepped in as her platonic man-about-the-house. During September he fixed her car for her (a small problem with the transmission), helped her paint her bathroom (apple blossom white on the walls and buttermilk for the woodwork) and even offered to loan her money (she was having difficulty paying her bills now that she was living alone). She had accepted help with her car and the bathroom but drew the line at money: she'd get by somehow.

Of key importance in this new stage of their friendship was the effort they put into being good friends and no more. They avoided all forms of physical contact, except a kiss on the cheek at the end of the night. They rarely spoke about the nature of their friendship, so that it didn't turn into an 'issue'. They always fake-gagged when they were out for a drink and accosted by ''rose-for-the-lady'' men, who constantly assumed they were a couple. As far as they were concerned, they weren't on the verge of falling in love but of 'falling head over heels in friendship' a fact to which the following moments in their relationship attested.

Moment one

It was ten to ten and Rob was half watching a Channel Four documentary about sex-change operations while he flicked through a copy of the *Evening News* that Jo had left on her coffee-table. She had disappeared a few minutes earlier, saying she was 'nipping out to the loo'.

Rob was wincing at some particularly gruesome footage of real-life gender reassignment surgery when Jo returned with a faded Adidas shoebox, which she handed to him.

'What's this?' asked Rob, with one eye on the TV.

'Take a look, you chump,' replied Jo. More to herself than to Rob, she added, 'This is like the worst thing in the world.'

Intrigued, Rob opened the box. 'Is this your book?' he asked.

'I have no idea why I'm doing this,' she said.

Rob, who had been lounging on the sofa, sat upright. 'Are you saying I can read it?'

'What do you think?'

'How come?' he asked. 'I thought—'

'Things change,' said Jo. 'You know pretty much everything about me that there is to know. Why should I keep this secret?'

'I'm flattered,' said Rob, taking the manuscript out of the box, 'and impressed. I can't believe you've written a whole novel. What made you do it?'

'I'll tell you,' said Jo, sitting next to Rob, 'but you have to promise me that you won't read it in front of me. I couldn't stand it.'

'I'll save it until I get home,' he said, then turned over the blank cover page to reveal: *The Backpackers* by Jo Richards.

She screamed and he put back the page, then closed the

box. 'Come on,' he said, 'it's away from prying eyes now. Tell me how it came about.'

'Okay. Do you remember me telling you I went travelling after I graduated? Well, when I got back to Manchester I decided to write a novel using some of the experiences I'd had while I was out there. I know it sounds like a cheesy idea but I was young and I loved reading and I wanted to do something different with my life. Anyway, one Saturday afternoon a few weeks after I started temping at the housing association I sat down at my old house-mate Gina's computer and started the story that ended up in the box in your hand.'

'*The Backpackers*,' said Rob.

'Yeah. The story that came out of my head was about Rosie Collins a twenty-three-year-old woman who splits up with her boyfriend – like me and Callum, my then bloke – as they're about to go travelling. She umms and aahhs about whether to go without him, then heads out to Thailand. All sorts of things happen to her involving drug-runners and murders.'

'And does she get back with her boyfriend?'

'No,' said Jo, looking scandalised. 'That would've been even more cheesy.'

'But she meets someone while she's away.'

'Naturally,' said Jo, grinning. 'His name is Jean-Paul and I based him on a French guy I adored on my course at uni. But, just like real life, it doesn't work out.'

'So at the end she's on her own?' asked Rob. 'That's a bit gloomy, isn't it?'

'If I thought you were serious, Brooksy, with your layman's lit crit there'd be trouble,' said Jo. 'In fact it's upbeat because Rosie learns loads of stuff about life and herself so she's a different person from the one at the start of the book.'

'You sound really excited about it even now,' said Rob. 'How come you never sent it to anyone even though your brother loved it?'

'I was a bit scared about a bunch of strangers reading it,' confessed Jo, 'so I started going to a writers' group at the local library. Most of the people who went regularly were right nut-jobs. One middle-aged woman carried round a notepad with just Biro scribble all over it, another in her sixties had written a novel about a talking willow tree and a heavy-metal type bloke produced something about a Utopian planet populated by fish-people. Fortunately a couple of others were normal and I got on well with them. Jean, in her late forties, told me how she'd written eleven historical romances without having one published and Edward, in his fifties, said that after five detective novels, all rejected, a collection of his poetry was about to be published by a small press based in north Yorkshire. But the guy who scared me was Alex. He was my age and had written a sort of comedy about two flat-mates in London. He'd sent it to agents and had no interest. Then he wrote a thriller – he took a year off work to polish the script. This time he found a literary agent but a year later he was still without a publisher. Out of curiosity I asked him whether I could read his manuscripts and, Rob, I was shocked. Both books were brilliant and he could write better than many published authors I'd read. It didn't make sense. I stopped going to the writers' group – the thought of being around all that creative futility was too depressing. I dumped my manuscript at the bottom of my wardrobe and almost forgot about it until one day Ryan asked if he could read it.'

'And he loved it?'

'He said I was mad not to send it to publishers. I was going to but I lost my confidence at the last minute, then Ryan lost his job, went travelling and you know the rest.'

Rob nodded. He stood up, put on his coat and picked up the shoebox.

'What are you doing?' asked Jo.

'I'm off home,' said Rob. 'I've got some reading to do.'

Moment two

The phone was ringing. Jo opened her eyes, reached out an arm from under the duvet and turned the alarm clock on the bedside table so that she could see the time. It was five to six.

'Who is it?' she said groggily, into the phone.

'Me,' said Rob.

'Do you know what time it is?'

'Look, I know it's early,' he replied, 'but with Ashley working last night I stayed up and finished your book.'

'You stayed up all night?'

'I couldn't put it down! When I started it just after midnight I was fully expecting it to be rubbish and that I'd be fast asleep within five minutes. But I haven't enjoyed a book as much as yours in ages.'

'I don't know what to say. I feel a bit embarrassed.'

'Well, don't. You should get a professional to read it.'

'That's sweet of you, Rob, but I can't see that happening. I wrote it back in the days when I believed I could do anything I wanted to do and be anything I wanted to be, before life knocked the stuffing out of me. I've worked in a housing office, Rob, for nearly ten years and, much as I hate my job, there's no point in me getting my hopes up.'

229

'Come on,' he pleaded, 'we both know why you didn't send it out last time – which is completely understandable – but why not give it a try now? What have you got to lose? I'll do all the legwork if you don't want to, and I won't charge you ten per cent.'

'Cheers,' said Jo, 'but if I'm going to do it I should do it myself.'

'So you will?'

'I'll think about it. But I'm not making any promises – so don't hassle me about it every time we meet up. I know you – you'll end up badgering me into it.'

'Fine,' said Rob. 'No badgering.'

Jo glanced at her alarm clock again. She had to get ready for work soon. 'Look, I'd better go.'

'Of course,' said Rob. 'See you later in the week?'

'I'll call you,' she replied. She was about to say goodbye when she added, 'Rob?'

'Yeah?'

'Thanks for . . . you know . . .'

'No problem,' said Rob. 'Just make sure that when you find a publisher I get to design your book jackets.'

Moment three

'Are you sure you're going to be okay?' asked Ashley, a few weeks later.

It was a quarter to eight in the morning and she was standing over Rob as he lay in bed beneath the duvet, curled into a foetal position.

'Yeah,' he said weakly. 'I'll be fine.'

He had thrown up two or three times an hour since three o'clock that morning and he was shattered. Ashley had diagnosed a twenty-four-hour sickness bug, of which a lot were going about. 'It won't kill you,' she reassured him, 'but there's nothing you can do except keep yourself hydrated and wait it out.'

Rob didn't care what the bug was called or from whom he had caught it. All he wanted was for it to go away. He had never felt quite as ill as he did right at that moment. He was weak from lack of sleep, his stomach muscles ached from dry retching and he was feverish. He also wanted his girl-friend to stay at home and look after him. He didn't want to be a man about it. After all, what was the point when there wasn't another man around to be impressed by his mastery of suffering?

'I wish I could stay and look after you,' she said, and glanced at her watch. She sat on the side of his bed and took his hand. 'I would if I could.'

'Stay,' said Rob pathetically.

'You know I can't. I'm a doctor. We're not even supposed to take time off when *we*'re ill, let alone our partners.'

'Can't you take half a day?'

'Honestly, Rob,' said Ashley, and stood up, 'I can't.' She picked up her bag. 'I've left you some water on the bedside table – make sure you drink it. Get as much rest as you can and I'll phone you at lunchtime – that's if I get a break – to make sure you're all right.'

'Okay,' said Rob, feeling guilty for having made *her* feel guilty. 'I'll see you tonight. I'll be fine.'

Ashley kissed him again, then made him promise to call her if things got worse or if he needed a chat.

For a few moments after she'd left the room Rob felt fine but as he heard the front door close another wave of nausea came over him and he was sick into the washing-up bowl that Ashley had thoughtfully left beside the bed.

He spent most of the morning dry retching, feeling sorry for himself and drifting in and out of sleep. Just before midday, after he had woken from a feverish sleep but before he was violently sick, the cordless phone rang. He reached across and answered it in the most miserable voice he could muster. 'Hello?'

'You sound awful.' It was Jo. 'What's up?'

'I'm ill,' said Rob, succinctly. 'I've been up with it since the middle of the night. I'm dying.'

Jo laughed. 'I bet you are.'

'No, really, I . . . I—' He had to stop speaking as another wave of nausea compelled him to reach for the washing-up bowl again. 'Sorry about that,' he said, after several minutes' dry retching.

'You're not dying, are you?' asked Jo, sounding troubled.

'Oh, so you believe me now?'

'Well, blokes always exaggerate about illness,' said Jo. 'How are we supposed to know when they're not faking it? Anyway, I'm sure Ashley's looking after you.'

'She's at work.'

'You mean you're on your own?'

'It's not her fault,' said Rob. 'She had to—'

'I'm coming round now,' said Jo, firmly.

'You can't,' said Rob. 'You're at work.'

'That's easily remedied. It's ages since I've had an afternoon off. I'll tell them I've got a family emergency and head over to yours. I'll come via the supermarket, if you like. Is there anything you fancy to eat? You must be starving.'

'No,' said Rob. 'I wouldn't keep anything down. Anyway, there's no point in you coming round here. I might give you what I've got. Who'll look after you when you're throwing up at three in the morning?'

'Dunno,' said Jo, 'but my mum always says I've got the constitution of an ox so maybe it's time I put her theory to the test.'

Half an hour later Rob answered the door in his boxer shorts and an old T-shirt. Jo was standing on the doorstep armed with a bottle of Lucozade, a bunch of grapes and a DVD of *Dirty Dancing*.

Rob spent the rest of the afternoon huddled under his duvet on the sofa while Jo topped up his glass of Lucozade, entertained him with tales about her work and sat quietly next to him while he drifted in and out of sleep.

When Ashley arrived home Rob could see she felt guilty for having left him alone all day, which put him in a difficult position: if he told her that Jo had been round to look after him she would feel even worse. But if he said nothing she might construe it as deceptive. In the end he opted not to tell her. He was glad that he had put the Lucozade and the grapes in his office, and cleared away the other evidence that Jo had been in the house. And when Ashley asked him what he'd done all day, he told what he considered to be a lie for the greater good: 'Nothing.'

Moment four

A few weeks later Rob made an impromptu trip to London to stay with Phil and Woodsy for the weekend. For the most part they had a good time, catching up with each other and bumping into a number of old friends they hadn't seen in a while, but things weren't like they had been in the old days. They were all busy Saturday. Ian One's wife had booked him for two dinner parties, Darren was away on business, Kevin was visiting his girlfriend's parents in Lincoln, and Ian Two claimed to be decorating his kitchen.

As a compromise they decided to meet up in the Queen's Head for lunch on Sunday, but Ian One pointed out that it was the weekend so it couldn't be boys only and he'd have to bring his wife. One by one the others confessed that unless their partners came it wouldn't happen, so what had started out as a boys' get-together was a much tamer affair. Ian One arrived with Danni, his wife of two years, quickly followed by Darren and Carmel, his girlfriend of three years. Then Ian Two appeared with Becky, his fiancée of three years, and finally, just after one, Kevin arrived with Rhona, his girlfriend of seven years.

It was odd for Rob to see his friends coupled up and cosy, older and supposedly wiser than the people he had met in London all those years ago. Suddenly he felt as if time was moving on so fast he hadn't appreciated that they were no longer a bunch of young tearaways. At some time in the last decade they had changed from boys into men with partners, proper jobs, and mortgages. Their lives were so packed with distractions that they no longer had time for each other. Rob couldn't recall the last time he had got them all out to the pub. The constraints of work, partners and life meant that time was now the most precious commodity of all.

When he returned from the bar with a round of drinks he took an empty seat next to Ian Two. He watched in awe as the conversations round the table spun off in all manner of directions. Rhona, Danni and Carmel were listening to Becky talk about preparations for her and Ian Two's wedding. Darren and Ian One were listening to Ian Two discussing Sam Raimi's *Evil Dead* films, which he'd watched back to back all the previous weekend. Woodsy and Kevin were deliberating on which animal would win in a fight between a shark and a tiger. With so many different conversations going on around him, Rob was free to talk to Phil about how odd their afternoon get-together had turned out.

'You think it's strange, too, don't you, that all of us are sitting round the table like this?' said Phil.

'Well, it does seem a bit . . . grown-up. I can't believe how much we've all changed.'

'I know,' agreed Phil, 'I liked things the way they were – this lot on the prowl for available women, Woodsy sleeping on our sofa and you and me doing *The Odd Couple* thing.'

Rob laughed. 'Were we like the TV series or the film?'

'The TV series,' replied Phil, 'which would've made you Jack Klugman – a.k.a. TV's *Quincy MD* – and me Tony Randall, who was far cooler.'

'We could argue that point all afternoon,' said Rob, 'because you know that you're way more like Oscar than I ever was . . . But that's not the point, is it?'

'Nope,' replied Phil. 'Things changed when you moved, Bobman. That was just the beginning.'

'More changes to come, then?' asked Rob.

'A lot more,' said Phil. 'I know for a fact that Ian Two and Becky are trying for a kid. Kevin and Rhona have put their place on the market and are looking to move out to Norfolk near Rhona's parents. Then there's Darren. I was in here with him last week and he told me his work are offering him a hefty promotion.'

'Good for him,' said Rob.

'Yeah, it is,' said Phil. 'But it'll have him based in Cambridgeshire, which isn't all that far but it's too far for him to come out for last orders in the Queen's Head on a Wednesday night.'

'And what about you?' asked Rob. 'Where are you off to?'

'Me? I'm staying right here, of course – Woodsy too. I can't see either of us ever leaving London.'

'But that's how I used to feel about London,' said Rob.

'And now?' asked Phil.

Rob shrugged.

'I think you did the right thing in getting out,' said Phil, quietly. 'Absolutely one hundred per cent. It could never have been worth losing Ashley for a bunch of mates who, sooner or later, were going to go their own way.'

As they sat drinking, talking and laughing, Rob couldn't help wondering what Phil had been getting at. Initially he thought his friend had simply been pointing out that Rob had done the right thing, but there had been something in his tone that suggested he'd meant more than that.

At just after three, everyone started getting ready to go home.

'Thanks for getting everyone out, mate,' Rob said to Phil. 'I can't believe we've been mates for a decade. We've had some good laughs.'

'The best. Although I don't think we ever quite realised that at the time . . .'

Phil looked wistful, and Rob finally realised what he'd been trying to say all along. It wasn't just that he thought Rob had made the right move in going to Manchester, he had been acknowledging that the things you take for granted should be appreciated. Indirectly, he was thanking Rob for his friendship.

Rob didn't know what to do with this information, so he said nothing. But on the train back to Manchester, with Phil's words still on his mind, he wondered if he was taking Jo for granted, and whether he should thank her for her friendship. He found himself calling her with no idea of how to put what he wanted to say.

'Hello?' said Jo.

'It's me. I just wanted to—' He couldn't finish the sentence.

'You just wanted to what?' prompted Jo.

'Nothing,' said Rob. 'It's all right.' He paused. 'What are you doing tonight?'

'Dyeing the grey out of my hair and eating half a tub of sour cream and chives Pringles while I watch Friday's *Corrie* on video.' Jo laughed. 'Are you on the train?'

'Yeah,' said Rob. 'It gets in at sevenish. Ash is picking me up and we're going round to Mia's for something to eat.'

'That sounds nice,' said Jo. 'I'll see you during the week.'

He ended the call, tucked his phone into the back pocket of his jeans and stared out of the carriage window.

Moment five

'Is this your local, then?' asked David.

'Not really,' said Jo. 'I've been in here once or twice.'

'How come the bar staff all know you?'

'I've got that kind of face. Familiar.'

It was ten past nine and Jo was sitting in the back room at the Lazy Fox with David Stockton, a fellow officer at the housing association.

David, who was six years younger than Jo, had been pestering her to go on a date with him from the moment she had split up with Sean. Two things had stopped her succumbing to his advances: first, she still wasn't shaving her legs, and second, if something happened between her and David it might cause more problems than it was worth. It wasn't just that the timing was all wrong – she still hadn't got over losing Sean – it was everything. She worried about how people at work would react when the news got out. She worried that he might like her too much and would want things to get more serious than she did – or the reverse. And now that she and Rob were such good friends, she worried about how he might react to her dating again.

While she understood that it was none of his business if she wanted to see someone, she felt somehow that she needed his permission to go ahead. She had floated the idea past him a few times, but he had failed to react at all. And although Jo knew she would have jumped down his throat if he had shown any sign of disapproval, part of her was disappointed that he seemed not to care. But the fact remained that unless Jo was going to remain celibate for the rest of her life, at some point in the future – regardless of Rob's opinion on the matter – she was going to have to go on a date.

So, after days of worrying about how an unavailable man might respond to the idea of his female friend going on a date, Jo concluded that she had to take action. The following day at work, she had approached David and asked him out for a drink.

'So,' said David smugly, 'here we are, finally out together.'

'Hmm.'

'I was surprised when you asked me out because . . . well, you know . . .'

'Hmm.'

David suddenly stopped looking smug. 'Are you all right? You seem a little bit distracted.'

'I'm fine,' lied Jo. 'I've just had a lot on my mind.'

'What like?' asked David. 'A lot of women say I'm quite good with problems.'

Jo stifled a laugh because she was quite sure that no woman in her right mind had ever said any such thing. David Stockton wasn't the problem-solving type: he was the cheeky, cocksure type that women like her were supposed to find attractive, and frequently did.

'Okay,' she began. 'Here's what's on my mind. I've been wondering if it's possible for men to be just friends with a woman.'

'No,' he replied.

'Why?'

'Because it just isn't,' he said. 'If you get on with a member of the opposite sex well enough to be mates with them, you might as well go out with them.'

Jo sighed heavily. 'But isn't that just lazy?'

'But people *are* lazy,' explained David, clearly pleased with his contribution to the debate. 'Men especially. We see an attractive woman and sex is the first thing on our minds.'

'Fair enough. Women do that too.'

'Yeah,' said David, 'but the difference is that you don't feel the need to act on the impulse.'

'I've heard that argument a million times and it always sounds daft. Are you telling me that just because the thought pops into a bloke's head he has to act on it? A million and one random things popped into my ex-boyfriend's head – things like wanting to go travelling around South America, or wanting to learn how to surf properly or building a house in the Canadian Rockies – but he's never done – and never will do – any of them. Why can't it be the same for being friends with women?'

'Three words,' said David rubbing his hands gleefully. 'Unresolved sexual tension – between most men and women anyway. I'm sure it's all to do with the propagation of the species but don't quote me on that. If you're talking about a man and a woman getting on *really well*, a by-product of that friendship has to be an increase in sexual tension between them. Men can't ignore it.'

Jo thought for a moment. 'But surely if they find a way to resolve the sexual tension they can be friends?'

'Absolutely.' David grinned. 'But last time I checked there was only one way to do that.'

Infuriating as he was, Jo couldn't help feeling that he was making a good point.

'But surely,' she went on, 'rather than just taking their clothes off they could talk it out.'

'Oh, yeah,' replied David. 'You've sat in on more custo-mer-relations training workshops than I have so you must know even better than I do that no one ever learns anything by talking. That's why they always get you to do those stupid role-plays – because the best way to learn anything is by experiencing it.' He laughed, then took a gulp of lager. 'Anyway, is this about you and me being friends because I was hoping for more than that?'

'No,' replied Jo, wishing she could call Rob for an excuse to leave her date early. 'It isn't about you and me at all.'

At the end of the evening Jo told David that, although she had enjoyed his company, she didn't think that anything would happen between them. She returned home alone to Levenshulme, dug out all of the pictures she had of her and Sean and pored over them for hours while she cried and tried to overcome the compulsion to call him. She was tired of being alone, eating alone and sleeping alone. She didn't want to be alone any more.

Popcorn and explosions (part two): exit strategy

'What did you think of that?' asked Jo.

It was now ten to eleven and Rob and she were sitting in Screen Three of the UGC Didsbury as the end credits to the 'high-octane thriller with a twist' began to roll.

'Normally I like to wait until I've left the cinema before I dissect a film,' replied Rob, 'because a million and one similar conversations are already going on in the auditorium, but that one was terrible.'

'It was the worst I think I've ever seen,' said Jo, as they stood up and moved towards the exit.

'Really?'

'The plot was ridiculous. The guy playing the police chief couldn't act his way out of a paper bag. And the twist with the serial killer was just plain silly.'

'But the *worst* you've ever seen?' said Rob. 'That's a bold statement to make in a world where there are films like *1492 – Conquest of Paradise*.'

'Gérard Depardieu as Columbus? I thought it would never end.'

'And if we're talking truly bad films let's not forget *Police Academy 7: Mission To Moscow*.'

'Yeah, you have a point,' said Jo, as they left the auditorium. 'You're right, but in its defence, if you've seen films one to six you might as well see the complete set.

And it might have been terrible but it was sort of satisfying too.'

'Okay,' began Rob. 'This is without doubt the absolute worst film in celluloid history and if I find out you liked anything about it I'll terminate our friendship forthwith.'

Jo laughed. 'Big words, small man.'

'Okay,' he said, and took a deep breath. 'Here we go. *Ace Ventura – When Nature Calls.*'

Jo let out a small scream. 'I wanted to go home three seconds after Jim Carrey started his rubber-faced gurning routine. The only thing that stopped me was that I'd have had to go home without Justin, the guy I was seeing at the time. I must be the only woman in the world whose sole reason for dumping a guy was that he'd taken me to a Jim Carrey film.'

'I doubt it,' said Rob, as they stepped on to the escalator and descended to the ground-floor lobby. 'Anyway, I haven't even got the excuse that someone else dragged me to see it. I went of my own accord.'

'*No!*' Jo was appalled.

'I thought the first one had its moments, but the second was too awful for words.'

'Did you walk out?'

'I fell asleep.'

They stepped off the escalator and Jo searched her bag for her car keys.

'We've missed last orders,' said Rob, looking at his watch.

'I've got a couple of bottles of Rioja at mine. It was on sale in Tesco. I had a glass out of one last night so we could finish off the bottle. What do you think?'

'I don't see why not,' shrugged Rob, 'but you're not going to persuade me to watch *Dirty Dancing* again.'

Jo laughed, then her face fell. Rob turned and immediately saw why. Sean was heading for them. Jo was staring at him, trying not to cry.

'What do you want?' she asked, when Sean stopped in front of her.

'I'm here with the boys,' he said, gesturing to some men beside a huge poster of Julia Roberts. 'We've just seen the same film as you guys.' His eyes flitted to Rob, then back to Jo. 'I saw you come in.'

Jo remained silent.

'How have you been?' he continued.

'Fine,' she said.

'Aren't you going to introduce me to your new boyfriend?' he asked.

The determined look on his face told Rob that Sean wanted to make a scene, if only to impress his friends. If it came to a fight they would be evenly matched, but if Sean's friends joined in he'd be in trouble. Despite the odds, though, Rob decided that he wasn't going to let Sean intimidate Jo.

'Just leave it, mate,' he said, meeting Sean's stare.

'He's not my boyfriend,' said Jo. 'He's just a friend.'

'I bet he is,' replied Sean. 'Doesn't say much, does he?'

'You're such an idiot, Sean,' said Jo, and tugged Rob past her ex-boyfriend towards the exit and outside, where a group of kids were playing on their BMXs.

'I can't believe he did that,' said Jo, as she stormed towards her car. 'I hate it when he acts like – like he's some sort of hard man. He's such a child.' Suddenly Rob realised she was crying. 'Why did he have to speak to me?' Tears rolled down her cheeks. She came to a halt and, without thinking, Rob put his arms round her, held her tightly and

told her not to cry, that everything would be all right. After a few moments the tears stopped and her arms dropped from his waist. He released her and they went on to her car.

'I'm sorry about that,' she said, as they left the car park.

'It wasn't your fault.' Rob paused, then added cheerily, 'So are we going back to yours to finish off the wine you were talking about?'

'Can we give it a miss?' said Jo, without taking her eyes off the road. 'I'm not feeling up to a late night now.'

'Of course,' said Rob.

Jo turned on the radio and the car was filled with the late-night chatter of Key 103. For the rest of the journey, until she pulled up outside Rob's house, they were silent.

'I'll see you whenever, then,' said Rob.

He undid his seatbelt and opened the car door, but before he could climb out Jo grabbed his arm. 'Wait,' she said. 'I'm sorry about tonight, okay? None of this was your fault and I shouldn't take it out on you. I don't suppose you're still up for polishing off that bottle of wine?' She smiled.

'All right then,' replied Rob, doing up his seatbelt.

'But if that *Dirty Dancing* DVD comes out of its case, I'm off.'

The living room

'For what it's worth,' said Rob, as he shared out the last drops of wine between their glasses, 'it's his loss, not yours.'

'That's very sweet of you, but it's not how it feels. It's *my* loss because I know he doesn't care about me.' She took a sip of wine. 'I miss him, Rob. Part of me thinks I would've been better off to have him around hating me than I am rattling around on my own.'

'You wouldn't,' said Rob. 'You just think you would.'

'But you have no idea how lonely it is living on your own.'

'Really? Well, Ashley's not at home very much these days, and I'm home alone all day every day.'

'I'm feeling sorry for myself, aren't I? I know you've had a tough time, but you always know that Ashley's coming home eventually. At least she's thinking about you even if she's not physically there. At the end of the day, I'm just not very good at being on my own, and seeing Sean tonight threw me. It's so much easier to get over people when you can pretend they've stopped existing – almost as if they've died. You feel sad rather than angry. You can grieve. And I think it helps you to move on. But it means that when you do see them it's that much more painful, a big fat reminder that they're out there, living their life, not giving you a second thought.'

A good night

'I'm shattered,' said Rob, stretching.

'Me too,' replied Jo, fighting to keep her eyes open.

It was now just after two. For the last few hours they had been drinking, listening to music and talking about nothing much. Now they were yawning. Rob stood up and rummaged in his pockets for his mobile phone.

'What's the number of that minicab firm you use?' he asked.

She didn't answer, so he asked again.

'I heard you the first time,' replied Jo.

'Come on, then, I'm knackered, mate. I need to get a cab home and go to bed.'

'Well, if you're that tired stay here.'

'On your sofa?' Rob laughed. 'You must be joking! My days of crashing on friends' sofas are well behind me.'

Jo looked Rob in the eyes. 'Not on the sofa . . .'

Rob swallowed hard. 'Look I know—'

'And before you start,' she interrupted, 'I promise this isn't some rubbish seduction technique. I'll wear my pyjamas and you can sleep fully clothed, with a coat and hat on for all I care. Rob, normally I wouldn't dream of asking something like this but I don't want to sleep alone tonight. I've had enough of it . . . more than enough. I promise I'll never ask again.'

Rob thought about it. Seeing Sean had upset her more than he had grasped, and her request not only seemed understandable but reasonable. It wasn't her he had a problem with. It was himself. Sleeping in the same bed now would be different from how it had been the first time. Then they had been strangers but now they were friends, and Rob thought this was a bad thing. Wasn't he putting himself directly in temptation's way? Wasn't he abusing Ashley's trust? Wouldn't it be easier for everyone concerned if he just went home? But he couldn't find it in himself to turn Jo down.

He kissed her cheek (in a warm, platonic, friendly way that he hoped would set the tone for their night together), then said, 'Yeah, of course I'll stay.' And without another word Jo disappeared upstairs. Rob finished his wine, then turned off the lights and made his way to Jo's bedroom. He sat on the edge of the bed and began to take off his clothes. Just as he was wondering what he should sleep in, Jo knocked on the door. 'Can I come in?' she asked, from the other side.

'Yeah,' said Rob. 'I'm decent.'

She was wearing a blue towelling dressing-gown. Her hair was pushed back with a headband and her face, now devoid of makeup, seemed to glow. 'I've got this for you,' she said, handing him a T-shirt.

'You like Motorhead?' said Rob holding it up.

'It was Sean's. An ironic fashion statement. It was in the washing basket when he left so he forgot it.'

She walked over to her dressing-table and began to put on some lip salve. Rob eased off his top and replaced it with Sean's T-shirt.

'Are you done?' asked Jo.

'Yeah,' said Rob.

Mike Gayle

'How weird is this?' said Jo, as she slipped off her dressing-gown.

Rob shrugged. 'Do we just get in?'

'I suppose,' said Jo, and pulled back the duvet. 'Are you still okay with this?'

'We're just two people sharing a bed,' reasoned Rob.

He climbed in, then Jo got in, and they arranged the duvet around them.

'How do you normally sleep?' asked Jo.

'On my stomach,' replied Rob. 'How about you?'

'On my side facing the window,' she replied.

There was a long silence.

''Night, then,' said Rob.

Jo leaned across him, kissed his cheek, then switched off the light. In the darkness Rob put his arm round her without a word. And there they lay, semi-spooning, feet touching, barely breathing and more wide awake than they had been all day until their self-consciousness faded and they tumbled headlong into sleep.

PART SEVEN

(Principally concerning repercussions)

The morning after: Jo's version

Jo's clock-radio alarm went off, blaring Manchester's Key 103 into her ear. She reached across to rouse Rob and found that his side of the bed was empty and Sean's Motorhead T-shirt was folded neatly on the pillow. She called his name but knew he wouldn't answer. It was like the first time they had shared a bed, but different. This time Rob had gone because they had overstepped the mark. A line had been crossed. And the blame for anything that happened next was hers. She had ruined everything, even though nothing had happened, because she was no longer sure that their friendship – at least on her part – was innocent any more. And lying there in bed alone it dawned on her that unless she did something to rein in her confusion about Rob, she might never see him again.

The morning after: Rob's version

It was a quarter past seven and Rob was in a minicab on his way back to Chorlton, trying to work out what last night had been about – for him and for Jo. Unable to make sense of it, he called, as ever, the one person he was sure could help him out.

'Phil, it's me,' he said, when his friend picked up. 'And before you say anything I know it's early but I need your advice, mate. I might have done something that I'm going to regret.'

'What now, Bobman?' Phil laughed. 'You haven't befriended lap-dancing twins, have you?'

'Look, it's serious. I spent last night at Jo's but this time it was different.'

'You didn't—'

'No. Nothing happened.'

'So, what's the problem?'

'I don't know.' Rob sighed. 'Nothing happened but it wasn't like before. We weren't drunk and it was deliberate. It was late and Jo just asked me if I'd stay over. I was sure it was innocent and yet . . . I don't know . . . it's freaking me out.'

'What are you saying? That you like her?'

'Not like that. We're just friends. I'm one hundred per cent sure of it. It's just that last night felt wrong.'

'Well, it was, mate. You went to bed with someone who wasn't Ashley.'

'But nothing happened.'

'I don't think that's true,' said Phil. 'And I'm not talking about sex.'

'You're right. What happened last night wasn't about sex. It was about . . . I don't know . . . I feel protective towards her. Almost paternal. I don't know, I wanted to protect her . . . to make her feel safe.'

'You're not falling in love with her, or anything daft like that are you?'

'No,' replied Rob. '*Definitely* not.'

'But you love her.'

'It's complicated. All I'm sure of is that even if I love her I'm not *in* love with her, like I am with Ashley. Do you see the difference?'

'Is there a difference?'

'Of course there is,' replied Rob. 'I love Jo in the same way I love Woodsy or Ian Two – even you – and it's not the kind of love you bang on about. It's just there. And sex has nothing to do with it.'

'Well, that's very noble,' said Phil, 'but you've still got a problem because, friends or not, you spent the night with someone who isn't Ashley. Now, I might not know much about women but I know enough to guess that if Ashley knew what had happened she'd be less than happy.'

'That's why I feel bad. It's like I've cheated on her even though I haven't done anything wrong.'

'Well, that's a matter for debate,' replied Phil. 'What are you going to do, mate?'

'Well, that's kind of why I called you – for advice.'

'I'm good,' said Phil, 'but not *that* good.'

253

'Well, then, it's up to me. I can't afford to do anything that might jeopardise me and Ashley, but at the same time, I can't lose Jo either. She's part of my life now. If I stopped seeing her it would ruin everything – not just for me but for Ashley too because I don't think I can make it work here without Jo.'

'Damned if you do and damned if you don't,' said Phil, sagely.

'Exactly,' replied Rob. 'But you've helped me decide one thing at any rate.'

'And what's that?'

'Until I come up with a solution there's no way I can see Jo.'

Time out

Rob didn't see Jo for over three weeks, although he spoke to her several times on the phone. The first call took place the day after the sleepover. Jo rang Rob on the pretext of arranging when and where they would meet up for a gig at Band on the Wall. The conversation was at best stilted and at worst filled with long silences, as though neither of them could think of anything to say. When Jo finally mentioned the gig, Rob replied, 'I don't think I can make it.'

'Why?'

'I've got a lot of work on. You know how it is.'

'Don't worry about it,' said Jo, sadly. 'I'm sure I'll find someone else to go with.'

'Cool,' replied Rob, then added, 'I'm sure things will be clearer by the end of next week. Maybe we can have a quick one in the Lazy Fox then.'

'That sounds good.'

'I'll call you Thursday,' said Rob, 'and see how you are.'

He didn't call her until late on Thursday evening and then only to say he couldn't see her as he still had too much work to do.

'Of course you should stay in,' said Jo. 'It must be horrible to have a deadline hanging over you and not enough time to get the work done.'

'It is,' replied Rob, and they talked for a little while until

255

finally Rob suggested they should try to meet up for coffee on Sunday afternoon in the Lead Station.

'That sounds great,' replied Jo eagerly. 'Shall I phone you or what?'

'I'll phone you,' said Rob.

Just after eleven on Sunday morning Rob sent her a text message:

Forgot. Parents dropping in on way to my uncle's in Sheffield, today. Sorry. See you early next week.

Rob knew that Jo would consider Monday or Tuesday 'early next week' but somehow still didn't get round to calling her. In the end she called him.

'It's me,' she said, when he answered the phone.

'I said I'd call you and I didn't, did I?' said Rob sounding uncomfortable. 'I completely forgot. It's my fault. There's absolutely no excuse for it and I'm sorry.' He paused. 'What are you doing tonight? Are you free?'

'Why?' asked Jo. 'Is all that work you've been doing suddenly finished?'

'Sort of,' he replied. 'I feel really bad, not seeing you all this time. I tell you what, why don't we catch a film tonight? We could meet in the bar at the Cornerhouse at about seven and then nip downstairs and see what takes our fancy?'

'Are you sure?' asked Jo.

'Yeah,' said Rob. 'Seven o'clock in the bar at the Cornerhouse. And I promise I won't be late.'

Talk to her

When Rob saw Jo sitting at the table near the window in the Cornerhouse the first thing that went through his mind was, She looks different. And she did. She seemed prettier and more confident. And, disappointingly, more serious. She was dressed in black, had a glass of red wine in front of her and was studying one of the cinema's film guides.

'Hey, you,' said Rob, as he approached the table.

Jo stood up and kissed his cheek, then gave him the kind of awkward half-hug people normally reserve for acquaintances they don't know well.

'How have you been?' she asked, as she sat down. 'Is all your work really done?'

'It was a bit stressful but these things are better finished than left to hang over you,' said Rob. 'Then you can get on with your life.'

'Look,' said Jo, pointing out of the window at Oxford Road. A man in an expensive-looking hooded anorak was walking in the direction of the university. 'That's Mani from the Stone Roses.'

'I missed his face,' said Rob. 'Are you sure?'

'Dunno. Half the guys in Manchester look like they might have been in the Stone Roses at some point in their life.' Rob laughed, and for a few moments he felt at ease, but then Jo was serious again. 'I've got a couple of things to tell you,' she said. 'Nothing big but I thought that, as we're friends and all that, you should probably know.'

'Fire away,' said Rob, 'because I've got news to tell you too.'

'Okay,' said Jo, and took another sip of wine. 'The first thing is that I've sent the book to a few agents. I decided you were right and I'd given up too easily. I printed out some copies at work – I'll be for it when they find out how much paper and toner I've used – and posted them yesterday.'

'That's great,' said Rob. 'I'm proud of you. It must have taken a lot of courage but I know it'll pay off.'

'Thanks,' said Jo, shyly. 'I would never have done it without all the encouraging stuff you said.'

'What's your other news?'

'It's like this,' began Jo. 'I've started seeing someone.'

'Wow,' said Rob, surprised. 'That's not small news that's big news – really big news. Who is it?'

'His name's David. Do you remember I went on a date with him a while ago and it didn't work out because, well, the timing was wrong? Anyway, recently he asked me out again and in the last couple of weeks we've been out quite a few times.'

'How's it going?'

Jo shrugged. 'Good, I think. But I can never tell with these things.'

'I'm really pleased for you—' began Rob, then cut himself short.

'What?' said Jo. 'If you've got something to say, then say it.'

'I was just wondering . . . Well, it's none of my business but . . . does this mean that you're going to start shaving your legs again?'

'I already have.'

'Oh,' said Rob, and laughed nervously. 'Happy leg-shaving day.'

Jo glanced pointedly at her watch. 'We'll have to go to the box office soon and decide what we want to see. Any preferences?'

'You choose. But before we do that I want to tell you my news. Ashley and I are engaged.'

'That's brilliant,' said Jo, without missing a beat. 'When did you ask her?'

'Last week,' said Rob. 'It's always been on the cards and I couldn't see the point in stringing it out if it was what I really wanted.'

'And is it what you really want?' asked Jo.

'Absolutely,' said Rob. 'She's the One.'

'Well, that's great,' said Jo. 'I'm really pleased for you both.'

'I knew you would be,' said Rob. 'And just for the record I think it's great news about you and David too. When you're a bit further on with things you should bring him over to us for dinner – I'd love to meet him.'

'That would be great,' said Jo. 'But you know . . . it's early days yet.' She paused, and smiled awkwardly. 'Any idea when the big day will be?'

'Not for a while,' replied Rob. 'We're both pretty good at saving so money's not the problem. It's the organisational stuff that's the pain. In the meantime we've decided that getting engaged is too good an excuse for a party to miss and so we're throwing a bit of an impromptu do at ours at the end of the month. Ashley's got it sorted on the catering front and the boys are coming up from London so you'll meet them. It should be a laugh.'

'It sounds it,' said Jo, evenly. 'I'll be there.' She looked at her watch again. 'Time's running out.' She knocked back the last of her drink and got up. 'Let's go and get the tickets.'

Together they made their way to the box office where they bought two tickets for a Polish film Rob had never heard of but Jo had seen a vaguely positive review about in a Sunday newspaper. As he took his seat next to her and the lights went down, Rob realised he didn't care about the film: he was just relieved to be in the dark watching a film in a language he couldn't understand because it meant that – for the duration of the film at least – he could be alone with his thoughts.

And by the end of the film Rob had come to the conclusion that the mistake of sharing a bed with Jo was no longer anything to feel guilty about. They had proved to themselves and each other that nothing was going on between them. He had moved on and so had Jo. And now they could get back to doing what they did best: being good friends.

Which was what they did. During the run-up to the engagement party they went to the Lazy Fox, called each other at work, made trips to the cinema and saw bands just as they had before. And as far as they were concerned everything was back to normal.

The engagement party

'Jo,' said Rob. 'This is Phil.'

'Pleased to meet you,' said Jo.

'Nice to meet you too,' replied Phil. 'Rob said you're an author.'

'He's exaggerating,' said Jo, grinning at Rob. 'I've sent a few copies of a book I wrote years ago to some literary agents but that's all. Rob seems to think I might get lucky.'

'Well,' replied Phil, grinning, 'never let it be said that Rob doesn't have a good eye for talent.'

'Ignore him,' said Rob, scowling at his friend. 'He thinks he's the Don Juan of Tooting.'

Jo laughed. 'How are you liking Manchester?' she asked.

'A lot,' said Phil. 'It's like London but more compact.' He laughed and then added, 'Has Rob told you about last night yet?'

'What happened?'

'It was a good night but it all got a bit lairy towards the end – you know what large groups of men are like when they get together. But it wouldn't have been like that if you'd come. What happened?'

'I've had a rough week,' said Jo, 'and I thought I'd better save myself for tonight.'

'Wise choice.'

'Do you want a drink?' asked Rob, noticing that Jo was without one.

'A vodka and tonic would be great,' she said.

'Right.' Rob turned to Phil: 'Can you look after her while I sort her out a drink?'

'Of course, mate,' said Phil. 'It'll be my pleasure.'

It was eight thirty on the evening of Rob and Ashley's engagement party. Their Victorian terraced house was now groaning under the strain of their immediate family (parents, brothers and sisters), their extended family (aunts, uncles, their various ex-wives and ex-husbands, cousins, second cousins and their partners). The majority of the guests, however, were made up of their friends – from school, college, university, work and elsewhere. Ashley had spent most of the evening introducing Rob to friends of hers whom he had only known by name, ranging from people she had met on her first day at Brownies to those she had come across during her medical career.

He was pleased that all of his London friends were there. They had arrived on Friday night (minus wives and girlfriends) armed with sleeping-bags. Once the living room had been turned into a makeshift campsite, Rob had ordered taxis to take them into town for what became known as 'The Big Night Out In the North'. Jo was supposed to have come too but just as the boys headed into the Old Wellington, she called Rob to say that she wasn't feeling well but promised to be at the party. Disappointed but buoyant, Rob had led his mates on a bar-hopping spree, and then to the best curry house in Rusholme. They had ended the evening with dancing, and more drinking, at Sankey's Soap on Jersey Street. And as they rolled up outside Rob and Ashley's just after six the following morning, they all agreed that it had been their best night out in years.

Friends of friends

'Rob tells me you and he are pretty close,' said Phil, giving Jo his full attention.

'Yeah, we are,' replied Jo, wondering if she was imagining that Phil was flirting with her. 'He and Ashley have been really kind to me.'

'They're a good couple,' said Phil. 'I was sorry when he moved up here but it all seems to have turned out well . . . Would you like to meet the rest of the boys?'

She followed him across the room to the hi-fi where a group of men were arguing over which CD to play next.

'Ashley made the mistake of telling them they could be in charge of the music,' explained Phil. 'You can't say that to five men and hope there won't be a major argument.'

Jo laughed. 'How come you're not arguing too?'

'And miss talking to you? Never.' He proceeded to introduce her to the others but then suddenly Woodsy, who had been carefully scrutinising the contents of the CD racks next to the hi-fi, pulled out a CD and waved it in the air. 'Problem solved, boys,' he said. 'I've just found *Queen's Greatest Hits*.'

Jo watched as Ian Two took it from him, scanned the CD's track-listing, then dropped it into the CD player and shuffled through the songs.

'Which one are you going for?' asked Woodsy.

'Which one do you think?' said Ian Two, with a grin, as his finger hovered over the play button. 'Gentlemen, prepare to rock!'

Within milliseconds of the first piano note of the intro to Queen's classic anthem 'Somebody To Love', an infectious grin had spread across the men's faces. And when Freddie Mercury sang the opening line, they joined in. Half-way through Rob came in and yelled, 'You should have told me we were doing Queen!' It was like one of those almost compulsory moments in modern romantic comedies where all the cast breaks into song, but now no one was in tune, only the boys were singing – everyone else in the room looked stunned – and it was happening in a living room in Chorlton instead of on a film set in Hollywood.

When the song ended, Phil wiped the sweat off his fore-head and turned down the volume. Then they composed themselves, tucking in shirts and adjusting waistbands.

'You lot are such good friends,' said Jo, still laughing. 'Good friends?' repeated Phil, 'we're not good friends. We're the best.'

Toast

It was ten o'clock and Jo had been dancing with Rob's friends for half an hour. She couldn't remember the last time she had had so much fun and met so many people with whom she had felt a rapport. She had already listened to so many of Rob's tales about them (everything from the origins of their annual golf day through to why Ian Two could no longer bend his little finger) that Jo had felt she knew them well before she met them, but she hadn't known how much she would like them. They made her laugh, they had interesting things to say and they were so laid back that she forgot she was the only woman among them.

She was about to take a breather from dancing (to yet another one of Woodsy's musical selections: 'The Only Way is Up' by Yazz) and roll herself a cigarette when the music stopped and Rob clapped his hands. 'Can I have everyone's attention for a few moments? I've got a few things I need to say.'

Everyone stopped talking and gave him a round of applause.

'Good evening, everyone,' he began. 'I just wanted to say a few words to put tonight into some sort of context, and to thank all of our friends and family for making the effort to be here. The first time I met Ashley I knew she was someone special but I didn't know how special until tonight – because if the way I feel now that she has accepted my proposal of marriage is any indicator of our future happiness, my life with her will be everything I ever hoped for.' He picked up the can of Carlsberg he had set down on a bookshelf. 'I know you aren't drinking champagne tonight – because my future wife and I are such cheapskates – but I'd still like you to raise whatever it is you're drinking, be it beer, vodka or even PG Tips, in a toast to Ashley. My future wife.'

The room broke out in spontaneous applause, then toasted Ashley. Jo, her eyes fixed on Rob, smiled and raised her glass too. But it was only when the music came back on and conversation got going again that she realised she was crying. She put her drink on the mantelpiece and quickly left the room, desperately wiping away the tears that were beginning to roll down her cheeks. She made her way to the front door and outside into the night. Once in the darkness of the side entry, she finally let the tears flow freely.

What's going on?

'Are you all right?'

Jo whirled around to see Phil standing a few feet away from her.

'I'm not feeling very well, that's all,' said Jo, wondering if he could tell that she was lying. 'I'll call a taxi in a minute or two.'

'Tell you what,' said Phil, 'why don't I take you home? I could do with a bit of peace and quiet.'

'I couldn't let you do that,' said Jo. 'Anyway, you've been drinking.'

'Half a can of Guinness,' he replied. 'I think I over did it last night with the boys . . . and, well, these days my ability to recover from a bit of a session is somewhat diminished.' He paused. 'So?'

'Yeah,' replied Jo. 'A lift would be great.'

All this and more

'Do you want to come in?' asked Jo, as they pulled up outside her house. 'I'm not really tired, are you?'

'I'm wide awake,' replied Phil.

Jo climbed out of the car and made her way up her front path, fishing in her bag for her keys to the front door. She heard the beep of the car's central locking system and turned to see Phil coming up the path behind her.

All evening Jo had thought Phil might be flirting with her but she couldn't tell why. Did he do it with all women, as a matter of course, or did he actually like her? In spite of her feelings for Rob she did find Phil attractive: it wasn't just that he was easy on the eye (although he was); it wasn't even that she found him charming (although she did). It was that being with Phil reminded her so much of being with Rob. Their personalities were different – Phil was far more laid back and exuded a lot more self-confidence than Rob – but she could see exactly why they were such good friends. And when Rob had introduced her to Phil something inside her had told her that they were on the same wavelength. It had reminded her of when she had met Rob at the party in Didsbury all those months ago, and felt as though she had known him all her life.

'Welcome to my bachelorette pad,' said Jo, opening the front door. 'I apologise now for any random items of underwear, piles of to-do ironing and washing-up that you might come across on your travels.'

'No worries,' said Phil. 'Sounds like Woodsy's and my place in London.'

Jo led Phil into the living room, took off her coat, kicked off her shoes and began to roll a cigarette on the sofa. Phil made his way over to the shelves near Jo's TV that housed her CD and vinyl record collection.

'You're such a typical boy,' she said as he began flicking through the music. 'That's just what Rob did when he first came round here.'

'We can't help it. I think we're both programmed that way. It's always been the first thing we do whenever we go somewhere new.'

'Like psychological profiling?' asked Jo, studying her now perfectly formed rollie.

'No,' said Phil. 'More like nosy neighbours.'

'Well, before you start criticising – as I know you will – can I just say that my ex took most of the good CDs. All he's left me with is the stuff from my student days that I didn't sell or give away.'

'It's the vinyl I'm interested in,' said Phil still flicking. 'It's like a blast from the past – you've got five Smiths albums.'

'I loved them *so* much,' said Jo lighting up her cigarette. 'Morrissey was my complete and utter hero back then.'

'And The Wedding Present's *George Best*,' said Phil, brandishing it eagerly. 'A classic.'

'They were my other favourites,' said Jo. 'At university I once went out with a guy just because he looked a little like the lead singer, Dave Gedge. He had the gruff Leeds accent too. But we split up after about a fortnight. The reality just couldn't live up to the fantasy. That's the thing about counterfeits – they're just not the real thing are they?'

'No,' said Phil. 'I suppose not.' He returned to flicking through the records. After a few moments he stopped and pulled out another album. 'Can I put this on?' he said.

'What is it?' she asked joining him on the carpet near the TV.

'The Sundays – *Reading, Writing and Arithmetic*.'

Jo took it from him, grinning inanely. 'I can't tell you how much I loved this album. It was the complete soundtrack to my late teens. I used to play "Can't Be Sure" all the time.'

'Well let's play it then,' said Phil.

'Can't,' said Jo, flicking the ash from her cigarette onto her makeshift ashtray – an old tea-stained saucer by the fireplace. 'I haven't got a record deck. Mine broke years ago and Sean took his when he moved out.'

'Never mind,' said Phil grinning. 'We'll just have to think of something else to do.'

Jo put down the record and carefully rested her cigarette on the saucer. There was now no doubting that he was flirting with her. But she didn't mind at all. In fact she was pleased because if she was thinking about Phil then she knew she couldn't be thinking about Rob. And so without saying a word she leaned in towards Phil and kissed his neck and then his chin and then finally she kissed his lips.

Rob at home

It was a quarter to nine on the day after the engagement party and Rob had just woken from a deep Sunday-morning sleep. Ashley was standing in the doorway with a smile on her face as if she knew something that Rob didn't.

'What's up?' said Rob, from the bed.

'Nothing, really,' said Ashley, who was wearing her early Sunday-morning attire of a long-sleeved white T-shirt and tracksuit bottoms. 'I don't think we should put two and two together just for the sake of it . . . because we'll only end up with five, but I've just been downstairs to see if the boys are okay and make them some tea and Phil wasn't there.'

'He's probably gone to the loo,' said Rob.

'Nope,' said Ashley. 'No one's seen him since last night.'

'I can barely remember last night,' said Rob, rubbing his head. 'Are you sure he wasn't there?'

'Well,' said Ashley, 'this is the thing. Darren saw him getting into his car just after eleven . . . with Jo.'

Rob sat up. 'Darren saw Jo getting into Phil's car?'

'Now, like I said, we shouldn't jump to conclusions,' said Ashley, 'but reports are that they were getting on *very* well last night.'

'Were they? I asked Phil to look after Jo for me and make sure that she didn't feel left out . . .'

'Well,' Ashley grinned, 'it looks like he gave her his full personal attention.'

'You don't really think that Phil and Jo—'

Ashley shrugged. 'Well, he *is* good-looking, and you know what a smooth talker he can be, and Jo's very pretty. I suppose anything's possible. But if you're that curious why don't you call him? He knows we're all meeting for lunch today so you've got a good excuse.'

'Can you do it?' asked Rob. 'I don't want him to think I'm checking up on him – them.'

Ashley laughed. 'But you are.'

'Yeah, but he doesn't need to know that, does he? Look, just call him and tell him what we're doing for lunch.'

'And what *are* we doing for lunch?'

'We'll go to the Lead Station,' said Rob. 'That'll do, won't it?'

'Fine,' replied Ashley, and picked up the cordless phone that was lying on top of the chest of drawers near the door and handed it to Rob. 'You dial his number and I'll speak to him.' His fingers tapped in the number and he handed it back to her as Phil answered.

'Hi. It's Ashley,' she said. 'I didn't wake you, did I?' She laughed, and moved on to the landing, chatting to Phil so quietly that Rob couldn't hear what she was saying. After a few moments, however, she was winding up the call in a louder voice. 'Right,' she said. 'We'll see the two of you at the Lead Station about midday.

'Well, that's interesting,' she said, as she came back into the bedroom and sat down on the bed next to Rob.

'What is?' asked Rob.

'Well, he said that he and Jo had talked until late and they didn't get much sleep.'

'They didn't get much sleep? What does that mean? Why not? Did he sound tired?'

'Doesn't everyone sound tired on a Sunday morning? And what does it matter if they've got together? You're always telling me that Phil usually goes out with completely unsuitable women – and isn't it about time Jo was seeing someone? Her ex went months ago?'

'She was supposed to be going out with some guy at work,' replied Rob, 'but she hasn't mentioned him much lately.'

'They're both adults, Rob. Let them get on with whatever they're doing.'

Rob kissed her. 'You're right,' he said, and pulled her into his arms. 'I should leave them alone.' But even as the words left his lips, he knew that he had just made the most empty of promises.

Late lunch

Rob, Ashley and the boys had been sitting round a large table in the café for half an hour when a sheepish-looking Jo and Phil came in.

'Morning, all,' said Phil, cheerfully, as he sat down in one of the two empty chairs between Woodsy and Kevin. 'How are we today?'

'Morning, everyone,' mumbled Jo, taking the chair next to Phil. 'Did you all sleep well?'

With the exception of Rob, who stared blankly at Phil, everyone responded in the affirmative to her question.

'What are you all having to eat?' said Jo, indicating Rob's menu.

'I'm not sure,' said Rob, drily. 'Here,' he said, handing it to her. 'Take this. I'm nipping next door to Londis for a paper. Anyone else want anything?'

'I'll come with you,' said Phil, standing up. 'I never know which paper I fancy until I see the headlines.'

In the shop Rob picked up a *Sunday Times*, an *Observer* and a *Sunday Telegraph*, took all three to the till, paid for them and left the shop without a word to Phil.

'Why don't you just come out and say it?' asked Phil following him.

'Say what?'

'Whatever you think you have the right to say to me.'

'Well, as you've just tacitly pointed out, it would appear that you're of the opinion that I don't have the right to say anything – so what's the point?'

'This is pathetic, Rob. Can't we just talk about it?'

'I'm all ears, mate.'

'I take it this is about Jo?'

'And?'

'Well, you're being like this because I stayed at her house last night.'

'It's none of my business,' said Rob, firmly. 'Why should I care what you two are up to?'

'Well, it would appear that you do,' replied Phil. 'Perhaps rather too much, considering you've just got engaged.'

'You're entitled to your opinions, no matter how off course they may be,' said Rob, 'but, just so that we're straight, let me tell you this has nothing to do with me liking Jo or any other daft idea you might be harbouring.'

'So what *is* it about?' asked Phil. 'I don't want to fall out with you, mate – we're better than that. If you want to know what happened between me and Jo last night—'

'Stop right there,' said Rob. 'I'm not the slightest bit interested because she's all yours. Whatever the two of you want to get up to is fine by me, as long as I'm well out of it. Okay?'

'The only time you ever act like an idiot is when a woman's involved,' said Phil. 'Did you know that?'

Rob thrust the *Sunday Times* into Phil's hands and headed back into the café. For the rest of the afternoon, until the boys climbed into their cars for the journey home, he barely said a word to Jo, and he said nothing at all to Phil.

A short talk about being friends

'I thought you'd be here,' said Jo. 'Can I sit down?'

It was ten past ten the following Sunday, and Rob was in the Lazy Fox sipping a pint and trying to make headway with a crossword when Jo interrupted him. He hadn't spoken to her since they were all at the Lead Station. Though she had phoned, sent text messages and emails he hadn't responded to her at all. He told himself it wasn't that he didn't want to see her any more, it was more that he needed a break from her and to be alone with his thoughts. During the week that had elapsed he had concentrated on his work, stayed in and watched TV, read a few books and spent some quality time with Ashley.

'I just want you to know that you've been a real idiot about all of this,' said Jo, sitting down opposite him.

'I know—'

'No, you don't,' interrupted Jo. 'You don't know anything because if you did it wouldn't have taken me getting a cab from Levenshulme to Chorlton every single night this week in the hope of finding you in here.'

Rob swallowed hard. 'Every night?'

'There's no need to sound so surprised. I did it because we're mates and I don't want to lose you over something stupid like this – that's how much I value what we've got. Even so, Rob, how dare you try to tell me who I can and can't spend time with. And I'm outraged that you thought you could get away with trying to control me like that.'

'You're right,' said Rob. 'I was well out of order.'

'Too right you were,' said Jo. 'You were acting like a spoilt child.'

Rob sighed heavily. 'I don't know what came over me.'

What good friends do

'Do you know what?' said Jo, as they stared blankly at the drinks Rob had bought as a peace offering. 'Phil thinks the world of you. We listened to some music, we talked – mainly about you – and, yes, we kissed briefly, but it didn't feel right. He was your friend. I was your friend. It was all too confusing. When the kiss was over I went to bed and Phil slept on the sofa. That was all that happened.'

'Why didn't he just say that?'

'Probably because it's none of your business. Why should Phil have to tell you anything about me and him? Why should *I* have tell you anything about me and Phil? You don't tell me things about you and Ashley, do you?'

'No,' mumbled Rob.

'And why not? Come on, Rob, if you feel like you have the right to get stroppy about me and Phil, shouldn't I have the same right about you and Ashley?'

'It's different,' said Rob. 'I'm not defending the way I acted . . . It's just . . . It's not like I don't want you to be happy or have a boyfriend. It's more like I feel responsible for your welfare. In a way, as much as I don't like Sean, I sometimes wish you were still with him because then I wouldn't feel like I had to protect you.'

'*Protect* me?' said Jo, surprised. 'From what?'

'From anything and everything that might hurt you,' Rob

told her. 'I can't help it. I know there's no logical reason why I should feel like this.' He laughed. 'You're a grown woman – what can I teach you about avoiding crap men that you haven't learned from experience? But I still want to save you from getting hurt by guys like Phil or David or anyone else who isn't good enough for you.'

Jo smiled and put her hand on his. 'I've always known that if Ryan had been alive he would've hated me going out with Sean, even though they were such good friends. He was protective of me too. But, Rob, I don't need another brother to watch out for me. I've got one, even though he might not be here. What I do need though is a good friend.'

'Okay,' nodded Rob. 'I'll be the best friend possible. Starting now. What are your plans for Christmas?'

'I've avoided thinking about it – for the last couple I was at home with Sean. I can't see myself spending the big day doing the blended-families thing with either of my parents . . . Maybe Kerry and Gary will invite me round if they're not going to her mum's in Devon.'

'Well, feel free to say no but I'd love it if you'd come to us.'

'That's sweet of you, Rob, but shouldn't you clear it with Ashley first? After all, this is going to be your first Christmas together since you moved in with her.'

'Of course I should, but I'm sure when I explain that you'll be on your own she'll be fine with it. After all, you're practically an orphan. And I'm pretty sure that it says in the rules that you have to be nice to orphans at Christmas. And you wouldn't be spoiling anything. Ash and I are going away on Boxing Day – she's booked us a few days at a resort in Gran Canaria so we'll have plenty of time to be alone then . . . and, anyway, I'm sure if one of her mates was contemplating spending Christmas Day alone she'd have them round to ours in a flash. And I wouldn't mind – even if it was Lauren and her annoying laugh – because I know how much her mates mean to her. But I'll run it past her first.'

'Okay, you're on,' said Jo, and kissed his cheek. 'Thanks, Rob. I have to admit I was getting a bit worried about being on my own over Christmas.' She paused. 'Can I ask a favour? It's just occurred to me that if I visit my mum on New Year's Day and go on to my dad's for a few days I'll be away for over a week. When you get back from Gran Canaria could you pop over to mine and water my plants? I'll leave you a set of keys.'

'No problem,' said Rob. 'Plus I'll keep an eye on the place. Watch out for burglars and that.'

'You're a real life-saver, do you know that?'

'It's nothing,' said Rob. 'It's what good friends do.'

Arrangements

When Rob got home that night all the lights were off. For a second or two he wished with his whole heart that at least one had been on, and that Ashley was in. It was just after eleven thirty and he wasn't tired. He turned on the TV and surfed the cable channels, then turned it off with a disgruntled snort, picked up the telephone and dialled Ashley's mobile. He needed to talk to her – now.

'Hello?'

'Hi, babe, it's me,' he said.

'I was thinking about you. How was your evening?'

'Cool,' said Rob. 'I met up with Jo for a quick pint in the Lazy Fox.'

'How is she?' asked Ashley.

'Good, I think. Nothing much to report. How's your night been so far?'

'Pretty busy. Drunks in need of patching up and a few victims of random violence – the usual pre-Christmas cheer. I can't wait until we go away. Talking of which, I know you're going to hate me for doing this without talking it over with you first – and I know I've been hinting that I wanted our first Christmas together to be just the two of us – but I've had to invite my family for Christmas Day, Mum, Dad, Grandma and Granddad, Michelle and her husband. I'm really sorry.'

'Look,' began Rob, 'about Christmas—'

'If you're angry, Rob, I wish you'd just say so rather than putting on that irritating voice. I'm sorry, okay? I'm sorry I've invited my family for Christmas without telling you. Now, can we move on?'

Rob laughed. 'There's no need to be so defensive, babe. All I was going to say was that it's fine.'

'Oh, that's brilliant! I'm sorry for being so mean.'

'It's okay,' said Rob, 'but I haven't finished what I was saying. It's just that Jo's going to be on her own at Christmas. Her parents are divorced and both remarried and, well, Christmas at either of theirs would be a night-mare, apparently, so I've invited her round for Christmas Day too.'

'So we've got my parents *and* Jo coming?' Ashley burst out laughing.

'What's so funny?' asked Rob, confused. 'You're not angry, are you?'

'Of course not,' giggled Ashley. 'How could I be? I know I wouldn't want any of my friends to spend Christmas alone. I'm laughing because my family won't get it.'

'What?'

'You being friends with another girl. My mother still can't get it into her head that there's nothing behind me and Neil being friends. It'll send her into paroxysms of confusion. I can hear her telling Dad, in her best shocked voice, "Well, we certainly didn't do *that* sort of thing in my day." She'll have a heart-attack.'

'Do you think I should tell Jo not to come?'

'No way,' said Ashley. 'You can't let her be on her own at Christmas. It would be awful. I've got a better idea. If I'm going to wind my mum up it should be done properly. Why don't I see what Neil's up to? If he's free I'll get him to come too. Think about it – me and my platonic male friend, you and your platonic female friend, and my parents. And it'll still be a special Christmas for us because it'll be done our way with our friends.'

Christmas in Chorlton

'Jo,' said Rob, opening the front door. 'Come in.'

'Happy Christmas,' said Jo, as she stepped into the hall-way. Rob kissed her. 'Season's greetings and all that other stuff too.'

Jo had never before woken up on Christmas Day in an empty house and it had unsettled her. It hadn't felt like Christmas at all. It had felt like the first Sunday after a nuclear holocaust – eerily quiet – or as if the world outside was covered with a blanket of invisible snow.

In the car she had worried about how dinner at Rob and Ashley's would go. She'd been horrified when Rob had explained to her that Ashley's entire family would be there too, not to mention her friend Neil. She had been much happier when she thought it was going to be just her, Rob and Ashley. Now it seemed all wrong. She felt incredibly self-conscious, as if none of Ashley's family would understand why she was there, and she was reminded of an article she had read in *Marie Claire* about an American man with two wives who lived with him in the same house.

As Jo took off her coat and hung it up she asked, 'Is everyone else here?'

'Neil's not arrived yet but my prospective in-laws are in the living room. And we've explained so everything will be fine.'

'Where have I heard that one before?'

Rob laughed. 'It'll be *fine*.'

'It had better be.' Jo grinned, then picked up the carrier-bag of presents she had brought and followed Rob into the living room.

'Everybody,' said Rob, 'this is my friend Jo.'

Jo looked at Ashley's family gave a little wave and immediately wished she hadn't come. An older man with white hair, whom she assumed was Ashley's father, was talking to a grey-haired elderly man, who had to be Ashley's granddad. Next to him on the sofa was a smartly dressed older woman, Ashley's mother, who was talking to an elderly lady in a lilac twinset, clearly Ashley's grandmother. On the sofa opposite a youngish man in a grey cardigan must be Ashley's brother-in-law and the attractive woman with chestnut hair could only be Michelle, Ashley's older sister.

'Hi, everyone,' said Jo. 'Merry Christmas.' She threw a look of panic at Rob, then said she was going to say hello to Ashley and scuttled off to the kitchen.

'Hi, Jo,' said Ashley, as she walked in. 'Happy Christmas!' She gave Jo a hug, and Jo delved into her carrier-bag, pulled out a parcel and handed it to her.

'You've brought me a present!' said Ashley. 'How lovely!'

'It's nothing, really. I just wanted to thank you for inviting me to spend Christmas with you.' She hoped Ashley wouldn't mind that it was only a selection of bath products from the Body Shop.

'These are great!' said Ashley, flung an arm round Jo's shoulders and planted a kiss on her cheek. She opened a bottle of shower gel and sniffed. 'Gorgeous! I've only got some stuff I bought in Superdrug by mistake. It's supposed to smell of figs – and who wants to smell of figs all day? Now I'll smell like fresh coconuts, which is infinitely more appealing.'

The doorbell rang and Ashley excused herself. She returned a moment later with Neil and Rob.

'Jo,' said Ashley, 'this is my friend Neil.'

'And, Neil,' said Rob, 'this is my friend Jo.'

'Look at us!' laughed Neil as he took Jo's hand. 'Living evidence that men and women can be just good friends!'

At the end of the day

Despite Jo's reservations, Christmas at Rob and Ashley's turned out to be a lot more fun than she'd imagined possible. Braced with several glasses of chardonnay she mingled with Ashley's family. She began by talking to Michelle and her husband and found common ground in fruit (Michelle, too, only bought it in Marks and Spencer) and cigars (she entertained Michelle's cigar-smoking husband with an embarrassing tale of how, after seeing Sharon Stone on the cover of the cigar magazine *Aficionado*, she had bought one to try and been violently sick). She then had an entertaining chat with Ashley's grandfather, who had failed to grasp why she was there but made her feel welcome anyway. Even Ashley's mother warmed to her, once Jo told her about her novel: it turned out that Mrs McIntosh had recently started to work part-time at her local library.

Her most interesting conversations, however, were with Neil. He had talked for a little while of the ups and downs of being a doctor but most of their conversation was about the things she and Rob chatted about. Neil knew about music, films and TV and he had an endearing manner. He wasn't what Jo had been expecting from Rob's description. She had had the impression that Neil was a bit 'wooden' – but he wasn't at all. He was fun and made her laugh, and with him

287

there she felt less of an intruder at Rob and Ashley's first Christmas get-together.

After dinner, more wine, present opening and yet more wine, she decided she'd had her best Christmas Day in years. Just after nine, she felt it was time to go and pulled out her mobile to call a minicab.

'I'll drop you home, if you like,' Neil offered. 'I'm ready to leave now too.'

'That would be great,' said Jo. 'I'll get my things together.'

With her coat on and the presents she had received, she kissed Ashley, then put an arm round Rob and kissed him too. Neil said his goodbyes, and they went outside to his Porsche.

'This is yours?' asked Jo, impressed.

He nodded. 'It was my treat to myself a while back.'

'My treat to myself is usually chocolate,' said Jo, laughing, 'but each to their own.'

On the journey over to Levenshulme they talked about the new year and what they hoped to get out of it. Neil told Jo that he was planning to take a career break and travel for a while because he was afraid that he was missing out on life by working all the time. Jo told him about her hopes for her novel, and that if no one was interested in it, she'd write something new: Rob's praise had inspired her.

'Well,' she said, as Neil pulled up outside her house, 'this is me.'

He leaned across and kissed her cheek. 'It was great to meet you.'

'You too.' Jo opened the car door. 'Have a great New Year.'

She stepped out of the car and was about to close the door when Neil spoke again: 'May I say something to you? It's more advice than anything else.'

'Of course,' said Jo. 'What is it?'

'I just wanted to say to you that I know it must be hard for you.'

'What's hard for me?'

'And I know too that, right now, your heart must feel like it's being broken apart . . . but it will heal . . . You will get over it. Time will help you to accept that in life there are things you can have and things you can't, and that's just the way it is.'

Jo was stunned. 'How did you—'

'It takes one to know one,' he replied. 'Just make sure you look after yourself.'

Jo closed the car door and watched as he drove away. Then she turned to her house and rooted in her bag for her keys. She opened the door, closed it behind her and cried as if she would never stop.

Brand new year

'Hang on, mate,' called the cab driver, as Rob slammed the door. 'I think you've forgotten something.'

'It's Chico,' Ashley told him, laughing. 'And don't think I don't know you've done it on purpose.'

It was now eleven o'clock on New Year's Day and Rob and Ashley had just arrived back in Manchester from Gran Canaria. The weather had been great (warm but not too hot, just the way Rob liked it), the hotel had been top class (he had been pleased not to see a single cockroach) and all they had done was lie around the hotel pool (Rob had read two books on graphic design and several dozen back issues of *Design Week*). As holidays went, he felt it had been one of the best he had ever had. And as a way for Ashley and him to reconnect after a fairly odd year it had been brilliant. They had made plans for their summer wedding, and to do things like see Manchester City – Ashley's newly adopted football team – play, spend a weekend at the health spa Hoarcross Hall and some time at Ashley's parents' holiday home in Paignton, Devon.

'Cheers, mate.' Rob reluctantly opened the cab door, and grabbed the sombrero-wearing straw donkey from within and tucked it under his arm. 'You're a real life-saver.'

As he picked up the suitcases, Ashley returned from opening the front door grabbed his lapels and pulled him close. 'Have I told you lately how much I love you?' she asked, looking into his eyes.

'Not since we landed at the airport.'

'Well, in case you'd forgotten since then, I'm going to tell you again. I love you very much.'

'Well, I love you too,' he said, and extricated himself from her grip – it had begun to rain. 'Come on, let's go inside before we drown.'

Work is a four-letter word

'I'd better go,' said Ashley, and drained the last of her orange juice. 'My shift starts in an hour and I can't afford to be late after a week away.'

It was just after six thirty that evening and they were sitting at the kitchen table finishing off a haphazard pick-and-mix supper of French bread, salad, Brie and hummus as though they were still on holiday.

'Do you have to?' asked Rob. 'Can't you call in sick?'

'Of course I can't. It's the sick who depend on me.'

'I suppose.'

'You know I'd love to if I could,' added Ashley. 'I'm already missing you, after all the time we've spent together, and I've got this stretch of night shifts to get through yet.'

'But we'll go out on Sunday night, eh? The cinema or something? How does that sound?'

'It's a date,' said Ashley. 'What will you do tonight?' she asked. 'Have a catch-up with Jo?'

'She's not due back for a few days,' he said, 'but I told her I'd water her plants and check that everything was okay.'

'Why don't you drop me off at the hospital now, and take my car straight on to Levenshulme?'

'Good plan. Do you know? I can't wait until you're Mrs Brooks.'

'And do *you* know?' laughed Ashley. 'Neither can I.'

Kitchen-sink drama

As Rob pulled up outside Jo's house he noticed that her Nissan was still parked outside and wondered whether she had come home early or had decided not to drive. He fumbled for her keys in his pocket, then thought he should ring the doorbell in case she was there. When she didn't answer, he let himself in, and noticed straight away that there wasn't any mail in front of the door, which was odd as she had left a couple of days ago. He touched the radiator in the hallway: it was hot, which, again, was odd – Jo wasn't the kind of person to waste money heating an empty house.

Just then he noticed a light was on in the kitchen; he could hear cupboard doors opening and closing. *Was it Jo trying to find her last box of teabags* he thought *or a particularly thorough burglar?* Silently Rob opened the kitchen door to see a naked man making a cup of tea.

'What do you think *you're* doing?' he yelled.

'What the—' The naked man turned round.

It was Sean. 'Since when have you had those?' he demanded, glaring at the keys in Rob's hand.

'Never mind that,' barked Rob. 'What are you doing here?'

'Why don't you ask Jo when she comes out of the shower?' said Sean, smugly.

Rob swallowed hard. 'But she told me—'

'Obviously she didn't go. So, why don't you drop off your

293

keys by the door on the way out, mate, and leave us in peace?'

Rob left the room and stalked towards the front door but was intercepted by a wet-haired Jo coming downstairs in her blue dressing-gown. It was obvious that she was naked beneath it.

'You've come to water the plants, haven't you?' she said, and winced.

'Look,' began Rob, surprising himself with his sharpness, 'I was on my way out.'

'Don't go,' she said. 'Not like this.'

'If he wants to go,' said Sean, from behind Rob, 'let him.'

Jo glared at Sean. 'Stay out of this.'

'He's right,' said Rob. 'I should go.'

'Let me explain,' pleaded Jo. She grabbed Rob's hand, pulled him into the living room and closed the door. Rob sat on the sofa next to an abandoned T-shirt and a pair of jeans.

'Well, this is a great way to start the new year,' said Jo, as she sat down next to him.

Rob didn't say anything.

'What's wrong?' asked Jo.

'Never mind me,' he snapped. 'What's the story?'

'Do you have to speak like that?'

'Like what?'

'Like I'm a silly little girl who's always getting into trouble and doesn't know what she's doing.'

'Well, what *are* you doing?' What do you think you'll achieve by getting back together with him? Why would you even want to hold a conversation with him, let alone share a bed with him?'

'Because part of me still loves him.'

'You don't love him.' He looked at Jo. 'You might think

294

you do but you don't. I can't understand why you don't see you're worth a million Seans. You deserve someone better.'

'Like you?' asked Jo, suddenly flaming with anger. 'Because I can do much better than falling in love with someone *like* you. How about *being* in love with you? Happy now?'

Rob couldn't believe what he had heard. 'You're in love with me?'

'There's no need to sound so surprised.'

'Look, I—'

'It's not your fault,' she interrupted. 'You didn't lead me on. I know that. I've learned that you can't help who you fall in love with. No matter how hard you try or what rules you set up, things happen. And being in love with you hurts far more than the worst times I've had with Sean.'

'But how long—'

'I don't know. I think I must have known on some level since the night we first met. But the last time you stayed here was when I really began to feel unsure. That was why I slept with David. I thought if I could do that it would mean that I wasn't in love with you – that we could go back to being friends – and it worked for a while. I suppose I'm good at fooling myself. Phil guessed how I felt that evening after your engagement party but promised to keep it to himself. That was when I knew I was in trouble but I didn't know what to do for the best.'

'I don't know what to say.'

'That's because there's nothing *to* say. Soon it won't matter anyway. I'm back with Sean now, and we're going to stay together for good.'

'When did all this happen?' asked Rob.

'Last night,' replied Jo. 'I stayed in, opened a bottle of

wine and felt sorry for myself. I even decided to go to bed early in the hope of sleeping through the whole thing but then the doorbell rang. I know it was silly but I convinced myself it was you. That you'd realised how I felt about you and had come back from holiday to tell me you wanted to be with me. I couldn't have been more surprised when I saw it was Sean. He told me he'd missed me. He told me he'd changed. He said he hadn't realised how much he loved me until now. And while I'm not sure I believe him, I'm prepared to give him another chance. I know I might not love him the way I love you but that doesn't matter any more. The truth is I just can't walk away from love – even the imperfect kind – any more. I don't feel I've got the luxury of choice. Sean's talking about marriage, kids, the whole works. He even suggested we move to London for a fresh start. How can I turn that down?'

'If he's what you want then I'm happy for you,' said Rob. 'And if he's really changed, well, he's what I want for you too . . . because friends want what's best for each other. And I do love you, as a friend. It's not a second-best kind of love. Or a consolation prize. It's the real thing but different. A different kind of love.'

'That would be fine if it were true for both of us,' said Jo, 'but it's not. I love you but not just as your friend. Anyway, none of this matters any more because we can't carry on seeing each other.'

'I know Sean and I have clashed quite a bit. But things don't have to be awkward between us – I'm prepared to apologise and start afresh with him,' said Rob.

'That's not it.'

'Then what? We can work something out, surely.'

'No, we can't,' said Jo. 'And I'd be fooling no one if I said we could. The fact is I'm in love with you. But the difference between today and yesterday is that the man I'm going to try to make a life with knows how I feel about you – which changes everything because I'd never be able to hide it from him. We can't be friends any more, Rob. It really is over.'

PART EIGHT

(Principally about a brand new friend)

A brand new friend

'It's a bit busy in here tonight,' said Neil, as he approached the bar.

'You're right,' said Rob, 'but that's Friday nights for you.'

It was eight o'clock on a Friday night in March and Rob and Neil had just arrived at BlueBar. Rob automatically scanned the room for any sign of Jo or Sean, as was now his habit, but they weren't there.

'I just remembered I've got these,' said Neil, and reached into his back pocket. He pulled out a pair of tickets and handed one to Rob.

'I can't believe it,' said Rob. 'I thought the gig had sold out.'

'Remember, it's not *what* you know but *who*,' said Neil, tapping the side of his nose. 'I've got a mate who's got a mate who works at the Academy and he sorted us out.'

'Well, tell your mate's mate that there's a beer with his name on it should I get to meet him.'

'It should be good,' said Neil, clearly pleased that he had impressed Rob. 'The queue's gone down a bit. Better get in there while it's quiet. Carlsberg?'

'Spot on the money, mate,' replied Rob.

The two men continued talking casually at the bar until they were joined by two others, whom Neil introduced as Gavin and Sanjiv. They all shook hands and said how busy

301

the bar was while Neil ordered more drinks. By the time they had been poured yet more of his friends had arrived and Rob was introduced to Daniel, Paolo, Johnny and Jonesy. While Neil added to his ever-expanding drinks order Rob listened politely to the others talk football.

'They've announced the England squad for next week's qualifier,' said Sanjiv.

'I saw it in the paper this morning,' said Paolo, 'and I was stunned. They couldn't have picked worse if they'd tried.'

'It doesn't matter anyway,' said Johnny. 'We're going to lose. You can just feel it.'

'How can you say that?' exclaimed Jonesy. 'We've done okay in the last couple of matches we've played.'

'You're joking!' groaned Gavin. 'All we've done is play teams on worse form than ours. It's the only way we ever win anything.' He turned to Rob. 'What do you reckon, Rob? Are you a football man?'

Rob gave his usual answer to the question: he was an armchair football fan but rarely went to the terraces. As the conversation moved on and he was then called upon to offer an opinion on the state of British rugby, the state of British music and even the state of British TV he suddenly realised that, after all this time and heartache in Manchester, he had finally found a group of men with whom he could have the conversations that mattered to him. And although Neil's friends weren't as rough and ready as his own in London, it didn't matter. They laughed at each other's jokes, held strong opinions on things that didn't matter and could tell anecdotes with all the skill and guile of professional stand-up comedians. In the first hour he spent with them Rob laughed, argued and harangued more than he had in months, and it made him feel good again.

Suddenly he saw himself on his birthday night, when he had been staring enviously around this bar at all the groups of male friends deep in conversation, and now here he was having conversations about life, sport, music and all the stuff in between without having to resort to asking people what they did for a living or bringing up the topic of rising house prices. And it was all thanks to one thing: a miraculous four-step conversion process.

Conversion step one: getting over Jo

After leaving Jo's on New Year's Day Rob had told himself that all she needed was a few days on her own to get herself together. He was sure she would come to her senses and dump Sean. Although he had told her he was prepared to give Sean another chance, he hadn't meant it. To Rob, the situation he found himself in was Sean's fault. If Sean hadn't done his about-turn, Jo wouldn't have told Rob she was in love with him and they could have continued as good friends.

He checked and double-checked as to whether he had led her on at any point in their friendship – and realised that their relationship had become a textbook definition of 'grey area'. They had shared a bed twice and he had lost count of the number of times they had touched (hand to face, leg to leg, arm to arm) in a manner that might have suggested to a casual observer that they were a couple.

Their problem, he reasoned, lay in their compatibility. They got on together too well to be just good friends. He could see how Jo might have found herself moving from 'Should I take things further?' to 'Why shouldn't I take things further?'

He, however, was not confused. He knew he could never betray Ashley, even if he had wanted to, because Rob believed in loyalty. Loyalty to his family, to his friends and to the woman he loved. To betray Ashley would be to betray something at the core of his belief: that you can only expect high standards from those you love if you give the same in return. And Rob had high standards for friends and lovers – which was why he could not compromise even when he was at his most desperate. He believed that the people in his life *were* the best in the world, and having them in his life reflected to the outside world exactly who he was.

He left it a week before he contacted Jo, and because she didn't return any of the messages he left for her he drove over to her place early on the Saturday morning hoping to talk to her face to face. He could tell she was in because her car was there, and when he was on the door step he could hear the radio in the kitchen, but although he waited for half an hour she didn't come out. As he drove back to Chorlton, trying to work out what to do next his mobile beeped. Jo had sent him a text message:

Please don't make this more difficult than it already is. j xxx

It had been hard to come to terms with the end of their friendship. Once again he had found himself in no man's land without a map, compass or guide. If Jo had been his girlfriend he would have known how to react (several evenings of excessive drinking and a revisitation of the musical canon of Leonard Cohen). If Jo had been a male friend he would still have known what to do (a bit of yelling and shouting, followed by a lifetime of ignoring the issue). But Rob's relationship with Jo was different: she wasn't his girlfriend and she wasn't a male friend. How was a man with a fiancée supposed to behave now that his girl friend was no longer in his life? His natural inclination was to fall into a depression because he missed her. But he couldn't grieve unless he accepted there was more between them than what he was prepared to admit to himself. When over a fortnight had passed and Ashley asked him what had happened, Rob told her a bare-bones version of the truth: 'She's got back with her ex-boyfriend and apparently he's not really into the idea of his girlfriend hanging out with another bloke.'

'Can't you explain to him that nothing's going on?' asked Ashley.

'I don't think he gets it,' replied Rob. 'At least, not like you do.'

Conversion step two:
A slight digression in a bar on Deansgate

After his conversation with Ashley, Rob determined to move his life on without Jo. The following Friday night, when Ashley was working, he showered, shaved and caught a taxi into town. He jumped out by the Corn Exchange and realised he hadn't put enough thought into how he would spend his evening. He didn't know where to go – it had to be lively enough to kick-start a good mood yet anonymous enough for him to be able to drink on his own without feeling like a loser. All Bar One – with its nice after-work buzz, its wooden floors and tables – sprang to mind.

An hour later the bar was heaving with people but Rob was the only one drinking alone. He occupied himself with a discarded copy of the *Evening News*, then looked around for a diversion and found one in the shape of two women sitting at a table near him. The woman on the left was attractive, wearing a short green and red striped dress and patent leather high-heeled black boots. The other was just as pretty but in a different way: her jet-black hair was cropped short and she was wearing jeans, a V-necked black cardigan and a black T-shirt. She glanced at Rob, half smiled, then looked away. It lasted a fraction of a second, but Rob decided that that was all the encouragement he needed. Before he knew it, he had set his drink on the bar and was walking towards them.

'Excuse me,' he said, kneeling beside their table.

Both women turned to look at him, bemused.

'Before you start,' said the first, 'we spotted you looking at us and whatever you want we're not interested, okay?'

'I thought you might say that,' said Rob.

'So why are you bothering us? We've just come out for a drink and a chat. And you're wasting your time with us because I'm married and my sister is off men for the foreseeable future.'

'Don't get me wrong,' replied Rob. 'You're both very attractive but I'm not trying to chat you up.'

'So what *do* you want?'

'To be friends.'

'Can you believe this guy, Leah?' She laughed. 'That's got to be the cheesiest chat-up line I've ever heard.'

'Give him a break, Marissa,' said the second woman. 'You have to admit it's a bit more original than ''Get your coat, love, you've pulled.'' Let's hear what he's got to say.'

'If it'll make him go away, fine.'

Rob pulled up a chair and sat down. 'Well, first off,' he began, 'my name's Rob, you're Marissa,' he gestured to the first woman, 'and you're Leah.'

'Tell me,' said Marissa, 'does this technique usually work with the sort of women you chat up? It's obvious you've done this a million times and I bet they really fall for it.'

'It's not a technique,' replied Rob. 'I used to have a good mate who was a woman.'

'Really?' said Marissa sarcastically.

'Really,' replied Rob. 'Her name was Jo.'

'And where did you meet her?' asked Marissa.

'At a party in Didsbury, then again in a pub in Chorlton, but it was complicated in the early days because my girlfriend—'

'You've got a girlfriend?'

'A fiancée, actually.'

'And she didn't mind you being friends with this woman?'

'At first it was awkward but it all got sorted.'

Marissa laughed. 'No woman I know would be happy about her boyfriend spending time with another woman.'

'Mine was fine about it because she had nothing to worry about. With me and Jo it was just about friendship.'

'Liar,' said Marissa. 'Of course you fancied her. If you're a bloke and you're hanging out with some woman who's not your girlfriend it has to be because you fancy her. Straight men aren't capable of being just good friends with women.'

'That's not true,' said Leah. 'I think they can . . . But it's hard.'

Rob looked at Marissa. 'Are you telling me you haven't got any male friends?'

She grinned. 'I've got plenty of male friends but there's always been a little frisson of sexual tension between us at some point.'

'I haven't got any male friends,' admitted Leah, cheerfully. 'I don't know why.'

A mobile phone rang inside Marissa's bag on the floor. 'It's John,' she said to Leah, as she answered it. 'I can barely hear him above all the noise in here. I'm going to speak to him outside. Will you be okay?'

'I'm fine,' said Leah, smiling. 'Just come back when you're done.'

Rob and Leah watched as Marissa left the bar, then turned to each other. 'Where are you from?' asked Rob. 'You don't sound local.'

'I grew up in a place called Nuneaton.'

'I know it,' said Rob. 'It's not far from Coventry.'

'That's the one.'

'When I was about sixteen I went on holiday with some mates to Málaga and I had a holiday romance with a girl called . . . what was her name? That's it! Corinna Massey. She lived in Hinckley, which isn't far from Nuneaton. Her idea of a big day out was to go into Nuneaton town centre. I fell madly in love with her and she dumped me for some guy who had left school and had a car.'

'The promise of a backie on some spotty youth's BMX is hardly going to compete with being driven to the Lakeside Superbowl in Alex Kennedy's Mini Cooper,' laughed Leah.

'Alex Kennedy, eh?' joked Rob. 'Did the two of you last long?'

'Put it this way,' she replied, 'it wasn't one of the best relationships I've ever had but it was a long way from the worst.'

'And which one would claim that title?' asked Rob.

Leah was about to answer when Marissa returned to the table. 'I'm really sorry, sis,' she said, 'but I've got to go. John's having problems with the kids. Molly's been screaming the place down since I left the house. I think it's her teeth again.'

'Poor John,' said Leah. 'Of course we'll go right now.' She looked at Rob apologetically. 'I'm sorry.'

'It was nice to meet you.'

Leah smiled. 'It was nice to meet you too. That whole let's-be-friends thing was a great chat-up line. If you'd picked someone a little less battle-scarred you might have been lucky tonight.'

'It *wasn't* a line,' said Rob.

'But it isn't how people make friends in the real world, is it?' said Leah. 'It's how people have one-night stands that they bitterly regret the next day.'

Rob watched them leave, and as the glass doors closed he realised she was right: making friends was all about context. If he'd met Leah at work or been introduced to her through mutual friends she wouldn't have had a qualm about seeing him again. But because they were strangers and had met in a bar it was never going to happen. People didn't make friends with strangers in bars, no matter how much they liked them. Especially when one was a man and the other a woman.

Conversion step three:
Two men and some red stripe

The following weekend Rob had planned to go to London to see Phil and whichever of the boys he could persuade to come out for a weekend involving drinking in the Queen's Head on Friday night, a house party in Camberwell on Saturday night and five-a-side football in Hyde Park on Sunday afternoon. At the last minute, however, he called Phil and cancelled, claiming he was 'feeling like he was coming down with something', even though he was fine.

Rob had come to an epiphany of sorts. He was sick of running away from Manchester and tired of depending on his old friends for a social life. He told himself that he needed to try to stand on his own two feet and find a way of making life work in Manchester.

On Friday night he stayed in with Ashley, a home-delivery pizza and *Top of the Pops* (when he should have been out with Phil and Woodsy in the Queen's). On Saturday morning, (when he'd planned to be sleeping off the effects of a night at the Queen's) Rob found himself in town with Ashley, in search of a new shower curtain, a set of wine glasses, embroidered cushions and cinnamon room spray. Around midday (when Rob should have been ordering a fried English breakfast from the Sunshine café on Tooting Broadway) he was in Stock on Norfolk Street, discussing potential honeymoon destinations over seafood linguine. And on

Saturday evening (when Rob should have been enjoying a pre-party drinking session at the Queen's) he was at home, surrounded by Ashley's friends, with an evening of drinking, finger food and board games ahead of him.

Among the usual crowd who came to Ashley's impromptu gatherings, like Christine and Joel, Luke and Lauren, Jason and Louise, Mia and Edwin and, of course, Neil, was someone Rob had never met before: Justine, Neil's relatively new girlfriend. At the beginning of the evening he had a chat with her. Justine worked in advertising in London and they knew some people in common. Rob would have talked to her for longer but he made the mistake of pausing to change the CD and when he returned she was discussing house prices with Mia and Christine. Disheartened, he left the room to get a beer.

Crouching over the fridge, Rob stared inside looking for inspiration: there were bottles of Budvar, which Joel had brought, Luke's cans of Boddington's bitter, Jason's Löwenbraü and Neil's Red Stripe, but there was no Guinness or Carlsberg. Rob hated Budvar, loathed Boddington's, balked at Löwenbraü and was scornful of Red Stripe, but the fact remained that he wanted a drink. He scanned all the bottles and cans again and found himself reaching for a Red Stripe. He promised himself that if it was too disgusting he would throw it down the drain and run to the off-licence even though it was raining.

Grimacing – as if he was about to be poisoned – he opened the can and took a swig, waiting for his taste buds to recoil. They didn't. In fact, the opposite happened. They practically purred.

'Didn't know you liked Red Stripe,' said a voice from behind Rob.

Rob turned to see Neil.

'Oh, it's you,' he said. 'You're right. I don't normally drink anything but Carlsberg or Guinness but, well, this stuff's all right.'

'Can you grab one for me?' asked Neil. 'I only came in to get away from Mia and Christine banging on about house prices but I might as well make the journey worthwhile.'

Rob handed him a can. 'I suggest we stay here until they've finished.'

Neil opened his beer. 'That could be a while. I'm pretty sure after Chorlton they'll be on to Didsbury.'

'And then Wythenshawe,' added Rob, grinning.

'And up-and-coming Withington.'

'Not forgetting highly desirable Crumpsall.'

'How long do you reckon it'll take them to do the whole of the north-west?'

'All night. And maybe into the early morning.'

'Well, we might as well make ourselves comfortable,' said Neil, and sat down at the kitchen table.

'That,' said Rob, 'sounds like a great idea.'

Rob couldn't tell whether it was the Red Stripe that they finished off or the Budvar and Löwenbraü that they started on, whether Neil was behaving differently because of his girlfriend or whether he himself was relaxed because he had drunk so much, but their mini drinking session was a turning-point for the two men. Suddenly the awkwardness between them disappeared. Rob laughed so hard at a few of Neil's jokes that he couldn't breathe. Riding this conversational high Rob discovered a host of things he hadn't known about him. Neil revealed, for instance, that the first record he'd ever bought was the seven-inch single of 'Welcome to The Rat Race' by the Specials and his first album was *Eat To*

The Beat by Blondie – which impressed him, and even more so when Neil revealed that he had been only eight at the time.

From this point the conversation went up a gear and the revelations came thick and fast. Neil, too, had a minor obsession with eBay but rather than collecting toys from his childhood he bought cult sixties and seventies first-edition paperbacks (everything from British pulp fiction to obscure novelisations of Italian horror films). He, too, thought that *Scarface* was one of the world's most overrated films; he, too, had given up buying Radiohead albums until they stopped being so wilfully experimental. But the moment when Neil finally stopped being 'Neil' and became someone far more interesting was late in the evening when Rob had insisted he should hear a song that would change his life for ever. He turned up the volume of the stereo and, air guitar at the ready, pressed play. Within three seconds of the intro Neil yelled, ' ''Dreams'', van Halen.'

'How did you know?' asked Rob, dropping his air guitar.

'Misspent youth,' explained Neil. 'Back in the day I had long hair and too-tight jeans.' He laughed. 'How do *you* know it? I'd never imagined you'd have a closet rubbish-rock-music phase to confess to.'

'No rock phase,' said Rob. 'My mate Phil sent it to me ages ago.'

'Well, tell him from me,' said Neil, grinning, 'he's got great taste in music.'

Conversion step four: Repeat step three

'Morning, babe,' said Rob, rubbing his eyes, as a fully dressed Ashley entered their bedroom with the cordless telephone in her hand.

'Afternoon, more like,' she replied.

Rob stared at the alarm clock on her bedside table. 'Is this thing right?'

'Do you mean, "Is it really four o'clock in the afternoon?" ' She laughed. 'If so, yes, it is!'

'I feel terrible,' he said.

'Really? I wonder why. Could it be that you and Neil were boozing downstairs until the early hours?'

'Last night is a bit of a blur,' he confessed.

'Hmm,' said Ashley. 'So I take it you can't recall promising your new best friend that you'd go for a drink with him tonight?'

Rob winced. 'He won't remember. We'd had too much to drink and got carried away. A one-nighter. Definitely not to be repeated.'

'Is that right?' said Ashley, grinning, and handed Rob the phone. 'So why is Neil on the phone to check that you're coming out tonight?'

Despite his thumping headache Rob agreed to meet Neil in BlueBar, on the condition that they limited themselves to a quick pint before last orders.

It was a repeat of the previous night: lots of laughs, good conversations and anecdotes. In fact, it was such a success that afterwards Rob went back to Neil's flat in Didsbury where they listened to a few CDs Neil had bought over the weekend. Rob didn't get home until a quarter past three when, to make matters worse, he remembered he'd left his house keys in his office. He had to ring the bell for Ashley to let him in.

When she opened the door with 'What time do you call this?' Rob laughed and fell over. And that night although he had to sleep on the sofa and was forced to spend the rest of the week apologising he didn't mind because he was sure he'd made a new friend. Soon he was seeing Neil regularly for a drink and spending the rest of his time with Ashley. And everything was great. His life was back on track. Jo was history.

Back to BlueBar

It was just after nine on Rob's big night out with Neil's friends and Rob was in his element. So far he and the others had discussed topics as diverse as 'Will there ever be peace in the Middle East?' posed by Gavin, right through to 'John or Paul? Which was the most talented Beatle?', Jonesy's offering.

'Okay, then,' began Paolo, 'who's the most attractive screen actress – living or dead – of all time, and in what film did they look their best?'

'I'm off to the gents, gents,' announced Rob, who had been resisting the urge so that he didn't miss any top-quality conversation. 'But that's a brilliant question Paolo, mate, and the answer, without any doubt, is Ingrid Bergman in *To Have and Have Not*. Women really don't get any better than her in that film.'

Paolo and the others laughed and immediately offered their own suggestions. As Rob headed across the room towards the loos he wore a huge grin. He was happy. He was enjoying himself. He even decided to come up with a few extra nominations in case his friends were still talking about actresses when he got back to them. As he entered the gents he wondered whether Jean Seberg in *À Bout de Souffle*, Halle Berry in *Die Another Day* or Maria Grazia Cucinotta in *Il Postino* would join Ingrid in his ultimate top three. In the end he concluded that although Seberg might beat Berry on the grounds that she had made better films, Seberg might ultimately lose to Grazia Cucinotta who really was a babe. Rob was so focused on his internal New Wave French cinema versus hot Italian actresses debate that when he came out of the loos he didn't see the woman coming towards him and walked right into her.

'I'm so sorry—' he began, then stopped when he realised that the woman in front of him wasn't a stranger. She was Jo.

For several seconds neither spoke. Instead they stared at each other, at a loss for something to say. In the end Jo broke the silence. 'Rob,' she said quietly, 'I was on my way to the loo.'

'It was my fault,' said Rob, making sure that his voice betrayed no flicker of emotion. 'My mind was elsewhere. Really, there's no need for this to be a big thing. You carry on doing what you were doing and we'll pretend it never happened.'

'How have you been?' asked Jo.

'Good, thanks.'

'I've put my house on the market and handed in my notice at work,' she said brightly. 'Sean and I are moving to London at the end of next month. I don't know what I'll do yet – anything but what I've been doing for the last ten years.'

'I'm pleased for you,' said Rob. 'Looks like everything's turning out right.'

'Not everything,' she replied, gazing into his eyes. There was a long pause. 'Just in case you were wondering, my book was rejected by every agent I sent it to – all ten. None had much to say beyond "This isn't for us", apart from a guy who called me to say he thought I had a "voice" – whatever that means.'

'Write another novel,' replied Rob. 'They obviously think you've got talent.'

'No,' said Jo, firmly. 'I've done with dreaming. I'm thinking about retraining – doing teaching or something. I need a fresh start.'

'So you're giving up just like that?' asked Rob. 'What happened to the woman who told me we all need creativity in our lives?'

'I don't know,' said Jo.

There was another long silence.

'Are you here with Ashley?' she asked.

'No.'

'But you're not on your own, are you?' she said, sounding concerned.

'And why would it matter to you if I was?' asked Rob. 'It's not like you're going to ask me to join you and Sean for a drink, is it?'

'Don't be like that.' Jo touched his arm. 'I know you think I've let you down and I'm sorry, okay? But there was no other choice.'

Rob shrugged. 'I'm with those guys over there,' he said waving to his friends.

'Isn't that Neil?' asked Jo. 'I thought you didn't like him.'

'Things change,' said Rob.

'I've missed you,' she said softly. 'You were one of the most important people to me in the whole world, Rob. I've never been as close to anyone outside my family as I was to you – not even Sean. The last time I saw you I—'

'Why are you saying all this when it's just not true?' Rob cut her short. 'How could I be more important to you than Sean when you chose him over me? Look, you've made your decision and that's fine. But it wasn't circumstances that stopped us being friends. It was you.'

Rob saw the hurt in her eyes and knew that his words had had the desired effect but he took no pleasure in it. It didn't come easily to him to be hard on her. All he wanted to do was put his arms round her and tell her that everything would be okay. But he couldn't find it in himself to forgive her for ending their friendship.

'How much do you hate me?' she asked, tears welling.

'About as much as you deserve,' said Rob succinctly. Then he brushed past her and crossed the room to his new friends.

321

Man to man

It was now twenty past nine and Rob was listening to Neil tell an anecdote about a weekend in Brighton with Justine when they had first got together. Although he was laughing in all the right places, his mind was elsewhere. His anger with Jo had evaporated, leaving intense regret. She hadn't deserved the way he had spoken to her, but he had needed to let her know how much he felt she had let him down. He was convinced she could have worked round her feelings for him – they would have faded in time. All it would have taken was patience and their friendship could have been salvaged.

As Neil came to the end of his story Rob decided to find her and apologise. He knew he had to accept that she hadn't made the decision lightly to end their friendship. Fully committed to his resolution to make amends, he looked over his shoulder to scan the room for her, And something stopped him in his tracks. A fist.

It belonged to Sean.

And it was heading for Rob's nose at an alarming velocity.

Rob had no time to duck out of the way as they do in films. Neither had he then time to even contemplate how much the blow might hurt when it landed. All he could do was wait for the punch to connect.

When Sean's fist reached its target Rob was surprised by how much it hurt. It was a shock to discover that something as simple as a tightly packed hand could deliver a blow akin to that of a mallet. And the pain was beyond ordinary pain: it was double-strength, super-sized, and made his head feel as if its contents were fizzing like the inside of a shaken can of Coke. He couldn't tell if he was still standing (he wasn't), he couldn't tell if he was bleeding (he was, profusely) and he couldn't tell if his nose had been broken by the blow (it hadn't, although it was quite a mess).

Suddenly there was a lot of commotion, and he could hear Jo yelling at Sean. After a few moments he felt hands pulling him to his feet. He opened his eyes to find that he had been helped up by two of the bar's weekend door staff, who ejected him, Sean and Jo from the premises and stood in front of the doors making sure no one could get in or out.

Sitting on the pavement outside, Rob tried to stem the flow of blood while Jo crouched next to him with an arm round his shoulders.

'Are you all right?' she asked. She pulled out a crumpled Kleenex and began to clean his face.

'I'm fine,' snapped Rob. His pride was far more damaged than his nose. 'Just leave me alone, okay?'

'I know you're angry,' said Jo. 'But—'

'It's just a nosebleed,' replied Rob, and glared at Sean, who was looking on passively.

'You heard him, Jo,' said Sean, grabbing her arm. 'He doesn't need your help. Let's go.'

Jo stared at him. 'Why are you still here? What are you? A six-year-old? You're such an idiot, Sean. You could've really hurt Rob.'

'That was his intention,' murmured Rob.

'This is so typical of you,' spat Sean. 'One minute you're in tears because of something this loser's said and the next—'

'I was upset,' interjected Jo, 'but I never meant this to happen.' She sighed heavily and began to cry. 'Will you go, Sean? Just go and never come back.'

'What are you talking about?' he asked.

'It's over.' She sniffed and wiped her eyes with the back of her hand.

'Because of him?'

'No. Because of you.'

Without a word, Sean walked away, leaving her to cry. Rob put his arms round her and Jo scrabbled in her bag for her tobacco and lighter. Then she threw them back. 'I've run out of papers,' she said.

'How about a trip to the off-licence?' asked Rob.

'You're on,' said Jo, and they stood up. Jo looped her arm through his and they headed along Wilbraham Road for Threshers.

'How's your nose?' she asked. It was raining now and she had to squint to see it.

'All right,' he said, touching it gingerly. 'It's stopped bleeding at least.' He turned his face side on to show her the damage. 'Do you think it's broken?'

'How should I know?' asked Jo. 'I've never seen a broken nose. Does it feel broken?'

'How should I know? I've never had a suspected broken nose.'

'I think the rain's easing off.' She wiped the damp off her face with her sleeve.

'I've missed this,' said Rob, as they walked.

'What?'

'You know . . . This . . .'

'That's as soppy as you get, isn't it?' said Jo, pulling his arm closer to her. 'But I know what you mean. Nothing's been the same without you around – not even *Dirty Dancing*.'

'You're kidding,' said Rob.

'I tried to watch it a few weeks ago and I got as far as taking it out of the case before I was in floods of tears. I just kept thinking, This is mine and Rob's film. And do you know what's wrong about that?'

Rob shrugged.

'*Dirty Dancing* isn't ''our'' film. It's *my* film. You'd never even seen it until I showed it to you.' She laughed, then sniffed again. 'You've done the impossible – you've ruined it for me.'

'I'm not sure *ruined* is the right word,' he replied, grinning. 'Surely it would have to have been half decent in the first place to be ruined.' Jo opened her mouth to remonstrate but before she could speak Rob was attempting to redeem himself. 'But if I did spoil your viewing pleasure I apologise.'

'Apology accepted. Joking apart, though, I've really missed you. Not seeing or talking to you has been the hardest thing I've done in my life. I've lost count of the number of times I've nearly called you, then lost my nerve at the last minute.'

'So, why didn't you?' asked Rob. 'I'm sorry, I didn't mean it like that, I meant—'

'It's okay. At least it shows you care.'

Rob smiled. 'It might not be too late for you to patch things up with Bruiser Boy.'

'After what he did to you?' said Jo. 'No, it's over. Really it is.'

'But I did sort of ask for it,' said Rob.

'Too right you did. But I don't think there's any point in me trying to build anything meaningful on such a shaky foundation.'

'But you said you loved him.'

'I do,' she replied, and then she corrected herself: 'Well, I *did*. I think the main problem with me is that, deep down, I just didn't want to be alone. You wouldn't have needed a crystal ball to guess what would have happened if I'd given up the life I'd made here just to be— The second I'd let down my guard he'd have been back to his old ways.' They stopped outside the off-licence. 'You'd better wait out here while I get my Rizlas,' she said, examining the dried blood on his face and clothes. 'You might scare the girl on the till looking like that.'

As Jo went into the shop Rob walked to the kerb and, although the ground was wet, sat down with his feet in the road. He rested his head in his hands and listened to the traffic. As the damp seeped into his jeans he concentrated on his throbbing nose and worried about how he was going to explain his war wound to Ashley.

'Feeling sorry for yourself?'

Rob opened his eyes to see Jo standing beside him with a packet of cigarette papers in one hand and a can of Pepsi-Max in the other.

'This is for you,' she said, holding out the can. 'I got it out of the fridge. It's ice cold. I thought you could rest it on your nose. It might help with the swelling.'

Rob took it from her and did as she had suggested. 'Cheers,' he said. 'Not only am I in pain, I now feel ridiculous.'

She laughed, sat down beside him and rested her head against his shoulder. Then she pulled out her tobacco and, with the newly purchased Rizlas, began to roll a cigarette. A minute later she said, 'All done,' and passed it to Rob. 'There you go.'

Rob was puzzled. 'What's this for? You know I haven't smoked in years.'

'I know,' said Jo as she began to make a cigarette for herself. 'Consider it a peace-offering. I never want to fight with you again.'

A silence fell between the two friends that neither felt inclined to fill. Instead they sat watching the traffic go by on Barlow Moor Road. Jo licked the gummed edge of the paper and rolled up the tobacco. She looked at Rob expectantly.

'What?' said Rob.

'I think you were right,' she said. 'I wasn't in love with you.'

'So what were you?'

'That's just it,' said Jo. 'I don't know.' She pulled out a yellow lighter and, shielding the flame from the wind, lit her cigarette, took a long drag and held her breath. As she exhaled, a stream of smoke billowed into the air.

'Do you want to hear an interesting fact?' said Jo. 'Eskimos apparently have over fifty different words for snow. Snow's really important to those guys – I suppose it's because sometimes the difference between one type and another can mean the difference between life or death.' She paused and laughed self-consciously. 'You know they've got words for dry snow and wet snow, fluffy snow and compact snow. They've got words for snow that comes down fast and for snow that comes down slow – they've thought of everything.'

'That's a lot of snow,' commented Rob as his eyes flicked to a scruffy-looking mongrel crossing the road in front of them, oblivious to the night bus hurtling towards it. It only narrowly missed being hit, but continued coolly on its journey to the bin outside the off-licence, which it sniffed studiously, then casually cocked a leg against.

'So what's your point?' asked Rob.

'Well it's like this,' replied Jo. 'If Eskimos can come up

with fifty words for snow because it's a matter of life or death, why is it that we've only got one word for "love"?'

She was gazing at Rob as if he might have an answer, but he was confused.

'The problem with you and me is that we haven't got a word for *this* . . .' She gesticulated with her hands in the space between them. 'We haven't got a word for what we are to each other. And that's a problem. If you haven't got a word for it, it's impossible to define, isn't it? We're not just friends, are we? And we're not lovers either. We're sort of platonic lovers. And although I thought I was in love with you I was wrong. Maybe I thought it was love because that was the only way I could imagine even half-way expressing how I felt about you.'

Rob watched the stray dog return to the edge of the road and wait for a break in the traffic. 'I get what you're saying,' he said, 'but at the same time I don't.'

'Do you remember that time ages ago when we were talking about all the great telly shows that went rubbish and you told me about that website – JumptheShark.com? Well, I was looking at it recently and it occurred to me that nine out of ten people on the forum thought that getting the male and female leads together was the kiss of death for a show. And they're right. I mean, look at the evidence. Sam and Diane in *Cheers* were never the same once they got together, and neither were Maddy and Dave in *Moonlighting* – oh, and don't get me started on Niles and Daphne in *Frasier*. It's as if TV writers can't put men and women in the same programme without having them get together or have a clear-cut reason why it'll never happen, like in *Will and Grace*. They're never just two mates who don't snog, are they?'

'No,' replied Rob. 'I suppose not. I take it you've got a theory on why this is?'

'Absolutely,' said Jo. 'It's about sex. Thanks to Freud, everyone in the world thinks that the motivation behind everything is sex – wanting it, not getting enough, getting too much. You name it, it's somewhere in the mix.'

'And?'

'Well, maybe it isn't.'

Rob laughed. 'I love this. This is so you – former politics and English student Jo Richards versus Sigmund Freud, the father of modern psychoanalysis.'

'All I'm trying to say is that maybe it's just a lazy way of looking at things. It's like going out with someone you don't fancy because you can't think of a good reason to say no. Sometimes I think people mistake love for a friend with love for a person they fancy because it's easier than trying to give a name to something that hasn't got one.' Her eyes narrowed. 'Do you understand what I'm saying?'

'I do . . . sort of . . .' he said, '. . . but the thing is I've got a bit of a problem with your little theory.'

'What is it?' she asked.

'It's this,' said Rob and he kissed her.

It had been a long time since Rob had kissed someone who wasn't Ashley. A very long time indeed. And while Rob kissed Jo and Jo kissed him back it was mainly Ashley who was on his mind. Part of him thought he might explode, or spontaneously combust. Or something else equally pyro-technical because he was kissing someone who wasn't his girlfriend. But he didn't.

'That wasn't what I was expecting,' said Rob, eventually.

'What *were* you expecting?' asked Jo.

'I don't know,' said Rob. 'I suppose I always felt sure that if

Mike Gayle

we ever did kiss I wouldn't feel anything. That it would be a let down and I'd realise I wasn't attracted to you after all. But that's not really the case is it?'

'No,' said Jo. 'It isn't. The truth is, you and I were never going to work being just good friends. Not that it's impossible for men and women to be good friends and nothing more, but it's impossible for us. I'm sure I knew it when we first met but I didn't want to face up to it. I don't know what you and I are, Rob, but we're definitely not just good friends, are we?'

'No,' replied Rob.

'We're lovers with terrible timing,' Jo smiled. 'I can't help but think that if we'd met years ago – before you found Ashley – we'd have been perfect together. I know I could've made you just as happy as she makes you now.'

'But we didn't meet first,' replied Rob, unable to look at her. 'We met second. And even though I know I shouldn't feel what I feel for you the fact remains that I love Ashley. I've never stopped loving her. Through all that's happened it's never occurred to me that she isn't right for me – because she is.'

Jo reached up and touched his face. 'I know,' she said, as tears formed once more in her eyes, 'and that's why it would never work between us. She owns your heart. What we have is special – I'll always cherish it – but the difference between our love and the love you have for Ashley is like the difference between knowing something in your head and knowing it in your heart. In your head you think you love me because we see the world the same way, we feel the same things – in a way we're almost like twins – but what you and Ashley have is much more special because it's not about what you have in common, it's about the way she makes you

330

feel in your heart. And the heart wins every time. It's how we're built. And I'd never want it any other way.' Jo stood up and Rob did too, holding her hands.

'So this is where we say goodbye for good,' she said.

'Are you sure there's no way round this?' asked Rob.

'No,' Jo said. 'This really is goodbye. It's for the best.' And then she placed a hand on either side of Rob's face and kissed him again. Rob wrapped his arms round her and held her tightly, unsure that he could ever let her go.

'See you in another lifetime,' she whispered. Then she turned and walked away.

PART NINE

(Principally about a letter)

Dear Jo,

I feel a bit stupid doing this. But I remember you told me once that you write letters to your brother even though he isn't around any more. I always thought it was a nice idea, but I never imagined that I'd ever do it myself. And yet here I am sitting at my desk in my office at home writing a letter that I know I will never send. I suppose I just want the opportunity to catch up with you for a little while, even if it's just in my head,

It has been over a month now since I last saw you. And though I do miss you I know in my heart that we did the right thing. After I left you that night I went home and told Ashley everything. Not just about the fight and the kiss, but about the two occasions when I stayed at yours, too. I know it would've been easier for me to keep quiet but I just couldn't. I felt as if I'd never be able to look her in the eye again unless I told her the truth – and I have to say it was one of the hardest things I've done in my life. To her credit she didn't freak out like I expected. Instead she was really calm and just listened to what I had to say. And when I was done talking she didn't kick me out of the house, tell me it was all over or even cry – she just said, 'Everything's going to be okay.' And for a few seconds I was really confused. I couldn't get my head around why she was being so understanding and then I realised what was going on – Ashley was standing in my shoes. She was seeing the world from my point of view. Somehow she understood that despite all that had happened I genuinely had never meant to hurt her. And in that single moment I realised that I loved her more than I ever thought possible. Ashley really is the one that I want to spend the rest of my life with. And I know now that I could never have any regrets knowing that someone like her was so resolutely on my side, even when I'd given her no reason to be.

Anyway, that's all I wanted to say. I don't think I'll be doing this again – I'm too self-conscious for this type of thing. Before I go though, I just want to say one last thing. You asked me why we've only got one word for 'love' when Eskimos have got fifty for 'snow' and I've been thinking about it ever since. Maybe you're looking at it the wrong way. Yes, it would be easier if we sub-divided and categorised it down to specifics – but would it really be as much fun? The way I see it is, we may only have the one word for love, but what a word it is.

Have a great life.
Love,
Rob

P.S. Don't give up on the writing

EPILOGUE

(Principally concerning Jo, two years later)

Reading, writing but no arithmetic

'On behalf of all of us at Waterstone's, Deansgate,' said the woman with the bright pink hair into the microphone, as the applause died away, 'I'd like to thank Ms Richards for joining us tonight – I'm sure we've all been entertained by what we've heard. And before we conclude this evening's event she has kindly agreed to answer questions, after which she'll be available to sign copies of her book for those who would like one.' She paused and smiled encouragingly at Jo. 'I'd like to put the first one, if I may?' she asked. 'Could you tell us what you consider your favourite part of being an author?'

Jo moved back to the lectern and the other woman stepped aside.

'What's my favourite thing about being an author?' she mused aloud, into the microphone. 'My favourite thing about being an author is that, unlike most people, on a good day I can go to work in a T-shirt and my boyfriend's boxer shorts and on a bad day I can sit in front of the computer stark naked.'

She got a reasonable laugh for that joke (much better than the response she'd had at the Library Literary Festival in the East Midlands, where it hadn't even raised a smile), then went on to expand on her usual writing day – missing out the endless trips to the kitchen to make cups of sugary tea and investigate the fridge.

Then she asked if anyone else had a question for her. A young auburn-haired woman in an expensive-looking leather jacket raised her hand. 'Hi, Jo,' she said. 'I read *Fifty Words For Snow* after I'd read a review of it when it came out in hardback and absolutely loved it. I've been recommending it to all my friends ever since. How did you get into writing?'

'Thank you for your question and kind words,' replied Jo. 'Before *Fifty Words For Snow* I wrote a novel in my twenties and I didn't think it was any good at all. A friend of mine read it some years later and encouraged me to send it out to a few agents. It was unanimously rejected and I was ready to give up but the same friend told me that instead of wallowing in self-pity I should get on and write another. For a long time I didn't take his advice and then one day, a few months after I'd moved to London, I thought about him and just started writing. At the time I had a bar job so any time I wasn't working or sleeping I was writing. Nine months and several edits later I sent it to a literary agent, who took me on right away. And a month later I found myself with a two-book contract with Cooper and Lawton. The rest, as they say, is history.'

She nodded to a scruffy-looking man in his twenties wearing a baseball cap and an old army jacket.

'I just wanted to ask this,' he said, grinning at Jo. 'I only read *Fifty Words For Snow* recently so it's still fresh in my mind but there's a bit in the book where the main characters – Ruth and Danny – talk about the world's most overrated films and Ruth nominates Brian De Palma's *Scarface*. Was that your personal choice or something you decided was right for the character?'

'That was my choice,' replied Jo, as the room erupted in

laughter. 'I mean, how can you take a gangster seriously when he looks like he's just stepped out of *Saturday Night Fever*?'

He laughed, and Jo looked out into the sea of hands before her and pointed to a dark-haired woman in her thirties.

'Hi, Jo,' she began. 'I work in Waterstone's in St Anne's Square and we've sold hundreds of copies of your book and it's still selling well. My question to you is a bit cheeky: I read in an interview that you lived with the novelist Matt Rose and I wondered what it's like being in a relationship with a fellow author.'

'It's great,' said Jo. 'The best ever. In fact, he's here with me tonight . . .' She waved at a smart-looking man with arty black spectacles and a grey suit, who waved back, looking a bit embarrassed. 'Matt and I have been together for nearly a year and have lived together for about nine months. It's really nice to be with someone who understands the ups and downs of writing – I'd recommend it.'

Question over, Jo gestured to a man in his thirties, wearing a black Led Zeppelin T-shirt.

'Hi, Jo,' he said. 'My girlfriend bought me *Fifty Words For Snow* because she said that the main relationship reminded her of how she and I got together – because we, too, used to be just good friends. I wondered if you were writing from experience.'

'No.' Jo grinned. 'I made the whole thing up – that's what we writers do – but I did draw on my own experience.'

'So does that mean you're Ruth?'

'Ruth and I share some similarities,' said Jo, 'in that we both drink too much, smoke roll-ups and have a predilection for locking ourselves in other people's bathrooms when we're upset.'

'Does that mean there's a Danny in your life?' asked the man, and chuckled.

'That,' said Jo, carefully, 'would be telling.'

Over the next twenty minutes Jo fielded questions such as 'Who is your favourite author?' (to which she answered, 'I'm a big fan of any Russian novelist who can write well about being miserable . . . which is basically all of them'); 'Have you had any film interest in *Fifty Words For Snow*?' (to which she answered, 'A few people have indicated an interest but there are no solid offers on the table yet'); 'Have you ever had a conversation about house prices in Chorlton and Didsbury?' (to which, once she had stopped laughing, she answered, 'Yes, lots, even though I lived in Levenshulme'); and finally, 'What's your next book going to be about?' (to which she answered, 'It's called *How Soon Is Now?* and it's about the impact that losing a brother in a car accident has on a young woman in her twenties').

She glanced at the audience to see only two hands in the air now. One belonged to a student-looking girl wearing a denim jacket who had already asked, 'Who is your favourite author?' and the other belonged to an old man with a matted beard, who had been clutching his plastic cup of wine to his chest all evening and mumbling to himself. Jo guessed that his question would be, 'Is there any wine left?' because he had asked it at regular intervals ever since he'd walked in off the street. She was about to point to the denim-jacket girl when another hand shot up from the back row.

'Okay,' said Jo, pointing, even though she couldn't see the hand's owner clearly. 'The person at the back – you can have the last question.'

'I'll stand up to ask it, if you don't mind,' replied the hand's owner, and a big grin stretched across Jo's face.

'Hi, Jo,' said Rob. 'My wife bought me your book for Father's Day on behalf of my little girl and I have to say, although I wasn't sure about it to begin with, I loved it. I've got one question, though, and it's about the ending. I don't want to spoil it for anyone who hasn't read it yet but I'm desperate to know what made you decide to let Ruth and Danny get together in the end. It could've gone either way, couldn't it?'

'Didn't you like the ending?'

'It's not that,' said Rob. 'But wouldn't it have been more true to life if they hadn't got together?'

'I can see what you're saying,' Jo said, holding Rob's gaze, 'and "true to life" was the way I wrote it in the first draft. But when I'd read it through I thought, Do you know what, Jo? This is your world and these are your characters and whether they're real or not I don't think I've ever met two people more deserving of a fairy-tale ending.'

Rob sat down, and the woman from Waterstone's stood up and thanked Jo for her talk, and the audience for coming. As she turned off the microphone, Jo scanned the room for Rob but a few people from her publishers came over to say goodbye and when they had disappeared she was escorted by the woman from Waterstone's to a table covered with copies of *Fifty Words For Snow*. A long queue had formed already and Jo had no choice but to get out her pen and turn on the charm.

Half an hour later, as she shook the hand of the last person – a fifty-something woman who had bought two copies of *Fifty Words For Snow* for her two twenty-something daughters – Jo had finished. She stood up and looked round the now empty room for any sign of Rob.

'Well, that went well,' said Matt. 'You had a great turn-out.'

'Thanks,' replied Jo, disappointed that Rob had gone. 'It was great, wasn't it?'

'There's a taxi downstairs,' said the woman from Waterstone's. 'It'll take you straight to your hotel.'

'Thanks,' said Jo again, as she picked up her Biro and dropped it into her bag. 'That's very kind.'

'Oh, and before I forget,' said the woman from Waterstone's, 'a member of the audience came up to me a while ago and said he knew you and wanted to say hello but that he had to go. He said to give you this,' she handed Jo a red plastic WHSmith's carrier-bag, 'and that you'd understand.'

Jo took the bag from her and looked inside. It was a DVD of *Dirty Dancing*, still in its shrink wrapping. Across it he had written in marker-pen: 'Another for your collection.'

'Who is it from?' asked Matt.

'No one, really,' said Jo, smiling to herself. 'Just an old friend.'